NOBODY,
SOMEBODY,
ANYBODY

NOBODY,

SOMEBODY,

ANYBODY

A NOVEL

KELLY McCLOREY

ecco

An Imprint of HarperCollins*Publishers*

HarperCollins books may be purchased for educational, business,
or sales promotional use. For information, please email the Special
Markets Department at SPsales@harpercollins.com.

Ecco® and HarperCollins® are trademarks of HarperCollins
Publishers.

FIRST EDITION

Designed by Paula Russell Szafranski

Library of Congress Cataloging-in-Publication Data
Names: McClorey, Kelly, author.
Title: Nobody, somebody, anybody : a novel / Kelly McClorey.
Description: First edition. | New York, NY : Ecco, [2021]
Identifiers: LCCN 2021002239 (print) | LCCN 2021002240 (ebook)
 | ISBN
  9780063002654 (hardcover) | ISBN 9780063002678 (ebook)
Classification: LCC PS3613.C3584 N63 2021   (print) | LCC
PS3613.C3584
  (ebook) | DDC 813/.6—dc23
LC record available at https://lccn.loc.gov/2021002239
LC ebook record available at https://lccn.loc.gov/2021002240

21 22 23 24 25   LSC   10 9 8 7 6 5 4 3 2 1

For my parents

ONE

On my first day as a chambermaid, two guests were in the hallway discussing the Commodore's Ball, and I heard one say to the other, "Why don't you ask that lady?" It took a moment for me to realize "that lady" was me, stooped over a trash can to replace the liner, but when I did, I felt proud and didn't mind that they had no idea who I was or that I had in fact attended college, a rather elite university. They never did ask me a question, but I quickly forgot about that, as I was too busy thinking *Lady with the Trash! I'm the Lady with the Trash!* because that sounded like Lady with the Lamp, nickname of none other than Florence Nightingale, hero of medicine and hero of mine, who stayed up all night ferrying her lamp from soldier to soldier, providing lifesaving care to the sick and wounded. Someday I hope to be known for that level of devotion.

As I finished with the trash, Roula appeared and told me to take my first break. I meandered down from the hotel floor into the dining floor, with the kitchen, offices, and trophy room, then into the harbor floor, with the lounge, ballroom, and deck, staked up on poles over the ocean. From the deck I had a brilliant view of the members' boats lolling about, all pristine and lovingly named, most with masts waiting to be draped in magnificent sails, as pure white as the sheets and towels I'd folded that morning. I settled with my arms dangling over the railing to watch as boys in polo shirts bustled about the T-shaped dock. One of them drove the launch boat that picked members up and towed them out to their own, bigger boats.

An elderly woman plodded down the dock, escorted by a man and a teenage boy. The man and boy had blond hair curling out of their heads and their calves, which were muscular and bronzed. She wore a whole rigging of jewelry so that I could hear it jingle from all the way up there and see it sing in the sunlight, flashing off her knuckles and wrists and the side of her head, where she must have pinned a fancy barrette. I was watching her slow, glittery progress when Doug, the general manager, sidled up beside me. "You don't want to be rich," he said, pressing the solid bulk of his belly against the railing.

The skin on his forearms burned with a deep rusty tan. "I knew this one guy. Had the most massive house I've ever seen—you'd want to call it a castle really. But he was so lonely up there, he went nuts. One night it got so bad, he spooned three thousand dollars' worth of caviar into a bowl of water. In hopes it would hatch!"

He gave me a serious, purposeful look. Apparently he thought I was dumb enough to believe there was a direct correlation between wealth and loneliness and, on top of it, that correlation implies causation, as though I'd had no higher education. Plus, didn't a place like this—an exclusive private yacht club created by wealthy people for the purpose of socializing with other wealthy people— offer evidence to the contrary? Still, I didn't intend to make sweeping generalizations. Florence Nightingale herself had grown up with two beautiful homes! One in Derbyshire, one in Hampshire.

"I was only thinking about sea squirts," I said. "They live under docks and boats." To convince him, I kept going. "Have you seen them around here? They can look kind of like fingers or flowers, or little tubes of jelly."

"Oh sure. We've got to scrape them off every few months," he said. "They can damage the equipment."

"Maybe. But did you know they also have compounds shown to be effective in treating certain kinds of cancer? I guess you never know about those things, what might be hiding just under the surface."

"I hadn't heard that." He fingered the perspiration on his forehead. "You are a fount of knowledge." He grabbed the face of his watch and grunted.

As he walked off, I noticed that the old woman and her two companions had made it into the launch boat. I watched the boat move away slowly, water opening and closing behind it like a curtain. Then Doug reappeared at my side, startling me. "One other thing, Amy," he said. "I'd prefer if you didn't take your breaks out here. The deck's for members only."

That evening, while the members enjoyed the Commodore's Ball—a special centennial edition to celebrate the club's one hundredth season, according to a flyer on the events board—I opened Florence Nightingale's biography. I reread all my favorite passages, dizzy with inspiration. She emphasized the vital importance of cleanliness: it was poor sanitation, not battle wounds, that had caused the vast majority of fatalities in the Crimean War, and she used data analysis to prove it, then illustrated her findings in an elegant coxcomb chart that made it easy for Queen Victoria to understand. She also wrote advice for ordinary people. Dirty walls and carpets can be as unhealthy as a dung heap, and tidying can't be done by simply flapping dust from one surface to another; dust should be removed completely with a damp cloth. All this reinvigorated me for my second day on the job, as did her many remarkable quotes. For instance: "I attribute my success to this—I never gave or took any excuse." I copied that down, as they were words to live by.

◼

Four weeks have passed since then, four weeks that I've been working as a chambermaid, which isn't technically my title, but I prefer it to housekeeper because of the rich history associated with the word *maid*. For instance, it was milkmaids who helped discover the smallpox vaccine. They noticed that those of them who had contracted cowpox from tugging on infected udders were later immune to smallpox, and their observation prompted Edward Jenner to extract pus from a heroic milkmaid's arm and inject it into an eight-year-old boy. History remembers them all, even the maid.

Although this is only a summer job, I strive never to treat it as such. I strive to treat each guest like family, or better than family, because isn't it true that we tend to treat our own family worse than enemies, believing we can get away with anything, and they'll never leave us? And since I'm about to become an EMT, once I pass the exam on August 25, I approach this job and everything else in my life with the knowledge and sense of responsibility of any reputable medical professional. The voice of Hippocrates, the world's first epidemiologist, came to me once as I flushed scum down a sink: "Is the water from a marshy soft-ground source, or is the water from the rocky heights? Is the water brackish and harsh?" He recognized water as one of the most important environmental factors when it comes to the spreading of disease, and right alongside water is cleanliness, which is why a job like this should only be undertaken with the utmost care. I've never been a germophobe—I can appreciate the value of exposure for building a strong immune system—but here I've become haunted by an open toilet lid (particles can travel up to six feet during a flush!) and, what's worse, a toothbrush sitting unprotected within that six-foot radius. I dunk unprotected toothbrushes in hydrogen peroxide, performing a sort of covert baptism. I'm extra cautious ever since Roula barged in and yanked the toothbrush out of my hand as though I were a child. "What are you doing, touching that?" she sneered. When I tried to explain, she cut me off, saying, "Just stick to the checklist." To her, a checklist is like God's final word.

The guests here are wealthy and tan and have a love of boating, and in order to stay in one of our rooms, they must be members in good standing or else have gone through the proper channels to be "introduced," which requires a member in good standing to accompany them to the clubhouse or write a letter or make a phone call on their behalf (but if there is only a letter or a phone call, they must wait at least fourteen days before being introduced again). We have only ten rooms on the hotel floor, though the workload varies depending on the number of stay-overs versus checkouts, with checkouts taking nearly twice as long. I always start by coating the shower and toilet with chemicals, allowing them time to penetrate while I refresh the dish of potpourri and swab the light bulb, a trick to instantly brighten any room. Once I have the porcelain and chrome glistening, the fumes stinging my eyes, I prepare to move into the bedroom by discarding my gloves and steeping my sponges in detergent. When it comes to making the bed, Roula taught me "The queen is always right," as a way to remember that tags on king sheets are on the left, while tags on queen sheets are on the right. Tags should always, always face down.

Roula and I share the housekeeping closet, where we store our cleaning caddies and hang our personal belongings on side-by-side hooks. There's a small table for our paperwork and a telephone, though she also keeps three potted plants there, to mark it as her domain. Although she holds the title of head housekeeper, she puts far more effort into caring for these plants than she does for any of our rooms, as far as I can tell. She dotes on them throughout the day, adjusting their positions as the sun moves across the window, spritzing and trimming their leaves, testing the soil with her finger. It can get isolated up here with just the two of us, so for a while I tried spending my breaks in the alley where the waitstaff hang out, smoking and using their cell phones and sipping on iced coffees they fill up for free in the kitchen. They're young except for one guy they call Shell, from his last name, Shelling. He must be at least two decades older than the rest; you can see it around his eyes, even though he's kept lean and has a full head of wavy brown hair. He works another job in the evenings, at a restaurant in Boston where the employees are paid to be rude to the customers—they write personalized insults on paper hats and place them on your head during the meal, and if you ask for a napkin, they throw it at you—but he's an actor first, I've heard him say that a few times. All because he once had a tiny role in a Bill Murray movie, a single line, something about the bricks being fake.

The last time I went to the alley, the lunch rush had just ended, and two girls I'd seen out there before, Liza and Bridget, were resting against the wall of the clubhouse. When I said hello, they nodded. Liza held a cup of ice and was munching on the cubes one at a time. Bridget kept fishing around in her purse, a repurposed rice bag sewed with leather straps. Shell sat on a crate and puffed smoke. Two other servers lobbed a tennis ball back and forth, occasionally doing tricks with it, slinging it from between their knees or behind their backs. One of them, Vinny, wore a Red Sox cap. I hadn't learned the other's name, though I recognized him by his uneven gait—he was pigeon-toed.

"You're a senior, right?" Shell asked as he scooched the crate closer to Liza.

She gradually tongued an ice cube to the side of her

mouth, annoyed by this inconvenience. "Going to be," she mumbled, her cheek bulging.

So she must be just a few years younger than I am, I thought, arranging myself against the wall beside the girls. Bridget spun the two bracelets on her wrist. I watched the rotations until I could make out the words engraved on them: WANDERLUST, SIMPLICITY.

"Aw. And I'm just a measly sophomore," Shell said. He turtled his head, trying to look shy.

"Ha, ha," Vinny said as he snatched the tennis ball from the air with one hand. "I thought you had to stay a thousand feet from any school."

Shell grinned. "Now, that's not very nice."

"What college?" I asked Liza.

"No," she said, "*high school.*"

Bridget's phone dinged in her palm. She leaned toward Liza and said in a low voice, "M is asking about the bonfire. What do you want me to say?"

"Did you say bonfire?" Shell said. "Now, that sounds like fun." He looked at me. "How about you, do you like bonfires?"

"I guess."

"What a coincidence! So do I. So, ladies, what time should we be there? Come on, now, it's not polite to whisper."

"Everyone's going to be in high school." Bridget typed on her phone without looking up. "I really hope you have better things to do."

"I don't! And what about poor . . . what was your name again?"

I hesitated, but saw no other option. "Amy."

"Right. And what about poor Amy? You're just going to exclude her too?"

"Leave her alone," the pigeon-toed waiter said, taking a step toward us.

I cast him a look, then turned back to Shell and the girls. "Yeah," I said. "Are you just going to exclude us?" I put my hand on my hip.

"Ha!" Shell was getting excited. "You tell her, Amy."

Liza spit her ice cube onto the pavement and said, "Jesus Christ. If you guys really care that much, you can come. This is depressing."

"Now, that's more like it," Shell said, and turned to me. "What time shall I pick you up?"

"I was just trying to do you a favor," I said. "Personally, I have better things to do."

"Oowee!" Vinny celebrated, raising his cap to the sky.

The girls clucked, and I tried to laugh lightly along with them, but I was feverish from the whole exchange, feeling bold and almost deranged, so that when Vinny pitched the tennis ball to his pigeon-toed friend, I sprang forward with my arms up, making a pocket with my hands, and heard my voice call out, "It's mine!" The ball landed inside. It was hot and woolly. They looked at me and I looked at them; we were all waiting. I wasn't sure what to do or why I'd caught it in the first place.

I faced the girls, the ball raised in my hand. "Let's all play," I said.

They gaped at me. The ball bore into my palm. I thought I could feel blisters forming.

"How about monkey in the middle," Shell whispered, just loud enough for everyone to hear.

I turned and chucked the ball blindly over my head toward the pigeon-toed one. It had too much force and bounced behind him, down toward the dumpsters. We all stood watching it. Shell laughed a little. Finally, the pigeon-toed boy said, "I'll get it!" but I didn't wait around for that.

Over the last four weeks, I've come to enjoy many aspects of the job, particularly the experience of scouring. Friction is a spectacular force. I am an extension of my sponge, absorbing the dirt and dust and grime and feeling them dissolve into me so that we, the dirt and I, become one. Together we sail from room to room, always moving top to bottom and clockwise to prevent the corruption of previously cleaned areas. Naturally, I'm curious about the items that belong to such wealthy, tan, boat-loving people, particularly the cosmetics. Each woman has curated her own collection to highlight her assets and cover her problem areas, and while I don't normally buy cosmetics myself, I appreciate this exposure to the cutting edge of high-end beauty. Just today, I stumbled upon a pot of 24-karat gold butter that, according to the label, should be applied with a vegetable sponge for luxurious exfoliation. I cupped the pot in my hand and squinted at the sparkly stuff inside, even twisted off the cap and took a whiff, but I would never go so far as to dip a finger.

The attention required to root out grime can be taxing, though, and I feel constant pressure to outdo the previous day's job in order to enjoy a sense of accomplishment and to please Roula, who has worked here ever since immigrating from Greece and so has the benefit of experience, even if she lacks initiative and shrugs it off when I bring up important issues like the invisible breeding ground on light switches and doorknobs. My small frame can be both a help and a hindrance: I must be a gymnast when I reach behind the sink, a weightlifter when I wrestle up a mattress. My back throbs from all the crouching, and when I creak up from my mashed-in knees, I often murmur with pain, and these murmurs sound honorable to my ears, and so urge me on. Imagine, I sometimes say to myself, the pain Roula must feel, given that she must be fifty years old or close to it, while I am lucky to be so young—not yet thirty and not yet tied down.

For a college course, I once read about a study in which researchers found that when hotel maids started to view their work as a form of exercise, they lost weight and became more physically fit, even though they were performing the exact same activities as before. That got me marveling at the power of belief: you never know what's possible when the mind and body agree to work together. Our guests probably spend a fortune on gym memberships and personal trainers, and here I am, the chambermaid, collecting their filth and dissolving it into myself and meanwhile burning enough calories to lose two pounds in four weeks simply by believing in my own movement. Whenever I scrub the grout between tiles, I feel the hump of my bicep growing more defined.

Each room has a wooden hutch that opens to reveal a widescreen television, and I often turn it on while I clean, since it doesn't distract me but rather sinks me deeper into the rhythms of my work. My only rule is no changing the channel—that way I'm connected to the guest and don't waste time searching for another program. It's usually *Oprah* or twenty-four-hour news or a soap opera or one of those shows in which everyday people sign up to get into an argument or receive relationship advice. Before long, the voices from the television seep into my brain, and not just my brain but my arms and legs, which begin to move with a different attitude and style, as though connected to someone new. Like this morning, while Eva pledged to make Jad pay for the death of her daughter, I plumped pillows and shook crumbs from a summer quilt with all the righteous anger of a vengeful mother. Sometimes I notice my voice following along, adding a snippet of commentary here and there, though if I hear any footsteps in the hall, I trail off and pretend to be humming a tune. Roula likes to remind me that I'm not allowed to turn on the television, it's unprofessional, but I know that if she could see the way I am there but not there, cleaning but not cleaning, exercising but not exercising, she would not only understand but emulate my routine. She probably wonders how on earth I've ended up here, seeing as I did go to college, which has a lasting impact on everything I do, even if I didn't graduate. I'll admit that sometimes I wonder the same thing, but then it's just for the summer, so there's no use dwelling on it.

This afternoon, after initialing all the items on my checklist and clocking out for the day, I began the walk back to my apartment, an in-law tacked to the side of a two-story house, with a separate staircase up to its own entrance. The first half of my walk follows the coastline, and I contemplated how both liberating and frightening it is to live on the edge of such an infinite expanse. Along two miles of that coastline runs a paved walkway where people pace up and down as though on the brink of action, and on stormy days waves crash and creep over, reaching out for them. I don't mind that it's mostly families who live here, affluent ones, and not people like me—in fact I prefer it, as they shift with the seasons more than young single people do. During springtime, the sidewalks were covered in chalk art, and the adults came out early with strollers and jogging suits and organized all kinds of creative events, like Make Way for

Ducklings Day, when they stopped traffic to parade a family of ducks through downtown. Even their houses change colors and moods. Now that it's summer, they have green lawns and colorful blooms and bright plastic pails stacked together on their porches with little shovels sticking out, and some have signs hanging on their doors that say things like "Gone to the Beach" and "Life Is Better in Flip-Flops," painted in a way that's meant to look rustic and weathered. I read one that said "If You're Lucky Enough to Live by the Beach, You're Lucky Enough"—my favorite so far. My landlord, who lives in the house connected to my apartment, has a sign that features a bronzed parrot in sunglasses under a palm tree and the words "Broke but Tan." My landlord is neither broke nor tan, and there are no palm trees in Massachusetts, but I get why he chose that one—something about the colors and the three-dimensional letters make you want to try to take a bite of it.

The second half of my walk zags away from the ocean, and as I left the salt air and crinkling waves and twirly kites behind, I was aware of the weight of the world's dust inside me, a tornado of it spinning within my abdomen, though it wasn't a burden but a privilege. From dust to dust, I thought; everything else is us kidding ourselves. I paused to pluck one ripe berry from the bountiful row of raspberry bushes outside 8 Magnolia Drive, as has become my habit. As the fruit burst in my mouth, my feet and back ached, and what a nice sensation that was, to be sore from hard work. I thanked not God exactly but some greater spirit for my body, all its organs and tissues and cells—over thirty trillion cells, most likely, significantly more than the number of galaxies in the universe—and how they've been assembled in the right way so that I might do hard work and every day strive to do better.

Also while I walked, I worked on my plans. August 25 is my last chance to pass the cognitive exam, and once I do, I will officially be a certified EMT, and I'll take all I've learned and will learn as a chambermaid—precision and observation and controlling my gag reflex—and channel it into saving lives. Then I'll go to work every day knowing that anyone who is afraid, anyone who needs help, will call me, trusting that I will come as fast as I can, ready and willing to do everything in my power. Like the rest of my team, I'll wear dark blue pants and a button-down shirt with the blue-and-yellow EMT patch stitched on the sleeve so that everyone I meet will recognize who I am and the impact I have on a daily basis. Some might stop me to say thank you or to exchange harrowing stories, and we'll get teary in our longing to preserve human life, squeezing our hands together as though we could squeeze out the very possibility of suffering inside us and everyone we love.

But for now I am alone in my apartment, though my landlord is just on the other side of the wall, maybe at his desk composing a letter to his Ukrainian girlfriend, and my exam book lies open on my lap so I can quiz myself on the first signs of anaphylaxis and the number of vertebrae in the thoracic spine. I sit by the window as the street outside grows dark and my face becomes reflected in the glass. Then I hear an explosion, a loud pop and a crackling, and another one. I rush outside to see great buds of red and gold in the sky.

Today is the Fourth of July, and I've forgotten it. I can't help banging a fist against my leg, I'm so angry with myself. For weeks I've watched streamers and flags go up on front porches and on the boats in the harbor, and somehow I still missed it. I breathe and try to forgive myself—I've had a lot on my mind, and I can still enjoy a partial view of the fireworks if I don't waste it with tears. I stand on the sticky pavement and watch through the trees, clapping for what I think is the grand finale, then for the true grand finale, which booms and sparks for two full minutes. Then it is dark and quiet again, and there is nothing to do but go back up to my chair by the window.

I am alone here, but not completely, because of the heavy book on my lap and the knowledge glowing within it and because of the fervent promises I made earlier today, which still hover in the air: promises to stay focused and to carry my book to the clubhouse to study at lunchtime and to never, ever give or take any excuse. Once in a while I get discouraged and slack off, but it's okay, because a part of me understands that it won't last forever and anticipates the time when I will study hard again and knows that when I do, like I am today, I'll feel renewed and recommitted, once again set on the correct path. Florence Nightingale said nursing is an art that requires as much devotion and preparation as painting or sculpting, even more so, because what is an old canvas or hunk of marble compared with the living body? Well, art also requires inspiration, and sometimes we must be patient and allow inspiration to arrive. Perhaps it's good that I failed my first two attempts to pass the exam; perhaps something deep in my subconscious even instructed me to fail, because now there will be more joy when I pass, euphoria even. And perhaps it's good I spend so much time alone, because whether I'm slacking off or working hard, I can still trust myself so long as no other eyes are burning at me, plus I'm inhabited by all the dust and grime and television characters I've absorbed during the day, so there's hardly room for more company. And if I need to, I remind myself how I am quite lucky and still so young.

T W O

Last time I took the exam, I had a degrading job at the call center of a credit union, though I started showing up less and less after I got the results back. I took refuge in my apartment all day and all night, until the difference between them no longer had meaning. I didn't care that I needed the money; eviction, starvation—I hardly flinched. I watched an exceptional amount of pirated television on my laptop. Whenever I did summon the courage to take out my flash cards or flip to a page of practice questions, loneliness would stomp its feet, demanding my attention—it had a fiery temper and didn't like to be ignored. It was the final stretch of winter, and mornings and early evenings I'd go to the window to watch my neighbors bolt between their driveways and their homes, all bundled up in heavy clothes and accessories. It inspired me to write a poem about the importance of togetherness based on the difference between gloves and mittens, the way mittens would always be the warmer choice, but when I reread it later, it only made me roll my eyes.

I dreaded spring, the harassment of a pleasant sunny day. But it came anyway, and with the trees budding outside my window, I said, Okay, time to live again. By then I'd been placed on disciplinary probation, with my hours cut back to two shifts per week, leaving me with a daunting amount of free time. On my off days, I forced myself out, right foot, left foot, right foot, left foot, crossing first through downtown in case something should be happening that might involve me, then branching off toward the woods, where peace and epiphany supposedly lived.

In the woods, fresh air would streak in and out of my nose and I had nothing to do but ramble and notice things, a patch of mushrooms, a mossy branch, the skeleton of a leaf lit up by the sun. I would make bets with myself about whether I could jump from this log to that log or how many Mississippis it would take to get from one tree to the next. I'd sit by a narrow stream and watch sediment float down, snag on something, then float free again, until my butt went numb and my skin turned yellow with pollen.

Some days the world was oblivious to me and the hours ticked by so slowly that I couldn't remember if it was today or yesterday or some time long, long ago, and I began to doubt what I was and had to touch my face to remember it. When a tree trembled with the spastic movement of squirrels, I would tremble too. The crows had many grievances, and they'd terrorize the rest of the woods with their bickering, until even the grubs punched their heads up through the ground in exasperation. But most days, the world was friendly and recognized me. Every stone gave the impression it had been placed on its back just for me to find and rub and flip over. What had I done to deserve this smooth round stone on its back? This little acorn in its checkered cap? Even the garbage I grew an affection for. In fact it was the garbage I often enjoyed most: Popsicle sticks and beer cans and plastic wrappers skittering in the wind, and each of them like a token of solidarity. They had been discarded by people, and here I was, a person just like those people—it could've been me to drop you, you Popsicle stick.

On those good days, I'd have to bribe myself to leave the woods by promising to stop at a certain supermarket where the deli workers knew my name and never required me to pull a number. On the way, I'd clear the dirt under my nails and pick the burs off my clothes, making myself presentable. My favorite deli worker was a woman with a faint mustache—the fluorescent bulbs illuminated every hair, though she never showed any sign of shyness—who immediately upon my arrival would launch into a description of whatever was on special. She knew how much I relished the details, the part of the cow such-and-such cut came from or the spices in this marinade, and I'd listen intently through the familiar haze of glass cleaner and freezer burn, revitalized by the peppy sound of sneakers squealing up and down the aisles behind me. When she finished, I'd watch the quiver of her mustache, the hairs in a neat line as though she had combed them in place, and say, "I'll take one. No, make it two!" She'd wrap whatever it was with care. As she handed the package across the counter, sometimes our fingers would meet and I would walk away feeling the ghostly residue of her touch and hearing the echo of my own voice, often for the first time all day: *Make it two, make it two.*

The truth was that I didn't always have a need for whatever was on special and couldn't usually afford to be buying two of it, so occasionally I had no choice but to abandon the package on a random shelf. It would break my heart to leave it behind, peeking out from behind a box of graham crackers or instant oatmeal, wondering where I was going and whether I'd be back.

Eventually I'd have to return home and loneliness would be waiting for me there—along with my landlord's mailbox. My own mail, when there was any, was dropped through a slot in my door and consisted of coupons, credit card offers, and occasional postcards from my brother in Burkina Faso with the Peace Corps. His postcards pictured the New York City skyline—he must have packed them in his suitcase—and they usually started by sug-

gesting I call or visit Dad and then turned breezy, telling brief anecdotes and ending with humorous requests:
*Please send king-size mattress; Please send high-speed
internet; Please send Starbucks latte, grande, no foam.*
My landlord's mail, on the other hand, was consistently
abundant. The mail carrier loaded so many mysterious
envelopes into the box that at times the front flap would
gape open, beckoning to me. Reading a neighbor's mail
would be illegal, and I never would've fathomed doing it a
few years ago, but I'd grown desperate to know someone,
not in the profound way like when people say "Can you
really *know* someone?" but just in the most basic sense.
Reading a neighbor's mail seemed better than marching
up to a door and knocking, since that door might open,
and then I'd be standing there with nothing to say except
"Sorry, wrong door."

I'm not shy by nature, but I've come to understand
that for many people a door is sacred. That's why they've
divided up the world with walls and fences; I see it every day as I walk through my neighborhood. Most of
the front yards are small and inviting, with a moat of
mulch or shiny white stones, but the backyards are different: sprawling, impenetrable fortresses. The walls are
made of tall wooden pickets or densely packed shrubs,
and they are solid, with only a few exceptions, such as
a bowl-like window built into a fence on Cliff Street so
the family dog can look out and bark at you. They don't
have barbed wire or high-voltage electricity, yet only the

occasional ivy plant is brave enough to scale them. Even the local movie theater, with its chilled air, is partitioned by fences, in the form of stiff armrests. I suppose people want to believe that all these walls and fences and sacred doors will protect them from outside contamination. But, as anyone with any medical training or knowledge of the biomedical sciences knows, the most important enemy is microscopic, and pathogens travel as they please, through a sneeze, a pipe, a gust of wind. They crop up when we least expect it, in a high five or an undercooked ham. And they've shaped far more history than any emperor or president.

One Thursday in March, I hurried from the woods to the deli, knowing my favorite woman was due back after a week-long vacation—I wasn't sure where, but I planned to ask. A vacation opened up new possibilities for conversation, and I'd planned a few questions in advance and let my refrigerator go bare so I'd have the confidence of legitimacy. I spotted her from across the store, extra color in her cheeks.

"Special's sold out," she said, so devoid of spirit that I looked around to confirm she was indeed talking to me. I almost said something goofy about whether she'd forgotten all of us after her vacation, but the fact that she'd brought up the special suggested that she knew exactly who I was. She blew air in my direction. Her demeanor was all off. "Why don't you just tell me what you came for?" she said finally.

I was speechless, almost frightened, imagining some imposter had taken over her body. "W-we," I stammered. When I feel ambushed, I have a tendency to say "we" instead of "I." "We need, um, a pound, one pound, of turkey. Sliced thin." I dashed off while she was still running the turkey through the slicer. I ran all the way home, scooped up my landlord's mail, and set a kettle on the stove. I held each envelope in the steam with a pair of tongs, doing a dance with my hips as I worked. I'd seen this steaming technique performed on a television show where a woman hired a team of investigators to find out whether her husband was having an affair with a teller from their bank. The envelopes wrinkled a little, but after some finessing with a butter knife, the flaps slipped open, discreet and inviting.

Over the next few days I perfected the technique, working as fast as possible, my adrenaline coursing, to allow sufficient time for the envelopes to dry, which was the most agonizing part. I never failed to get the envelopes resealed with fresh glue and returned safely to their positions well before my landlord's car pulled into the driveway. Though the process was exciting, the results were flatly underwhelming—mainly bills and special offers on credit cards or car insurance. But just as I began to lose interest, a thick, notebook-sized envelope arrived, conspicuously plain, the typeset return address a PO box in Houston. I had a weightless feeling as I slid a packet out from inside. It had a stock photo on the cover, a light-haired woman and a dark-haired man, and the heading "Sincere Romance's 10-Day Singles Tour Experience: All you need to know before you go!" Then a letter on the first page:

> *Congratulations on your purchase of the 10-Day Singles Tour! We hope you're ready for an unforgettable experience meeting hundreds of attractive single women as you travel through Odessa, Nikolaev, and Kherson. The information provided in this packet will help you make the most of your time and get the results you're hoping for.*
>
> *Remember, there's a reason our international dating service has become so popular—it WORKS! On our "Testimonials" page, you will hear from men just like you, who took the leap of faith and joined our thousands of satisfied customers. We hope you will be our next success story!*
>
> *Sincerely,*
> *Ken & Oleksandra Bryant*
> *Travel Directors for Ukraine (Married for Fourteen Wonderful Years and Counting!)*

I was gripped, immobilized, my finger turning damp on the page. I read through the whole packet once, then again. There was a list of dos and don'ts, like *DON'T:*

- Stop yourself from approaching a woman because you think she's out of your league. Ukraine is home to some of the world's most beautiful women, but their strong family values is what really sets them apart. You'll find that many of them care more about qualities like stability, maturity, and intelligence than outward appearance or age.
- Take her shopping. It might sound fun to spoil her, but it's important to put off making large purchases until you have a relationship commitment. This will avoid any misunderstandings and help you both feel more secure about the relationship in the long run.
- Allow her to make arrangements for a date, particularly location.

But *DO:*

- Start now! With your purchase, you enjoy unlimited access to the thousands of profiles in our database. If you haven't already, we encourage you to begin reaching out to any women you have interest in and forming connections. Through the website, you can send invitations to our social mixers or set up a private date, with on-call interpreter services available.

- Be selfish and have fun! You've put your own time and money on the line, so leave your hang-ups at home and don't walk away with any regrets.

The testimonials page featured quotes from men identified by first name and last initial, along with photos of the women they'd fallen in love with. The last page had a list of frequently asked questions about currency, plug adaptors, the metric system, and suggestions for small gifts to pack: "Perfume and dark chocolate are universal." It took all my self-control to eventually close the packet. As I shuffled the envelopes back inside his mailbox, my conscience tugged at me for the first time. I knew something I had no right to know, and no matter how bad I might feel, I could never unknow it. When we crossed paths in the front yard a couple days later, I kept my eyes down. But then he stopped me to ask if I'd be willing to collect his mail and water the lawn while he went away on vacation, so I decided to take that as a sign of forgiveness and permission.

Watching from the window as he stumbled into a taxi with a rolling suitcase and an oversize backpack, I shivered, unsure how to feel. I pictured him and his broad stomach undulating under the blinking lights of an Odessa nightclub while he told himself, *Be selfish, have fun, don't walk away with any regrets.* Some people might laugh at my landlord for purchasing a ten-day tour from Sincere Romance, but I didn't want to be one of them. Why should I be so quick to laugh? Who knows what will be funny in the end? At first you might find the suffering of a loved one funny because it seems so overdramatic; then, by the time you finally stop laughing, it's too late.

I didn't feel sorry for him either—as quick as people are to laugh, they are even quicker to pity. Take me now, these few months later, as a chambermaid. The other day a guest watched me lug a trash bag down the hallway, leaving in my wake—unbeknownst to me—a trail of brown juice from a leaky corner, and he must have known that once I'd hurled the bag into the dumpster and brushed my hands off in triumph, I'd return to find the trail of brown juice, and this idea probably made his heart want to burst. Probably tears came to his eyes as he thought, Poor thing, with her trail of brown juice, what a pity she didn't get to go to an elite university like me. And how far from the truth! Since the truth was that I met that trail of brown juice with a sunny resolve, for I would scour and eradicate it, ruminating all the while on Florence Nightingale's suggestion that we view diseases as conditions, the same as dirty and clean, and just as much under our own control. I happily blotted and rinsed, blotted and rinsed, and I'd gone to an elite university besides. It never occurred to him that at the end of the day, I'd be going home to study for the EMT exam, and that in the future, when he experiences the first sign of a stroke or takes a sudden fall from a ladder, I might be the only person standing between his life and death—me, the one he felt sorry for!

A couple weeks after my landlord returned from his trip, an envelope arrived from an Irina Mezhebovksy. The tongs shook as I positioned it over the hot kettle. She called him her true love, her one and only. She still couldn't believe that he'd actually come all the way there to meet her, and she already missed him terribly and wouldn't be happy until they were together again, but in the meantime, she thought it'd be romantic to send handwritten letters, like in a movie. She wanted to send a little piece of her country—a scattering of dried petals at the bottom of the envelope, from a sunflower. This was more than I'd ever envisioned. They were engaged to be married! She included a photograph of herself in a red sleeveless turtleneck, and even though she wasn't smiling, she was beautiful, somehow both severe and alluring at the same time, with light hair and dark elaborate makeup on her eyes and lips. I soared with hope that she would soon move into my landlord's house. How could we not become fast friends when she didn't know anybody else and I was conveniently located right next door, on the very same property? It was the ideal situation, and she was the ideal candidate. She looked close to my age, closer to mine than his, and I could invite her to teach me aerobics—she said she couldn't wait to taste his cooking, but she'd have to double her aerobics classes so she didn't "blow up." Soon after that, packages from Effortless Epicurean began arriving on his porch, each box stamped with a cartoon frog in a chef's hat.

I no longer waited for the mailman to disappear around the corner. The moment he descended from the porch, I raided the mailbox, frantically searching for more news from Irina. I tried to remind myself that they had email and texts and video calls. Even if she *had* sent another letter, it might take a week or two, even three, to finally reach us.

One evening I heard a knock. Without checking the peephole, I knew it was him. I dropped to my knees and scooched back against the wall, my heart thudding. I'd let myself get careless. What could I possibly do now? Deny ever touching his mail, pretend to be shocked, offended that he'd even suggest I was capable of something so illegal and unneighborly? But it might not be convincing, and he might have evidence—fingerprints or an abnormality in the envelopes. Without a plan, I groped desperately for the windowsill above my head, thinking I might as well jump. Something on the window latch tickled my finger, and I yelped at the surprise. A harmless spider. My landlord called my name once, then we were both quiet, in a kind of standoff, and I closed my eyes and thought of nothing, and after a long moment like that, he fiddled with some keys and opened the door.

"Oh!" he said when he saw me hunkered under the window.

"Sorry," I said, hugging my knees on the floor. "I didn't recognize your voice."

"No, I'm sorry. I didn't mean to barge in. I was scared you might be hurt or something." He seemed unsure of what to do or where to look, like someone plotting his line of attack. But then he said that he knew someone who was looking to hire summer waitstaff at a yacht club, they'd happened to run into each other and it had come up in conversation, and so he'd thought of me, since he knew I'd been having some issues getting all the rent together on time. Meanwhile I waited for him to get to the part about the police being on their way, waited for it even as he finished and I squeaked out that sure, okay, I'd be interested, he could leave the contact information on the table. He closed the door behind him, and I sat, processing. It was bittersweet. He had gone out of his way to offer me a job and to wonder whether I was hurt and to care enough to barge through my door as though it were nothing sacred, but this meant I'd no longer have any way to monitor what was going on with Irina, since I couldn't ransack his mail anymore, not after he'd done all that.

The person my landlord had run into turned out to be Doug, the general manager of the clubhouse and now my boss, and although Doug told me later that there was a mix-up—all the server positions had been filled and the only position still available was in housekeeping—I accepted anyway. I don't believe either of them meant to be deceitful. It pays $2.50 more than the state minimum wage, and I can work with that, since I limit my expenses and keep my student loans on an income-based plan, which means I pay nothing now, though ultimately it will add an extra fifteen years and associated interest. Whenever I pass Doug's office, I aim to appear serious and enthusiastic, calm but not casual, so he won't believe he's slighted me. Most days his door is open and he's hovered over a plate of food, moaning with pleasure. One time he called me in and turned his plate 360 degrees so I could behold the consummate slice of meatloaf. "Can you believe when I was a kid, I thought *pepper* was too spicy?" he said while pouring sugar all over the meatloaf. The sugar sits next to his computer in a ceramic camel whose humps have been hollowed out to form a container. He puts it on everything. He doesn't bother to use the tiny silver spoon, just tips the camel over and lets the sugar tumble out.

Since accepting the job as chambermaid, I haven't opened a single letter from my landlord's mailbox, and with no sign of Irina, I've begun to wonder if she was only leading him on, or if he's screwed things up, or if the distance itself has torn them apart. When we happen upon each other outside the house, we nod as usual and I search for any clue, good or bad, in his body language, finding none. For my part, I try to show my appreciation through the expression on my face. Even though there was a mix-up and the only position still available was in housekeeping, I believe the job was meant as a true gift. The same as the guest who opened a tin of peppermints and, despite having no obligation, made a motion to offer one to me—the chambermaid. I was so taken aback that I just stood there, and so she carted that peppermint all the way down the hall to the palm of my hand, which at some point must have opened itself in expectation. Then she continued on her way without pausing for recognition, while I cradled the green gem in my palm, rolling it this way and that.

On the other hand, some people like to torment you with their so-called generosity and use it to exploit your weaknesses. It happened to me back in middle school, when I fell under the spell of a pair of boots, the most perfect boots I'd ever seen, with a cuff of fur, chocolate leather, and gleaming silver buckles that hooked around each ankle. My neighbor Angela was the lucky owner of these boots, and though I never voiced it, she no doubt noticed my gazing at them—she sat next to me in class and liked to tap the leg of her desk in a rhythmic taunt. One day, when we met as usual to walk home from school, she announced out of nowhere, "Here, take them." She unbuckled the boots, pulled them off, and handed them to me.

She set off walking down the sidewalk in her socks, so I followed after her, the boots swinging from the notches of my fingers. She wanted me to feel bad, but her socks seemed plenty warm, plus she'd only given up the boots to make herself feel superior and because they were old news to her; soon they'd pass right out of style. She probably would've thrown them away otherwise. Her father owned all the Dunkin' Donuts franchises in the area. Every year for her birthday, they would set up clotheslines in the living room and string powdered doughnuts along them, then hold a competition to see how many you could eat with your hands tied behind your back. Afterward everyone would be walking around with beards of sugar, trampling crumbs into the carpets, and her parents didn't even care.

Still, the cuff of fur felt as soft and luxurious as I'd imagined, and as soon as Angela disappeared into her house, I sprinted upstairs to finally have a moment with them in private. But my mother burst in. Though I quickly tried to drain the giddiness from my face, she'd already clocked it. Now she'd have to get involved, take over. She wore me down until I disclosed where they'd come from, and then she wouldn't stop purring over them and exclaiming how generous Angela was, we were so fortunate to have her as a neighbor and I to have her as a dear friend. She chose to ignore the light scuffs, the faint smell—any evidence they were pre-worn. At dinner she said, "Did you show your father the boots? They're top quality, and it isn't even her birthday! Just a thanks-for-being-my-friend present from Angela. Isn't that nice? We've got to write a thank-you note tonight." She nudged me. "Well, what are you waiting for? Go put them on."

"They're already going out of style!" I fled to my bedroom and tried to tear the boots apart, yanking on the fur cuffs, then the buckles, then the sole, but one thing was true: they were top quality. I couldn't resist putting them on once more and admiring myself in the mirror. My mother's meddling had ruined it, though, and I carried them outside and dumped them in the trash can.

In the morning I dug them out again. I decided to ditch them on Angela's porch along with an underhanded note, one that seemed witty on the surface but would burrow into her brain, force her to brood over every nasty implication, until she felt ashamed for ever thinking she could manipulate me with fake charity. I spent hours with my notebook searching for the right words, but at the end of the day, all I had were pages and pages of sketches of me and the boots in various places all over the world: the Eiffel Tower, the Great Wall of China, the top of Mount Everest. So I packed them in a box and traded them to a woman in a consignment shop for thirty delicious dollar bills that proved I'd won. Later, I saw them all polished up on display in the window, selling for $75 to any passing moron.

When my mother realized they were gone, she moped around the house, saying "I'll never understand you." This struck me as odd, for I was just as understandable as the next person, and this was my own mother speaking, the person who'd created me and known me my whole life. Though we had little in common, I believed I understood her, and everything else, for that matter—there were no mysteries to me at that age. I'd presumed it was her disappointment talking: she could no longer go on obsessing about the boots; she'd have to find something else to do. But she said the same thing—"I'll never understand you"—many times after this, so that it stopped surprising me and began to infuriate me, until finally I snapped. It was a stupid disagreement, over what I needed to pack for college. Really, she was just desperate for any sign that I would miss her. But when she felt small, I could always crush her smaller. I can remember exactly where I was standing in my room—*I'll never understand you*—and how I slammed the suitcase and sharpened my voice: "Well, I guess now you can do us both a favor and stop trying."

THREE

On the fifth of July I had a meeting scheduled with Doug after my shift. I'd requested the meeting myself after compiling an extensive list of recommended changes for the hotel floor, informed by Florence Nightingale's writings and some more contemporary literature. I carried my proposal down to his office in a handsome leather folder, passing Roula in the housekeeping closet, who made a point of setting down the fertilizer she was sprinkling over her plants so she could give me a skeptical look.

Doug was engrossed in something on his computer, his head zoomed in almost touching the screen, so I helped myself to a chair opposite him. He banged a few keys, then finally popped his head out to acknowledge me. "Hey, you're my resident genius," he said, and squinted back at the screen. "Any good with computers?"

"Not really. Sorry."

"A Toshiba," he said. "So what should I expect. Brought to you by the same people who brought you Pearl Harbor." He laughed with his shoulders, while the rest of his body stayed still. "Now there's another winning example of diplomacy. Ha." He pushed his keyboard so it retracted into his desk. "Don't get me wrong, I like diplomats. They make great hostages." Again he laughed, his shoulders heaving, then leaned back with his fingers cushioning his head and his belly on full display.

Just as I opened my mouth to begin, his telephone rang. He snorted at the caller ID. "You're lucky you don't have to deal with this swarm of mosquitoes," he said. I gave him a look meant to show I didn't understand but also wasn't overly curious; I was hoping to get on to the purpose of the meeting. "Came up with that myself," he said proudly. "The perfect word, don't you think? All those little bloodsuckers trying to worm their way in here without going through the proper channels. Mostly new money, if you catch me."

"It's actually only female mosquitoes that suck blood," I said. The phone kept on ringing. "And they can carry serious diseases. Malaria, West Nile—"

"Of course, even better! I knew I liked you. You've always got something going." He held a button to make the ringer shut off. "Now, when are they going to make a mosquito net that's big enough?" His gaze shifted above my head. "Oh, good." I turned to see Roula in the doorway. "I thought Roula should sit in for this. Seeing as she's head housekeeper. Best one we got," he said, then loud-whispered from behind his hand, "Also the only," as though this would entertain us. I should've known Roula would find a way to interject herself—she was intent on policing me at all times. "In any case," he went on, "I've got a tee time in twenty. So brass tacks, if you will. What's on your mind?"

I breathed and tried to refocus. He would never be expecting such a studied and thorough proposal! And perhaps Roula would take something valuable from the experience. I opened my folder and passed a copy to Doug. "I only brought two," I said, then slid the other one halfway, a little less than halfway, between Roula and me. "Someone with my educational background is in a unique position here." I couldn't help peeking at Roula from the corner of my eye; though I hadn't aimed it at her, this was how I'd always planned to start. "I'm able to offer some guidance on how we can elevate the standards of health and sanitation on the hotel floor. To this end, I've put together a list of some high-priority items that should be addressed. I'll go through a few of them now to flesh out the details."

Doug didn't say anything, so I went on like I'd planned, my enthusiasm building. "You'll see that the first item is carpeting. A dirty carpet literally infects the room."

This was a direct quote from Florence Nightingale, and I twitched as it sailed out of my lips. "The ideal course of action would be to remove all carpeting and replace it with wood or tile, but, as you'll see here, I've taken into account both long- and short-term goals. I'm aware that it can be difficult for organizations like this to implement large-scale changes. In the meantime, the recommendation is to shampoo regularly, with a deep clean at least once a month."

While I explained the advantages of replacing wallpaper with oil-based paint, I noticed Doug check his watch and had a flare of self-doubt. I tried to speed up. "So, skimming down here, you'll see most of the instructions are self-explanatory. And some can be done in tandem, like with the ventilation fans and air-conditioning units. Or with some simple coordination among departments. Like putting our vacuum filters through the dishwasher once the kitchen's closed."

"I see," Doug said. His eyes traveled the page. "This sure is comprehensive. Feels like I'm back in school, getting homework. No, but in a good way."

All at once I felt drained and started to regret the whole endeavor. "I hope I didn't overstep my bounds. It's just, I feel a sense of responsibility to our guests, seeing as I'm going to be an EMT. I couldn't have a clear conscience if I didn't try to do everything in my power to protect them."

"I appreciate that. And we'll do the best we can with this. Right, Roula?" She made a noise, but I refused to look over. "Yep, we'll see what we can do. You put a lot of work in here, I can see that."

"It wasn't too much."

"You're going to make a dynamite EMT, that's for sure. And we're lucky to have you on board till then. Most of the servers can hardly string two words together, they're so used to staring at their phones twenty-four seven." He dropped the paper inside a drawer and knocked it shut with his knee. "Anyway, I better get going, or I'll never hear the end of it. But thanks, Amy. I appreciate this."

I traipsed home with mixed feelings—he had been receptive, but not quite as animated as I'd hoped. He'd always been impressed by my knowledge and he liked me, though perhaps only in the sense of "I get a kick out of her." Sometimes I got the feeling people actually wanted you to be as passive as Roula. My list of recommended changes might sit in that drawer forever. When I got to 8 Magnolia Street, the owners were outside laying mulch in the garden, so I had to bypass the raspberry bushes. "Sorry," I whispered to their hopeful ruby faces. "I'll be back tomorrow."

I found my landlord out on his porch, fumbling with a package from Effortless Epicurean. As usual I waved from a polite distance and continued toward the stairs to my apartment, but I could sense his presence behind me, lingering there. He called out, "Hey. Uh, Amy?" My heart sped up.

He waited for me to retrace my steps, but I'd lost the instinct for walking and had to focus on bending my knees at the right time.

"This might seem kind of out of the blue," he said. "But . . . any chance you'd be interested in a meal?" He gestured to the package in his arm. "See, I'm trying to test out my cooking skills before my fiancée gets here. She's moving halfway across the world for me. So I could really use a second opinion, if you're up for it."

I must have managed to nod my head because he held the door open and said, "You can just hang out, put the TV on if you want. It should only take twenty minutes."

I paced in a circle around his living room as if in a trance. Twenty minutes passed, then thirty, then forty, while he banged around in the kitchen. For almost three years we'd lived under the same roof without ever sharing more than a few words, and now this? Any moment now, I might wake up from a dream or find myself detained by local police, under investigation for tampering with the mail. *Before my fiancée gets here.* So Irina was coming after all! And I was here to help with preparations for her arrival, which meant that everything might work out even better than I'd imagined.

His belongings were close enough to touch—a plush armchair with a dent in the middle, a giant television, a desk with a laptop and printer, three leaning stacks of video games. I refrained from inspecting them too closely; I didn't want this to feel like just another guest's room at the clubhouse. Circling the room put me in an almost meditative state, and listening to the turmoil in the kitchen, the clanking and muttering, somehow lulled me as well. Here, *I* was the guest, and a welcome one. I had received an invitation, without even having to press for it or devise some convoluted scheme.

"Sorry, sorry," he said, panting. He transported napkins and two sets of silverware to the coffee table. "I don't know how they get away with calling these twenty-minute meals. Please, have a seat."

I sat on the sofa beside a black gadget, some kind of headset. The coffee table was low and pushed close so that even after shifting a few times, I still couldn't find a satisfying position for my knees.

He paused, surveying the room. "Do you think she'll like it okay here—my fiancée? I haven't had company in a while, if I'm honest. She's all the way in Ukraine. She wants to decorate, you know, make it her own, but that will take time. I want it to at least feel comfortable when she gets here."

"I'm sure she'll like it." I squirmed, trying to rearrange my knees again. "Though you might think about getting a dining table."

"Never had the need before!" He seemed agreeable and kept looking around, as if to say, What else?

I eyed the three leaning stacks of video games, wondering whether Irina would be a fan of them. He followed my gaze and poked one of the stacks with his toe. He was wearing socks; I was in his home, and he was wearing socks. "It can be a nice way to kill the time," he said softly. "But I guess I won't have to worry about that anymore."

I picked up the gadget next to me. "What's this do, by the way?"

"VR. Virtual reality."

"Oh, right. I've seen that on TV."

He took it from me and turned it over in his hands. "It's actually pretty cool. You can basically go anywhere you want without ever having to leave your house. I used to love going to the movies. But with this, I can watch any movie like I'm in my own private theater. And you don't have to worry about anyone making noise or blocking your view. The technology's come a long way. The old ones, you got a lot of space between pixels, the screen-door effect. This one has double the field of view and lower latency, so there's less motion sickness. They sent it for free to anyone who donated to help fund development. It's not even on the market yet."

"Wow. That's like a foreign language to me."

"Yeah. It might seem weird. But in a few years, everybody's going to have one." He set it on his desk and returned with two teetering plates. "Chicken piccata with angel hair and chives."

"Looks delicious."

"I'll bet you could balance all this on one hand."

"What? Oh. Actually, I'm a chambermaid, not a wait-ress. At the same place, just, that was the only position still available."

"I didn't realize." He pulled the table out, and it stam-mered over the carpet. Now my knees were free, but the gulf between sofa and table was too wide, and I struggled to reach my plate without lifting my butt. "I don't know Tripp all that well," he said. "I knew him when we were kids."

"Tripp?"

"I mean Doug. I guess he doesn't go by Tripp any-more."

"Was that because he was clumsy?"

"It stands for the third. Douglas something Yarusso the Third. Makes him sound like some kind of king, doesn't it? Probably acts like one too, if he's anything like he was in high school."

"He's not too bad. Anyway, it was no big deal. Pretty soon I'll have my EMT certification, so I'll be getting a new job anyway."

He reclined and rested his plate on the mound of his stomach—it was as large as Doug's but looser, more blub-bery. I followed his lead, balancing my plate on my jittery thighs. "You're not eating," he said. "Does it taste okay? Be honest—don't worry about hurting my feelings."

I had zero appetite, but I scarfed some down while he

watched. "It tastes good," I said. He hadn't brought cups or offered any beverage.

"My fiancée, she was concerned, because cooking isn't really her thing. So I may have exaggerated my skills a little. But I figure it can't be that hard to learn the basics. And they say cooking is one of the most romantic things you can do for someone. Not if it doesn't taste good, of course."

"Well, this definitely tastes good." I chewed and nodded vigorously. "Although it's not like I'm an expert or anything. I don't cook much myself."

"That's okay. I don't need an expert, just someone with taste buds. I've gotten pretty used to heating up frozen meals."

He watched me eat as though searching for any clue that would expose my true opinion. I needed to offer something valuable so he wouldn't regret inviting me in. I invoked Florence Nightingale, who wrote about the importance of a patient's diet and the idea of intelligent cravings. "The truth is, every stomach is like its own chemist, guided by its own principles. So you should pay close attention to her likes and dislikes—observation is key."

I could hear him chewing slowly, swallowing hard. "Observation is key," he said, considering the words. "That's good advice."

It sounded genuine. We ate a few bites in silence. I saw us sitting there with Irina, playing cards or watching a movie, each with our own headset so that we were in our own private theater where no one else could bother us, and then he gets up and goes into the kitchen to micro-wave popcorn and meanwhile Irina and I huddle close together, whispering about this or that, and he rushes back in, tossing the hot bag from one hand to the other, because he doesn't want to miss out on a single moment. Then again, it wouldn't work that way, because if we each had our own headset, we would all be in separate the-aters, divided from the others, and that wouldn't do. I hoped my landlord was wrong about the future; I hoped they would discover that the headset caused brain dam-age and he'd have to throw it away.

"So how does it feel to be engaged?" I asked.

"It's weird being so far away. I just can't wait for her to actually *get* here. She's perfect, like you wouldn't even believe. She could be in movies." He'd nearly cleared his plate, and I scrambled to keep pace, wishing I had some water to wash it down. "Anyway, thanks for being my guinea pig," he said. "I'm hoping to be a decent chef by the time she gets here."

"When will that be?"

"Ding ding, that's the million-dollar question! You wouldn't believe what a process it is just to get her visa. First you have to file all this documentation to prove your relationship is real, which is demeaning enough in itself. These government people going through all your personal stuff. They want to see your photos and receipts, even your phone records. Basically everything short of sleeping in bed between the two of you."

"That sounds terrible."

"And that's just step one. Once it's approved, you've got to wait a month just for it to get to Kiev, as if this isn't the twenty-first century. Then there's more paperwork plus an interview—oh and the fees. There's a fee for everything. A medical exam fee, a processing fee, a fee for processing the processing fee. And none of that includes the plane ticket, of course."

"Jeez. Well, at least you know Irina is worth it."

"I-ri-na," he repeated, drawing it out slowly.

He hadn't told me her name! I froze. My fork quivered in midair, one noodle hooked and trembling. I stared at the noodle. I pictured falling out of my chair, faking cardiac arrest. But by some miracle he seemed to distract himself, forget to pursue the line of thought. "I love to hear her name," he said to the ceiling. "Isn't it beautiful?" He nodded. "You're right. A hundred percent worth it."

"If you want," I said, feeling gutsy again—why should I be on edge when I'd been invited here? In fact *I* was the one doing *him* the favor—"I could come back, to test out another dish."

"Actually, that'd be great. Maybe we could make it a regular thing, a few nights a week or something, until she gets here. You get a free meal, and all I ask in return is your honest opinion."

"Sounds like a plan."

■

There was a time when I ate all my meals in a dining hall across from Nnenna Okafor—who also came from overseas, not Ukraine, but Nigeria, by way of France—though it feels like a lifetime ago now. Nnenna lived across the hall sophomore year. She was the type to avoid doing things on her own, due not to self-consciousness but to a genuine preference for company, and she never altered her personality, no matter who the company included. We began to meet for breakfast, lunch, and dinner, sometimes joined by other people, sometimes just the two of us. I was the better student, so I took her to the library and helped her make study guides, and though she was more often invited to parties, she preferred to have me by her side, mostly so we could rehash everything that happened over breakfast the next morning. She would ask for my take on everyone we'd met and then relay some juicy tidbit about them, always prefacing it with "I know you couldn't care less about gossip, but . . ." Though I did start to care, because she cared.

When it came time to choose housing for junior year, it was a given that we'd room together; we didn't even need to discuss it. And those first few weeks living with her were among the best of my life, our only obstacle being her new boyfriend, Nick, who wasn't a student there, or anywhere—he lived with his parents and didn't seem to have any plan for the future, meaning he was always available and eager to stay over. Nnenna and I agreed that our dorm walls looked sad and prison-like, so I suggested we buy a roll of massive paper and paint pictures to fill the space, almost like our own wallpaper. Nnenna came up with the idea of eating pot brownies first, which turned out to be crucial. We spent an entire Saturday convulsing with laughter and covering the walls with inexplicable portrayals of each other and the people we knew, whimsical creatures, jungle and desert and underwater scenes. The walls became our kind of trademark, with random people stopping by to check them out for themselves.

When I had to leave school, and Nnenna, and everyone else I knew there, my father and brother pleaded with me to move back home. But the more they did, the more impossible it became. To think I could walk around that house like I was one of them, look them in the eye, allow them to waste even one more drop of their grace and kindness on me. They were the only two people in the world who would welcome me in and the only two I couldn't allow to, at least not until I'd done something to deserve it, even marginally. So I was alone, but I figured that would be temporary. I moved into a tiny studio apartment in a large building on a busy, urban block full of people to meet. I employed every conceivable tactic: offering a hand with groceries, attending events advertised on telephone poles, memorizing questions and anecdotes, positioning and repositioning myself near the front door, in the stairwell, by the dumpsters before trash day. But I didn't understand that the state of friendlessness has more inertia than any other, which is why it's also the most dangerous. Over time, you forget what it was like to exist before it, you begin to doubt there ever was a before. My confusion grew so intense, it would make me physically ill. Sometimes it turned into rage, and I would slide my mattress up the wall and pummel it with my fists. I became so helpless that I'd turn off the lights in my apartment on Friday and Saturday nights, as though I owed it to my neighbors to pretend I was out living a life. Then I'd lurk at the window and try to study their comings and goings, what they said, how they moved, in the hope that if I could learn to imitate them, they might mistake me for one of their own. Now I can see that it didn't matter what I did or didn't do. The inertia can only be overcome by a powerful external force, initiated at just the right moment by an independent party, such as a person standing on a porch with a package, asking if you'd be interested in a meal. It can take years for a force like that to come along; indeed, it had.

After we'd finalized our dinner plans, I went up to my apartment and lay in bed, though I had no intention of sleeping. He was no longer just my landlord, he was

Gary—and that couldn't be easily undone. For a few minutes I allowed my imagination to run free, and it constructed all kinds of scenarios, activities Irina, Gary, and I would do, trips we'd take, sights we'd see. I would help with arrangements for their wedding, maybe even participate in the ceremony; what with her family being so far away, I could be the one to calm her nerves and zip her dress. Then I cut my imagination off and sobered up, tried to scrub those fantasies from my head before they went and wrecked everything. But after a while my imagination wrestled free again. So I let it go for another few minutes, then cut it off once more and sobered up again—it went back and forth like that all night.

FOUR

I got out of bed at dawn, a clawing in my large intestine. I sat on the toilet with my exam book spread across my thighs. The condition of my bathroom—sour laundry, mildew, stray hairs, a smell like a dirty fish tank—didn't help the nausea. But who could be expected to spend their days washing and tidying, just to come home and do the same? I wondered whether it was the weight of the world's dust or Gary's chicken piccata that had clogged me up and left me so constipated. *Gary's* chicken piccata. It was still digesting inside me, proof that I hadn't concocted it all in my mind.

Soon all that dust would be Roula's burden again, and I would be an EMT—a *dynamite* EMT, even Doug could see that. Gary and Irina would appreciate having a friend who was a medical professional, who they could call to dress a burn or examine an insect bite.

I gazed down at the page of multiple-choice questions: *0.66 mg; open-book pelvic fracture; all of the above; administer oxygen by non-rebreather mask; prepare for rapid transport.* I knew it all, without even having to think. So then why was it so hard to pass the exam? I'd easily passed the practical part on the first try, but this cognitive one was entirely different. You had to sit alone in a stall across from a cold screen, the only noise coming from your own brain. The instant the silence had settled in the room, my heart tremored and my mouth went dry. I would see the answers in the distance, their distinct edges and shapes, and chase after them as fast as I could, but they kept shrinking smaller and smaller until they dissolved completely. In their place came a storm of unwelcome voices and images, memories I couldn't control or ignore; it only inflamed them when I tried. Then my brain went dark so I could barely read one word after another. The second time, my nose began to bleed.

I'd never had this issue with tests until the point in junior year when I lost it, whatever *it* was. That first time when I signed into the student portal and saw the grade by my name, I wanted to believe it was a typo, the numbers had gotten reversed. I'd hunted down the professor—he went by his first name, Peter—in the hall and rambled about how there had to be a mistake, I'd studied nonstop and memorized all the material, inside and out, front and back. Even though he was on his way out, wearing gym shorts and hugging a basketball, he listened thoughtfully. "How about you try this next time," he said. "When you first get the test, stop and take a few deep breaths. Breathe in, breathe out. When you notice a negative thought crop up, turn it into a banana, and stack them up one by one, until you have a big pile. Then imagine a monkey comes along, and he hasn't eaten in a week." Peter bounced the ball a few times, right there in the hallway. "It might sound silly, but that kind of visualization can work. It doesn't have to be bananas. You've got to have some fun, some perspective, that's what I'm saying. Relax a little." On the way back to my dorm, I repeated to myself, "Turn them into bananas, then a monkey comes along; turn them into bananas, then a monkey comes along."

Nnenna and I had decided to take a random 101 class together, to mix things up and because we'd never get to be classmates otherwise, seeing as her major was film and media studies and mine quantitative economics. She won the series of coin flips and chose Psychology 101, taught by Peter, who turned out to be the most remarkable professor I ever had, so I am at least indebted to her for that. Whenever Peter spoke into the microphone at the front of the lecture hall, I became convinced he was speaking directly to me, that somehow he knew everything about me, every feeling and problem, every question and struggle and dream, knew them better than even

I. Though he appeared to be simply reviewing a chapter from the textbook, he always had a hidden message for me to decode, and he'd fix his gaze on me, particularly during the parts he knew would hit the hardest. Nobody could tell stories better than Peter. He'd get everybody stirring in their seats, while I for one could get so moved I'd have to spring from my chair and exercise my legs at the back of the hall. After, Nnenna would laugh at me affectionately, calling me a Disciple of Saint Peter. Though psychology had never been my favorite subject, I planned to take every course he taught, maybe even add it as a double major or a minor—though I never got that far.

I closed my exam book and schlepped out of the bathroom, the knot in my gut growing and twisting. The National Registry of Emergency Medical Technicians gives you three chances to pass; after that, your only option is to enter a humiliating remedial program, and that would be no option for me, emotionally or financially. I needed to ensure that this time would be different. Knowledge can't leak out of a person's body like brown juice from a trash bag, so I just had to find a way to coax it to the surface and lock it there. I needed help, guidance from someone I could trust.

I opened my laptop. I had an email from my father. The subject line read "Urgent," so I knew the content by heart: please get in touch with him right away, he understood that I still needed space, but I had promised not to go so long again without checking in; he couldn't help but worry and just wanted to know I was okay and hear how things were going. My brother was included on the email too. I despised myself for clicking away, but I didn't have the capacity right then. I would come back to it later, as soon as I could.

I pulled up the university website. The sight of it made the breath clot at the back of my throat. But with just a few clicks, I discovered that the most remarkable professor I ever had was teaching two classes during summer session, including today, at one o'clock. A drop of blood fell onto my keyboard. I found I had bitten all the nails off my left hand and was chewing on them. I sucked the blood from my finger. I hadn't stepped foot on campus in almost six years; I hadn't planned to ever again. But one o'clock today—that had to be a sign. After all, he was the person who'd led me, however indirectly, to Florence Nightingale, and thus to my calling,

I left a message for Doug, saying I couldn't make it in as I was suffering from a digestive issue, though that seemed to have cleared itself up. I took the bus to the train to the shuttle, a two-and-a-half-hour journey in total, and stepped onto campus. I walked full speed toward the lecture hall with my head down, passing what I knew to be broad leafy trees and wrought iron benches and brick buildings padded with vines but refusing to look up and let them suck me into the past. But just the smell in the air and the sound of my shoes on the pavement were enough. Soon Nnenna was beside me, the two of us power-walking as fast as we could without breaking into an embarrassing all-out run after we'd snoozed the alarm too many times. Racing, occasionally sticking a leg out as an obstacle or giving a light push to throw the other off. Once we'd made it to our seats, she'd peel back the neck of my shirt to see how damp and flushed my skin had become, while she was still as cool as could be—she always got a big kick out of that.

I was early. I chose a seat toward the back, regularly checking over both shoulders for anyone who might question me. I sat through a lackluster art history class, waited for those students to file out and new ones to file in, and then Peter finally made his way down to the podium. I almost got up and ran. I tried to concentrate on him, imagining we were alone in another place and time, another planet in another galaxy. He looked the same, just with more gray in his hair. He was attractive but had these ears that stuck out from his head and made his attractiveness more approachable; he called them his propellers. I'd never seen him in a short-sleeved shirt before. His upper arms were wide as loaves of bread, filling his sleeves.

While the last stragglers trickled in, his eyes tunneled into me just as they had when I was a student. My back and shoulder muscles bristled. Today they were discussing process theories of motivation: reinforcement theory, equity theory, goal-setting theory, expectancy theory— when he reached this one he abandoned his PowerPoint and began pacing, which meant he was about to get to something good. "Now, here's an incredible study for you," he said. "So, our team of fearless researchers gets three hundred people together. Regular Jacks and Jills, except that they all suffer from chronic arm pain. The researchers randomly assign them into one of two groups." He drew two large circles on the whiteboard. "Now, this group, they're going to try a new experimental pain medication. While these guys will be getting acupuncture treatments." He drew a giant pill inside one circle and in the other, a body with massive cartoonish arm muscles, a bunch of needles sticking out of them. "This guy works out a lot, you know, when he's not suffering in pain. So, they sit each group down and go through the details of the treatment they'll be receiving, along with any possible side effects, like, say, fatigue or swelling." He tried unsuccessfully to make one arm look swollen. "Well, this guy was already swole, what can we do." We chuckled. "Over the next ten weeks, both groups report a reduction in pain levels, though many also report experiencing side effects, the very ones they'd been told to watch out for. And—every pharmaceutical company's worst nightmare, a direct threat to Western medicine as we know it—the acupuncture group reports even better results than the pill group." He drew stars around the acupuncture circle. "But, my friends, that is not the incredible part. The incredible part is that the pain pills were made of corn starch, and the acupuncture needles were shams that never even broke the skin." He drew a big X through both circles and wrote "SHAM!!"

The placebo effect, of course—it was one of Peter's most beloved topics. He shot me a look and paused to sip from his water bottle; he wanted his message to land. I worked to unravel it while he went on with the lesson.

Those people with chronic arm pain just needed a little outside help—a regimen of pills to swallow or acupuncture appointments to attend—in order to get their mind and body to agree to work together. That was all I needed too. A regimen, a prescribed therapy, working from the outside in, inspiring my mind and body to join forces. A placebo activates your expectations for results, and then you experience results. Expectations, results. Just like with chronic arm pain, the healing would gradually begin to feel imminent, unavoidable. By the time August 25 came around, my test-taking problem would be cured.

It might not be common practice to placebo oneself, but why not try? Weren't we all doing it to some extent every day anyway? Telling ourselves mind over matter, think positively, visualize, manifest, fake it till you make it. Delusion was an accepted part of life. So why not take a more formalized, clinical approach?

When class ended and the students had shuffled out, it was only Peter and his new TA left up front and me in the back. I knew I should leave, but something compelled me to stay. The two of them climbed the stairs, toting folders and laptops. Peter paused at the end of my row, while his TA carried on alone. Suddenly my bladder felt full, and I had to squeeze my thighs together. "Amy? I thought that was you. Wow, it's been what? A few years at least. How are you doing? I hope you've been taking care of yourself."

I had to push my mouth open with my tongue to get it to move. He had recognized me and remembered my name. "Yes."

"So, you're back on campus. What are—is that okay, you being here?"

The TA stood lurking by the door. He had a patchy beard and a staring problem. "It was just a quick visit, just this once," I said. "I'm leaving right now." I rooted my feet on the ground and set my hands on my thighs.

"Well then, I'm glad to see you, see you're doing well." He rearranged the items in his arms as if to get a better grip, though they already looked secure. "Let me just say." He stepped closer and lowered his voice. "For what it's worth, that was an incredibly difficult time back then, I know. The things we do during a time like that, they don't define us."

My head was full of a thousand hot bricks, but I finally managed to nod it, and Peter nodded in return. Then he climbed the rest of the stairs to where his new TA stood, pretending not to eavesdrop. As they passed through the door, they laughed, and the laughter felt pointed and vicious. I told myself it was just some inside joke that had nothing to do with me, but I still felt ashamed of my existence.

On the train ride home, I was surrounded by a mob of lanky young girls. They wore leotards with shorts pulled over and slick buns in their hair, and some carried gym bags printed with the words "Boston Ballet." I figured they must be part of a summer program for gifted youth—the luckiest thing in the world to be—and as I contemplated what it must feel like to balance on the very tips of one's toes, it came to me, the reason why the laughter had sounded so pointed, so vicious. It was that new TA. He'd grown a patchy beard, but it was certainly him, August Eccles, a student from my class and not even an exceptional one, one who was always more eager to speak than to listen, who regularly overslept and bragged about how little he'd studied. Once, after class, August and his friend had been walking up the stairs while I was walking down—to ask Peter a follow-up question about something in the lecture—and as they passed me, I heard August whisper to his friend, "Hope Peter's ready to get his dick sucked."

Back home, I tried to forget about August Eccles and focus solely on following Peter's guidance. I remembered him describing the importance of details in a placebo treatment, how the size and shape and color of a sugar pill all make a difference when it comes to activating the right expectations, such as blue for a sedative, red for a stimulant. We have an innate preference for bright colors and brand names, for capsules over tablets, the bigger the better. Some doctors use the term *obecalp—placebo* spelled backward—for a little extra nudge. As my own prescriber, I had to ensure that my patient's obecalp had the proper appearance, official and authentic. I spent a while searching Google and the NREMT website, gathering information, copying down language. In a new Word document, I typed a letter dated September 1, a week after my exam date.

Dear Amy Hanley,

Congratulations! We are pleased to inform you that you have passed the National Registry of Emergency Medical Technicians EMS cognitive exam and have successfully obtained your National EMS Certification at the NREMT-B level. You have demonstrated your competency as an EMS professional and your commitment to protecting the health and well-being of your community.

Your certification will remain valid for two years. You are responsible for completing the recertification process before the expiration

*date, and can find all pertinent information and
instructions on our website, www.nremt.org.*

*Please note that your current certification allows
you to use the post-nominal notation "NREMT."*

*On behalf of myself and my colleagues, I
would like to commend you on this significant
achievement and extend my best wishes for a long
and distinguished career.*

Sincerely yours,

Randall A. D'Souza, MS, NRP, LP, AEMCA

Executive Director

I left space for his signature and pasted in the NREMT logo to create a letterhead, getting the formatting just right. It looked legitimate. Now I needed a printer.

How lucky to have a door to knock on! It was no longer intimidating, now that I'd been on the other side of it. I stood there knocking for quite a while, so long that I started to feel hot and wonder if I was an idiot for thinking he would open the door just because we'd shared one dinner and made plans to share more, or for believing that he ever intended to follow through on those plans. But no, when the door finally swung open, Gary of course was happy to help—it was only that he'd been wearing his VR headset and hadn't heard me knocking.

I hovered close by as his printer sputtered out a neat, professional copy. "This is just some paperwork," I explained. "Since I finally passed my EMT exam. Officially a certified EMT. Though I still have to wait on a couple things in the mail and get my state license, then find a job and all that. I'm still going to finish out the summer at the yacht club."

"Congratulations," he said. "Wow. That's great news." He was holding the headset, fingering the strap.

"Were you watching a movie in your own private theater?"

"Actually, I was driving a race car." He laughed. "I thought I was going to puke."

I escorted the letter back up to my apartment and positioned it over my computer screen so I could trace Randall D'Souza's signature, channeling him as I swooped my pen through his big, confident *R*. I typed an email back to my father and brother, sharing the fantastic news that I was officially a certified EMT—things weren't just okay, they were better than ever—and promising to write again soon and visit too, once I'd settled into a position and had some exciting stories from on the job. I hesitated before pressing send. But plenty of doctors and researchers have used a little deception to achieve amazing results, so I shouldn't feel guilty about doing the same. For my obecalp to be effective, I had to convince myself that it was real, and I would be more convinced if other people were convinced too.

I slid the letter into an envelope and placed a stamp

in the corner. I'd drop it in a mailbox tomorrow so I got the thrill of having it arrive at my door. That would signify the official start of Phase I. Before I sealed the flap, I read through it one last time. *Congratulations, congratulations, congratulations.*

FIVE

When I knocked for our second dinner, Gary opened the door straightaway, as though he'd been waiting on the other side, hand poised over the knob. "Ah," he said, with an air of mock formality. He had a dish towel thrown over his shoulder in a deliberate way, and now he whisked it off, bowing slightly. "Table for two? Right this way, please." He ushered me into the kitchen and stood back so I could take it in—a brand-new table, just as I'd suggested the first night. He'd decorated it with a maroon cloth and a glass vase of fake roses. There were two sets of silverware, two glasses of water, two chairs with upholstered seats, waiting for us. I got choked up when I saw all that.

"So? Big upgrade, huh? And these look just like the

real deal, don't they? Irina loves flowers. She said she's always wanted a house with flowers in every room. Smell." He lifted the vase to my nose. "They spray them with this special perfume so they even smell like the real thing. Only $6.99, and these will last forever. A much smarter investment."

The roses were stiff and too shiny, and the perfume made my nostrils burn. "The table is perfect, I love it. But I'm on the fence with these. Don't you think she might prefer real ones? It's just, the smart investment isn't always the most romantic."

He set them down. "I don't see what's so romantic about watching something shrivel up and die." He went to the counter and picked up the recipe, a plastic-covered sheet with large color photographs. "But I guess you might have a point." He dumped green onions from a pre-portioned bag onto a cutting board and chopped them. "Just look at her." With the tip of his knife, he pointed to a framed photograph set on top of the microwave, Irina in her red turtleneck. "You wouldn't think in a million years that someone like me could end up with someone like her, right? I mean, it's like I drew her up in my head. But it's not just that. She really cares about me, you know. I never met anyone like her. Oh, have a seat, make yourself comfortable. You'll be the first to try out those chairs. I think maybe it's partly because women in her country tend to be more traditional. They really *want* to have a husband and a family, they value those things over everything else. We all deserve love, and you never know where you're going to find it.

"Sorry, I'm feeling kind of sentimental tonight. I don't get the chance to talk about her much." His phone chirped, and he pulled a pan from the oven, breathing heat into the room. "This has to sit for a few minutes." He reset the timer on his phone. "I haven't told anyone at work. People always have their opinions."

He hadn't told anyone at work, but he had told me. I grasped the edge of the tablecloth and screwed it tight around my finger. The thing to do was not dwell on such a marvelous confession in the moment but to return to it later when alone, celebrate it then. In my breeziest voice, I said, "And what is it that you do exactly—for work?"

"Oh, I'm an architect. I guess I never mentioned it."

No, he hadn't mentioned it, and I'd never come across any evidence of it in his mail. He'd received a notice about a change in health care benefits from a company with an ambiguous name where I'd always imagined him doing something like accounting or IT support. He brought in his laptop to show me a 3D rendering of a house. He made it rotate and zoom in and out, revealing each room and surprise features like a staircase that unfolded from a wall. "A micro house I'm working on," he said. "People are really getting into the whole micro house thing. It's more sustainable for the environment, and more afford-able. They want to, you know, simplify. I wouldn't be able to stand it myself. But I figure it makes some sense. Plus it's kind of fun, trying to come up with ways to fit everything inside a few hundred square feet."

I was mesmerized, watching the rotating house. He could form a vision in his mind and then use some special computer program to make that vision come to life. "Amazing," I said.

"This is just in my own time. Most of what I do at the office is commercial stuff. This is more for fun." His phone chirped again, and he closed the laptop. "Don't get me wrong, I like my job and the people I work with—I'm really lucky in that way. But I'm not sure they'd understand about Irina." He divvied up the food and brought our plates to the table. "Cheesy enchiladas rojas with cilantro cream and a side of black beans. That's why you seem like a good person to be helping me out. You're more positive, open-minded. Most people aren't like that, in my experience at least."

"People can be quick to make assumptions."

"And they love to gossip. It starts to eat at you after a while. You can't help it."

"You can't judge a situation from the outside."

"Exactly. That's what I always say." He sawed his enchilada and watched the steam waft out. "When I'm designing, there's a level of certainty there. I just have to focus on being precise, thorough. Those are the kinds of problems I like to deal with."

Now that we were sitting across from each other at the new kitchen table, I noticed how his teeth were a polished white, straight, and perfectly aligned, though not in a phony way. I ignored the sag of flesh under his chin and instead looked forward to the next glimpse of his teeth, the flash when he took a bite or pronounced a certain word. They seemed resistant to food particles. Perhaps this was what it was like to see Gary through Irina's eyes, her true love, her one and only. I wondered what else she saw.

"So dealing with something like *this*, when it's all out of your control . . ." He flicked his hand to say forget it, impossible. "I mean, somehow I found Irina. I can't believe how lucky I got. But then you're forced to put the fate of your relationship into someone else's hands—and it's the government's, at that. They get to decide when she comes, *if* she comes. And then when she finally gets here, they only give us ninety days."

"What do you mean?"

"Like an expiration date," he said. "We have to get married within ninety days, or else she has to go back. To Ukraine."

"But you'll get married, right?"

"God, I hope so. That's the plan. But we never lived together before. I only ever spent a few days with her in person, which probably sounds crazy." His eyes flickered up at me, then quickly away. "But we'd been talking a lot before, video chatting for hours. There was something different with her, right from the beginning, like it just flowed. Then as soon as I saw her in person, I knew that was it, I had to propose. But you can just imagine the kind of pressure I'm under. Ninety days to figure everything out, convince her to spend the rest of her life here, away from her family and friends, everything she knows. But I have to have faith. That's what she tells me. And I do, I have faith." He chewed with his eyes fixed on the photo of Irina on top of the microwave. "I hope you don't think I'm too crazy now."

"I think you're the perfect amount of crazy."

He smiled and ate another few bites. "So," he said. "What made you decide you wanted to become an EMT? I'm always the one dominating the conversation. I never even ask you about yourself."

"It's okay, I like listening. I want to be someone who listens, and cares and helps. That's what it means to be an EMT. You get to do good deeds every day. You don't have a choice, even if you're feeling selfish or tired, or whatever. I think of it more like a calling than a job."

"It's good to have a calling."

"Florence Nightingale—she's a hero of mine—she heard her calling at a young age, but at the time she didn't know exactly what it meant. She didn't start training as a nurse until nine years later. That's sort of like with me. It took some time for me to figure out the details. But now I'm finally at the finish line."

His fork clattered to his plate. "These are soggy, aren't they? But I followed everything exactly. And I took it out at fifteen minutes on the dot."

"They aren't too soggy. They taste just like in a restaurant. The only thing I'd say is the black beans might have a tad too much salt."

"You know what, these recipes, they give you exact measurements for everything except salt and pepper. For that it just says 'to taste.' Well, what happens if you go and taste it, and it's already ruined? The whole point is for them to tell you the measurements. Or what am I paying them for?"

"It's not ruined, just the teeniest bit salty. And that's just me, everyone's different. Irina, she might think it's not salty enough."

"You can't tell me these aren't soggy." He rocked himself to his feet. "See, right here. It says three-fifty for fifteen minutes." He slammed his palm down on the counter. I wasn't sure if he wanted me to respond or disappear, but I understood where his outburst was coming from: we needed Irina to be comfortable, to be happy, to stay. And we would only have ninety days.

"Twenty-three dollars per meal," he said. "I don't like to feel I'm being taken advantage of."

"You're doing a good job, really. And it will only get easier."

He returned to the table, and we kept eating. I leaned my head over my plate to avoid dripping on the new tablecloth. When it seemed sufficient time had passed, I said, "Irina loves you. That's the most important thing. She won't care if everything isn't perfect. But . . ." I paused.

He looked dejected but not unreachable. "But if she sees you get so upset over some tortillas, she might get worried, or blame herself. She probably prefers it when you're calm, cool, and collected."

He sighed. "Yeah. You're probably right." He took my plate and stacked it on top of his. "And no matter what, this will be a whole lot nicer than where she grew up. She took me to her parents' house . . ." His tone implied something harrowing, something that he couldn't even begin to describe, though he seemed to cheer up thinking of it. "I should stock up on wine, to go with dinner. She'd like that."

"Wine might help you both relax."

After we said good night and I'd started for the front door, I heard a rustle behind me. I turned just in time to see him dumping the fake roses into the trash can under the sink.

At my refrigerator, I read my congratulations letter aloud. *Congratulations, congratulations, congratulations.* The letter had promptly made its way back to my apartment, delivered by the unsuspecting mail carrier, and was now fixed to the refrigerator door, where I read it aloud every morning and evening, whether or not I was in the mood. Ritual and repetition were key. I'd received emails back from my father and brother. They were proud of me and not at all surprised by my success and glad to know I was keeping busy, though I had to keep my word this time about not going so long without checking in, especially since they couldn't wait to hear about my new job and all the exciting things I was up to.

Over the next couple weeks I became a regular at Gary's, someone who knew her way around and could make herself comfortable—how ironic, I thought, that the word *regular* should describe something so extraordinary. This new routine with Gary gave me a bolt of energy that I channeled into being both a chambermaid and an EMT, which were even more complementary than I anticipated. The other morning, for instance, I entered room 3 as though responding to a 911 call and practiced procedure for a scene size-up, estimating the general extent of the incident (or mess) and scanning for potential hazards, which could be conspicuous, like a spill of gasoline (or mouthwash), or inconspicuous, like the fumes from an industrial tank (or a can of hair spray). In room 4, I honed my visual memory and clue-probing skills with an exercise. Stepping inside, I looked around and took note of the guest's belongings, storing every detail up in my head. Then I closed the door, listed everything I could remember, and reentered to judge my accuracy. I had easily retained the entire dresser top: one monogrammed handkerchief—folded; three hard candies—yellowish color (caramel? choking hazard); sunglasses—one pair, no case; one hook of single-use dental floss; one tin of shoe polish (cap screwed on? potential toxicity?); one flag-shaped pin (sharp point hidden); one vial of artificial tears. I couldn't help but rejoice when my list turned out to be impressively accurate and thorough.

They'd left the toilet in a gruesome state, but that offered another opportunity for practice. I approached it as an obstructed airway, offering a simple introduction to reassure the patient and judge her responsiveness: "My name is Amy Hanley, and I'm a certified EMT. I'm here to help you." I held up the certification card that I'd printed on cardstock and laminated at an office supply store and then mailed to my apartment to initiate Phase II of my obecalp. I'd assigned myself a registry number, E4068211, and spent hours replicating the font, the layout, the shades of blue. I found all the information I needed on Google Images, even what text to overlay in small print across the logo on the back, such as "This card is the property of the NREMT and must be surrendered upon request." This new phase involved not only starting and ending each day reading my congratulations letter but also carrying the card with me at all times and occasionally presenting it to myself or a "patient."

Once I sank the plunger into the swamp, I had to forget about all that EMT stuff and focus only on breathing through my mouth. I pumped and pumped while the swamp gurgled and sloshed. When at last the clog broke free, I held my nose under my shirt and sprinkled bleach, scouring the bowl with a hard-bristled brush as though I were responsible for a crime and not a valuable service. Extraordinary people didn't seek recognition. Florence Nightingale sometimes used a pseudonym: Miss Smith. Still history remembers her.

Halfway through cleaning, I turned on the television— it was now my policy to wait until at least halfway through, a well-deserved treat. A woman on a reality show was hosting a glamorous fundraiser for a children's hospital, and after surveying the event she turned to a friend and said, "This is my city." She cackled. That phrase and that cackle rattled around my head as I Windexed the mirror, so that I couldn't help catching my own face in the glass and feeling that this face owned not only the mirror but also the bed and the curtains, the whole building, and every last boat out in the harbor.

I felt so invincible that, after making sure Doug was busy in his office, I snuck out onto the harbor-floor deck. A few of the servers, Vinny and Bridget and the pigeon-toed one, were making rounds to the tables out there. I had successfully avoided all of them for weeks and still wished to, though it felt less urgent now. I wedged behind two women standing in the far corner drinking martinis, their bright manicured fingernails spiraled around their glasses, their hair flapping a bit in the breeze. Every so often they reached up to smooth a piece of it down. I wasn't particularly interested in these women, I only wanted to take in some of the salty air and see who was on the dock and watch the water cradle the boats, but there they were, discussing diet trends in intrusive, actressy voices. "They just hook you up to an IV so, you know, you get all the essential nutrients. That way you don't actually have to eat anything. Avery did it before her wedding, Mel's friend? You have to be kind of insane, but it does work."

My lips parted. It was an appalling misuse of medical equipment and personnel, but I didn't intend to speak up because I wasn't particularly interested in these women, plus I wasn't supposed to be on the deck in the first place. However, they seemed to think I *was* interested because one of them said, "She probably thinks we're out of our minds," and the "she" was me.

"No." I tried to sound good-humored, but they'd included me in the worst kind of way, and I had the sudden urge to cry.

"Don't mind her," the other one said, uncurling a finger from her glass to point at her friend. "She's high off divorce."

"Heather!" the first one said, slapping her friend's arm.

"Watch it! You're going to make me spill."

My lips trembled and I darted away, blocking my face from Vinny as he delivered fresh martinis. I understood why the deck was meant for members only. But it wasn't just that. I found myself unsteady on the stairs, leaning on the banister and thinking of Nnenna, feeling her absence like a cave beside me, like I might fall into it. Whenever we were laughing, really laughing, she'd go limp on my arm and say, "Save me, save me." She was a toucher and a hugger, and it had surprised me how much I enjoyed that, the sensation that my body was just an extension of hers. In an alternate universe, it could've been us standing there drinking martinis, or doing something else, whatever we wanted.

To console myself, I made some minor adjustments to the next room. I gave the lampshade a playful little tilt, as though it were tipping its hat, then opened and closed a curling iron until it became a mouth chatting with me. A cardigan with pearl buttons had been tossed on the dresser and I folded one of its sleeves across so it could hold its own heart. In the bathroom I retracted the fangs of an electric shaver and swished the belt on a robe, the tail of a pet eager to greet me. As I worked the toiletries into a group pose, I spotted *chitin* among the ingredients on a label, and that one word gave me the fuel I needed to finish the day. Chitin comes from the exoskeletons of horseshoe crabs and has moisturizing properties, but it is hardly the true contribution of the horseshoe crab. The true contribution is its blood, which has the rare ability to detect and trap bacteria and so is used to test the safety of our doctors' injections. We pluck these medieval-looking creatures from the ocean floor to harvest their blood, and while most survive and are returned to their habitat, some inevitably lose their lives. I like to believe they are willing participants, despite their hard-armored appearance, because they understand that nothing of value can be accomplished without sacrifice. It can't be avoided. Even Marie Curie—for years while she studied, she survived on tea and buttered bread.

■

That evening I was back at Gary's front door, which he'd started leaving unlocked in anticipation of me. I could hear music drifting out from inside. Gary had never played music before, and I entered hesitantly, inching through the living room toward the kitchen, where I spotted the silhouette of a woman. She sat at his kitchen table pressing the end of a cigarette into a dish. Irina? She could have arrived early and been kept secret, a surprise for me. I had the impulse to run back upstairs to check my breath and change my clothes. But as my eyes adjusted, I realized she bore little resemblance to the woman in the red turtleneck. "Oh, sorry," I said as a way of announcing myself.

Gary turned from the stove, a wooden spoon in one hand. "Amy!" He cupped his other hand under to catch a drip. "Come in. Meet my mother. A surprise visit. I tried knocking on your door, but you must not have been home yet."

"Oh, sorry. That's all right," I said, taking a step backward. "I'll just see you next time."

"No, stay. She isn't even hungry, for some reason. I made two servings."

"Yes, stay," his mother said. "We're better when we have a third party."

"Ignore her," Gary said.

She laughed, so I did too. I liked the hearty sound of her laugh and the look of her. She wore long earrings and three beaded necklaces that came alive as she moved. She was thin and didn't seem to share any physical traits with Gary. She took up one of the kitchen chairs, which left the other empty, for Gary, so I dragged in an armchair from the living room. It sank me down low and set my head adrift above the table like a balloon. The music came from a vintage-style radio set on top of the microwave, where Irina's photograph used to be. It was tuned to classic rock, the Rolling Stones.

"You might splurge for another chair," his mother said, watching me.

"You're lucky I even have a table. You have to thank Amy for that. I'd be lost without her. We'd all be sitting on the floor. Surrounded by ugly fake flowers. Those really *were* ugly."

"Well then, thank god for Amy."

"Yes, thank god for Amy." Gary poured glasses of water and wine for the three of us with a steady, confident hand. "Lamb and beef tagine with herb couscous and labneh," he said, leaving his mother's place empty.

"Labneh?" I asked, inhaling the delicious aroma.

"The white stuff. It seems kind of like yogurt. But I didn't have a chance to read the description. What with my dear mother showing up out of the blue."

Gary and I began to eat. It felt odd with his mother just sitting there, watching and sifting the beads of her necklaces through her hands. "So . . . is it that you're scared of Gary's cooking?" I said.

He laughed emphatically. "She once ate a soup made of bird saliva! I'm not kidding."

I chewed slowly, unsure whether a punch line was coming.

She dismissed him with her hand. "He loves bringing that up, just to get a reaction. Bird's nest soup. I paid good money for it at one of the best restaurants in Hong Kong, and I loved every bite. It's known as the Caviar of the East, actually."

He snorted.

"And why not?" She finished her wine and went to the counter. "Everything's arbitrary." She filled her glass with ice, vodka, and tonic water.

"She's a relativist," Gary said.

"Gold—why not apples? Or vodka, or wampum beads." She sashayed back to the table, drink overflowing, and slurped the drippings off her hand.

"Wow, Hong Kong. So have you done a lot of traveling?" I said.

"More countries than I have fingers and toes." She grinned. "He hates when I say that."

"She's a citizen of the world," Gary said sarcastically. He patted her arm.

"As we *all* are. Or should be. There's nothing more arbitrary than borders. And yet we like to act as though they were ordained by God himself." Gary groaned. "We better change the subject or my son will pop a blood vessel. He says I try to make traveling seem like some noble act, when the truth is I'm just—what was it? Bored and self-righteous, I think it was." She thumped her empty glass down onto the table. "And he's not completely wrong," she whispered, "but don't tell him I said that. What's the difference anyway? It makes me feel alive— kind of like *video games* do for other people." Now she patted his arm. They were needling each other but in a toothless way, as though this was how they showed affection, and it was nice, witnessing that, but also left me with a hollowness in my gut. I wondered if it had always come so naturally to them or if it was a later development, one that all adult children eventually reached with their mothers.

"My brother's in the Peace Corps," I said. "In Burkina Faso."

"How exciting!"

"But for who?" Gary said. "Sorry, I just wish people would be more honest about that kind of thing. They might do some good here and there, but mostly they're just patting themselves on the back and paving the way for more Coca-Cola products. It's arrogant, if you ask me.

Not to mention completely counterproductive. I read that some people are actually giving up their kids to orphanages, just so more volunteers will come to town and bring their tourist money—" He cut himself off. "No offense to your brother."

"Expert cynicism. Perfected over many years," his mother said. "So, do you plan on visiting while he's there?"

"We aren't that close anymore. Not that I don't want to be, I do . . ." I could sense my lips wavering and moved my hand in front, pretending to have an itch under my nose. I knew my detachment was hard for my brother, and my father, though they tried not to show it, so as not to scare me off more. This had always made me feel guilty but also more certain of my obligation to protect them from what they didn't understand: that it would be much worse to have me around. I'd told myself I would rejoin their lives just as soon as I could trust myself not to destroy them. But now, as I imagined explaining that to Gary and his mother between bites of tagine, it all sounded so flimsy.

"But I'd like to visit, maybe, one day," I said. Those thoughts would drown me right here at the table if I let them. I sipped my wine and searched for a new topic. "So, are you happy Gary's marrying someone from another country?"

They both laughed. "Sure," she said. "Even if I *did* just find out about it. I mean, not because of where she's from. That makes no difference to me. I have some concerns about the whole thing, of course. But any parent just wants to see their kids happy and getting what they want, whatever that is." I felt my eyes cut away, as though she meant it as an accusation. "And for Gary, that's always been the traditional life, white picket fence, station wagon, two and a half kids. I was worried he'd never put himself out there again. He's very talented and he's got a big heart, but he's always been sort of a late bloomer." Gleefully, she plucked a chunk of lamb from Gary's plate and dropped it into her mouth.

"I'd say I'm doing pretty well," he said. "For someone who was raised by the 'gravy lady.'" He looked at her expectantly, and a laugh shot up her throat so fast that she had to clap her hand over her mouth to keep from spitting out the bite.

"Oh my god," she said. "I haven't thought about that in years."

I shifted my focus between them, realizing they weren't going to explain anything for my benefit but still content to be among them and feeling soothed by the radio and its steady churn of music, one song leaking into the next. This was a new side of Gary. No more agonizing over what Irina would think of this or that or blabbing on about how perfect she was; he was relaxed and comfortable, he had opinions and interests, he was sure of himself—and being around his mother and me had brought that out of him. Maybe Irina wasn't such a positive force in his life after all.

"I almost forgot," Gary said, standing. "Don't fill up."

He got a square box from the fridge and held it so I could look through the plastic window on top. "Store-bought, obviously. So I couldn't mess it up." Inside was a cake with icing piped into the shapes of a stethoscope and a Band-Aid and cursive letters that read *Congratulations, Amy!* "I know it was a while ago—I kept meaning to pick one up. Better late than never, I guess. I told them just to draw whatever medical stuff they could. Though I can't imagine you'd use too many Band-Aids."

I gaped at it, my mouth completely dry. Even my eyeballs felt dry when I blinked. "It looks amazing. Wow. You really didn't have to do that."

"And what are we congratulating exactly?"

"Amy passing her EMT exam."

Gary had ordered this magnificent cake just for me and shared my news with his mother, and that meant it was all working, better than I could have hoped. There was no room for hesitation or second thoughts now. Simply feel, believe, soak it in.

"Congratulations," she said.

"Thank you," I replied. Feel, believe, soak it in. "Here, I can cut it." I took the knife from Gary. I was no different from any other newly certified EMT cutting a cake a proud friend had purchased in recognition of my significant accomplishment, one that marked the start of an exciting and fulfilling new life that I'd worked hard for and deserved to celebrate.

"I could never handle all that life-and-death stuff on a daily basis," Gary's mother said. "I do everything I can to avoid thinking about mortality. Especially my own."

"Nobody *likes* to think about mortality," he said. "But we're lucky that some people are willing to confront it. For the sake of the rest of us." He tipped his head to me in deference. The two of us ate big slices of cake, while his mother shooed it away. "She knows everything," he said to her between bites. "Seriously. Ask her. Any medical question."

"You know I get all my medical advice from traditional Chinese healers." She got up and tousled the hair on Gary's head. "And *The Today Show.*" She planted a playful kiss on his cheek. "We don't agree on much, but I wouldn't change a thing. My baby." She tugged on the skin she'd just kissed.

She wheeled the dial on the radio through blips of static and voices and tunes until she found Kiss 108, a pop music station. "Top Forty countdown. My guilty pleasure. Gary's a real music snob, as I'm sure you've figured out by now. Has he shown you his record collection upstairs?"

"Right, because having any kind of taste automatically makes you a snob. I can appreciate *plenty* of music, just not this crap. Makes me feel like my teeth are rotting."

"Why mess with a formula if it works? Give the people what they want!" She turned up the volume and swayed and grooved to a sugary song. She moved naturally, like someone who knows she's magnetic. From what I could gather, the song was about staying up all night and having no regrets and being addicted to somebody's love. It switched to a commercial for a local water park, and she took a pack of cigarettes from her bag. "Quick smoke," she said, and went out onto the back deck, the screen door rasping closed behind her.

"That's probably what's killing her appetite," I said.

"I think that's the point."

"Doesn't it concern you, though? Smoking's responsible for one in five deaths in the United States."

"She's heard it all." He licked frosting off his fork and scraped it across his plate. "It's not any more dangerous than carrying all this around." He caught the flab of his stomach between two fingers, jiggled it.

"Well, that's—maybe." I looked down at my own stomach, invisible behind the drape of my T-shirt, my cheeks flaming. Of course I nitpicked parts of my body and my face, especially as a teenager, but I'd always been smaller than average, without trying.

"Yeah. I used to try out a new diet every couple of years. But it never stuck and then I'd wind up feeling even worse than before. Then when I met Irina, it turned out she liked me the way I was. She says in other countries, being overweight can be kind of a good thing, especially for men, since it's a sign that you're probably well off. Hopefully she doesn't change her mind once she's living here."

"What did that mean, 'gravy lady'?"

"Oh, that's just an inside joke, from a million years ago. Long story." Gary huffed as he got to his feet and cleared our plates.

"The cake was delicious, thank you so much. That was so nice of you."

"I'll put some in a Tupperware for you. I shouldn't be left alone with the rest of it."

A song with a catchy, upbeat chorus came blaring through the radio, and we could hear Gary's mother outside singing and stamping her foot to the rhythm. "Your mom is cool," I said.

"I know." He watched her through the screen door. "I think coolness always skips a generation. It's like they have to balance the scales or something, cosmically. Make sure things even out over time."

"I don't think that's true." In my observation, coolness seemed more like a dominant trait, passed down as readily as brown eyes or curly hair. But as I watched him watch her, it occurred to me that this idea was gravely important to him, one he'd spent years willing himself to believe, and I regretted contradicting it. "Anyway, a lot of the time I think being cool looks better than it really is," I said.

"No, I don't mind. Really. It just means my kids will have it easy. They'll fit right in." He sounded resolute, if not especially cheerful. Still, I couldn't help smiling—I felt honored to have a friend like him.

SIX

The next morning marked exactly four weeks and four days until my exam. So, after I read my congratulations letter and tucked my certification card in my pocket, I ordered the supplies for the third and final phase of my obecalp treatment. I strutted to the clubhouse feeling like the mastermind behind a brilliant, trailblazing therapy that would be discussed in textbooks for years to come. "Can you believe it," I said to the plumpest raspberry on Magnolia Street, its tiny hairs tickling my palm. "Can you believe how this summer is just flying by?" As it turned to sugary juice on my tongue, I realized I'd forgotten what that felt like, for time to "fly by." It could be nerve-racking, but I recognized that above all, it was a privilege.

Room 1 was currently being occupied by the same old woman I'd watched stride down the dock with her clanging, singing jewelry during my very first week on the job. Some of that jewelry now sat, I assumed, in the heavy box on the dresser, secured by a combination lock. You could feel the delicious secrets inside it straining for air. The lid had a large gold scallop shell in the middle, rising up like a crown, which meant she shared an impulse with Florence Nightingale, who, when she wasn't saving lives, enjoyed strolling the beach to collect rare shells that she polished with oxalic acid and cherished for years.

I'd learned that the old woman's name was Valerie Calvano—a beautiful, singsongy name—and I'd seen her up close while she stood in the hallway examining the rosewood clock, one face for telling time and another for tracking the hours between high and low tide. She had soft, spongy cheeks painted with rosy circles of blush and two ripe pearls dangling from her earlobes, and I thought, Here is someone who deserves to say "This is *my* city," and probably has said it at least once before. I was so captivated by her face that I had to remind myself of what Florence Nightingale believed: you can't trust a face like you can trust a kidney or a lung, since the face is the part of the body most exposed to outside influences.

After Valerie had finishing examining the clock, she walked to the staircase, then backpedaled to the clock again, at which point she looked over at me—I was pretending to contemplate the dirty linens in my basket—

and said, "I take a few steps and the numbers have already floated right out of my head! It's a wonder I ever make it anywhere on time anymore. Sometimes I say to myself: Now, Valerie, you're leaving the room. Where on earth are you going?" She glided off again before I could respond.

Instead of turning on the television, I tuned the alarm-clock radio to Kiss 108 in honor of Gary's mother. The music instantly perked everything up, even the alarm clock itself, which blinked its festive green light and seemed to almost bop along from its spot on the night-stand. In recent years I'd listened strictly to instrumental music or music sung in a foreign language so I couldn't get too emotionally entangled, the further from English the better, nothing too easily deciphered. A melody could be overwhelming in itself. But now I understood why Gary's mother considered pop music a guilty pleasure. She was right, the formula worked. It filled you up just enough to make you hungry for more. I wondered about Gary's record collection, when I might get the chance to see it, and why he'd never mentioned it before—probably because he was always so preoccupied with talking about Irina. It would have been nice to spend more time with his mother, to hear more about her tastes and her travels, and about many other things, but that was just our initial introduction. Gary had wanted me to meet her, had invited me to stay, and so there would be plenty of other chances for us to get to know each other better. She might even let me persuade her to quit smoking, and she'd have to start calling me at all hours of the day and night to talk her through her cravings, and I would be patient, never indifferent or unbelieving, not even for a moment. She'd tell me I was like the daughter she'd never had, and we'd start making plans, just the two of us, if Gary was busy—I'd forgotten to ask where she lived, but it probably wasn't far, seeing as she'd shown up out of the blue, but even if it was, she loved to travel, she would go a distance if necessary. She'd stick her fingers in her ears whenever I tried to tell her about what I'd seen on the ambulance that day, saying "No, no, no! I prefer not to think about mortality," teasing me the same way she teased Gary, and I would tease back, and soon we'd have our own set of inside jokes to make us laugh and reminisce.

As I stripped the bed, the pop songs roused something else inside me. Soon I was swaying around the room and longing to be in love, to call someone my baby and touch his body, or even to find myself heartbroken, devastated yet determined to prove that I was better off now, I was stronger and sexier and never looking back.

I had almost been in love once, before I left for college, with a boy named Quinn. He was an all-star cross-country runner but the slowest walker, constantly stopping to massage a thigh or brace a foot against a telephone pole to stretch. Randomly he'd get a spurt of energy and accelerate, sprinting off in one direction without warning, then a few minutes later he'd come striding back with no explanation and a smile on his face.

Once, before I knew him well, I'd spotted him in a crowded park sprawled on his back on a picnic table, hiking up his legs in an abdominal exercise, while a family loitered nearby with baskets and coolers, waiting to sit down. That was what had drawn me to him at first. He cleared a place for himself, blind in his passion, and saw the potential in every object, how it could be manipulated to meet his needs. His body was just another piece of equipment, and he was both intimately in tune with it and detached from it, treating it as a separate entity to be monitored and cultivated and catered to, so that any odors or waste it emitted could only be a source of curiosity and never a source of shame. In fact, he once lost control of his bowels while running a marathon—I was rooting him on from behind a rope near the finish line— and just kept on running, even with that mass swinging inside his shorts and brown stripes trickling down his legs.

But after a while, that grew tiresome. He turned out to be more oblivious than bold. The idea that he could do or think or care about anything else never seemed to cross his mind. He had an athletic scholarship, which he valued only for the opportunity to compete, and showed no interest in what my or anyone else's plans might be, not to mention what was happening on the news or out in the world. He was definitively uninspiring, and I couldn't love a person who didn't inspire me. Florence Nightingale turned down numerous proposals and remained single her whole life, believing marriage would only stunt her ambitions. Still, it didn't have to be that way—take Marie Curie and her husband, Pierre. Together they discovered a radioactive element and won the Nobel Prize, and for their wedding, Marie chose a practical blue dress so that afterward she could wear it to work in the laboratory.

After I broke up with him, Quinn parked his car outside my house every afternoon for weeks and sat there, with no indication why, maybe hoping for me to come out, or building up the courage to come in, or simply monitoring my whereabouts. Soon my mother got in my ear, cooing about how romantic it was and demanding to know how I could be so cold. "I'll never understand you," she said for the umpteenth time.

"Don't you get it?" I said, pulling back the curtain and gesturing outside to emphasize how unimaginative and pointless it was, sitting blankly in his father's station wagon until it came time to leave for his evening jog, then repeating it again the next day. "This is the best he can come up with: absolutely nothing!"

My mother sighed, one of her most hopeless-sounding sighs. "It's amazing you were born with that turned-up nose," she said. "Like God was already doing the work for you." She must have felt guilty afterward because for the rest of the night she was my pet, tiptoeing around me and rushing to agree with anything I said.

I left Valerie's bed half made and went to the mirror. I studied the turned-up swoop of my nose, then smashed it down with the heel of my hand. I pressed so hard my eyes watered. It struck me as rather poetic now, what my mother had said about my nose and God doing the work. It made me wonder if she'd had it preplanned. Maybe she'd had a hundred other lines like that stored up in her head and in a diary hidden under her pillow.

A pounding on the door interrupted me. I glanced at my red nose and wet eyes in the mirror and tried to quickly fan my face, imagining Valerie must have returned to collect something. But the pounding turned more furious, much too harsh to come from Valerie's knuckles. I seized the handle of my dustpan just as the door sprang open. Roula. I'd never seen her in shorts, and her bare legs were a grisly sight, covered with squiggly purple varicose veins. As she barged into the room, they seemed about to erupt, to tear through her skin and spill across the floor.

"How many times," Roula said over the music. She went to the television, assuming the sound came from there, then halted, the pressure building in her veins as she stood looking around. Finally she figured it out and hit the power button on the radio. "How many times do I have to say it. You attack the room, in and out, then on to the next. Going down the checklist. You're not getting paid to watch TV. Or listen to the radio." She shook her head and narrowed her voice. "You're lucky, you know. I could walk down right now and tell Doug about what happened last week." She gave me a searing look and disappeared, leaving the door ajar so she could spy on me—that was what humiliated me most.

I retreated into the bathroom and collapsed in the tub. The week before, I'd neglected to swap out the sheets for a new check-in, and though I'd remedied it as soon as the guest arrived, it was a careless mistake that I lamented and that Roula insisted on holding over me, even though she'd probably made the same mistake or worse a hundred times over. I made fingernail marks up and down my thighs. Why hadn't I shown her the way I'd dug every last cobweb from the air-conditioning unit, or how I'd thought to carry up an extra set of fresh towels, just in case Valerie had a need for them? I never got the chance to redeem myself, she made sure of that.

Roula had no idea what it was like to have a calling. Not many people did. Even when I'd finally saved up for an EMT training course, I glanced around the classroom and saw yawns, cell phones, absentminded doodling. I wanted to shake them and scream "The precious gift of life will be placed in your hands!" During breaks, I'd follow them out to where they chewed loud snacks from the vending machine, licking their fingers and shaking the bags over their mouths to get every last crumb. I went along to try to understand them and how it was possible we could share the same goal and yet be so different, but I could never understand, and sometimes I'd catch myself wishing that I would be the one to change. But all the most successful and inspiring people—Florence Nightin-

gale and Marie Curie and Peter—vowed to be conscien-
tious, devoted, indifferent to nothing except the opinions
of others. I would choose suffering over indifference any
day. As Florence Nightingale said, out of nothing comes
nothing, but out of suffering might come the cure—give
me pain over paralysis!

From the bedroom came a terrible, jingling thud. I
dashed out to find Valerie's heavy lock box capsized on the
rug. With my certification card displayed in my palm, I
took a deep breath and pronounced, "My name is Amy
Hanley, and I'm an EMT. I'm here to help you." I couldn't
do a proper top-to-bottom assessment without first moving it, so I lifted the box with all the care I would give a
patient, wincing as the precious items inside shifted and
chimed, and set it back on the dresser. The combination
lock was secure, but the scallop shell had a chip missing
and a horrifying jagged line running down the middle
of it. I could not be held accountable here—it wasn't the
music but Roula that had disrupted the flow of my work,
and she'd disturbed Valerie's belongings with her unnec-
essary pounding as well. She kept saying I should attack
the rooms, in and out and whatnot, but this kind of work,
even if just for the summer, should be approached like an
art, not an invasion. I was the one who'd gone to college
and who strived to treat the guests like family, only better, and meanwhile she continued to ignore all my advice.
Maybe Doug would have something to say about *that*.

I felt around the carpet until I located the chipped

gold piece, not much bigger than a kernel of corn. If it had been an amputated finger, I would've sealed it in a sterile bag and kept it on ice on the way to the hospital, but in this case there was no hospital to rush to and no obvious course of action. The rough edge of the gold piece cut into my palm, reminding me of all the ways I'd let myself down. Without an exact plan, I slumped down to Doug's office, meditating on the sacred Hippocratic oath, which demanded I preserve not only the finest traditions of my calling but also a measure of humility: *Above all, I must not play at God.*

As usual, his door was open. I could hear him saying "Personally, I always wanted three girls and a boy. I figured you need the one boy, but girls are what you want. My very own Niña, Pinta, and Santa Maria. Of course it turned out the exact opposite." I veered away as quietly as I could.

"Amy!" he called. Reluctantly I entered, avoiding eye contact with him and the man he'd been talking to, who lurked in the corner. "You look like you've seen a ghost," he said. "Tell me I don't have to add *that* to my list. I've got enough trouble here with the living."

"No." I fiddled with the sweaty gold piece in my pocket.

"Did Roula give you the rundown of events for August? Feels like the Fourth of July was just yesterday, yet here we are. It's all up on the events board. The main thing is the regatta coming up in a couple weeks, then we finish out with the big Centennial Cruise—our humble little operation hit a hundred years this summer, if you can believe it. Nothing gets you in the festive mood quite like figuring out the logistics for a massive three-night private charter that you will not have the pleasure of attending. At least I get to be quality control for the rum tasting." He struck his knuckle against a fat amber bottle on his desk. "Maybe Peter here will give you a taste. Best in town. You look like you could use it."

The name startled me, and my eyes darted up and over to the man in the corner. Of course it wasn't *Peter* Peter—why would the most remarkable professor I'd ever had be in the clubhouse giving Doug samples of rum?

"Amy here," Doug said, wagging his finger at me. "Don't let this quiet act of hers fool you. You wouldn't believe all the stuff she's got in her head. Like a walking encyclopedia. You remember those?"

"I remember." Peter's hand trembled as he suspended the bottle over two glass tumblers and filled them one glug at a time.

Doug dumped sugar from his ceramic camel into both glasses. "Keeps it smooth," he said. "We deserve this." I clinked mine against his and threw it back, thankful.

I paused at the events board to glance at the flyers for the regatta and the Centennial Cruise. Roula hadn't given me the rundown of events—she must really want the worst for me. I wanted her to know what that felt like.

Back up in Valerie's room, the rum whirling in my head, I crafted a letter in which I took full responsibility for what happened to her shell, expressed my sincerest apologies, and declared that if she wished for me to leave my post, I would do so willingly and immediately. I signed my full name, including my postnominal letters: Amy Hanley, NREMT. Thankfully it was time to go home then, so I trudged to the closet to collect my things.

Roula had taken her purse and left her caddy of cleaning supplies in the corner, meaning she'd left for the day. She and I were the lowest people at the clubhouse, yet she acted like her position as head housekeeper gave her an advantage over me, rather than what it actually meant: that this was the best she could ever hope for. Her three plants sat on the table by the window, lush and green in their ceramic pots. A breeze came through the window and set their leaves into an obnoxious, hyper little dance. I watched them, a wrenching in my chest, until I couldn't stand it anymore. I picked up a pot and squeezed, my fingers turning white. Before I knew what I was doing, I'd lifted the window screen and tipped the pot upside down, shaking until the dirt released in a block and fell into a patch of grass outside. I rushed to do the same with the other two, reveling in the sudden change in weight as the dirt went tumbling out.

When my frenzy had passed, I looked down at the three empty pots and felt surprised, as though the principle of cause and effect wasn't meant to apply here. In a panic, I sprinted outside, a wall of hot air rushing back at me. One of the waiters, the boy with the pigeon-toed feet, was standing next to the pile of dirt. I peered down at it, unable to find my voice. "Was that you?" he said. "I thought the sky was falling."

I stared at the ground.

"I was just out here waiting for my ride," he said.

"It was an accident," I said, scooping up whatever leaves and roots I could find intact. What had I expected?

"How's everything up on the third floor? You don't come around on your breaks anymore."

"Fine."

"It seems like it's nice and quiet up there. There's always stupid drama going on with the servers. Sometimes I wish I could switch places with you."

"It's not like it's easy."

"No, I know. I didn't mean that."

"I've got to go," I said, and took off back up the stairs, my hands cupped together with dirt and plant remains. Maybe I could still reassemble them somewhat, get some fresh soil, prop the stems upright.

Valerie poked her neck out of room 1 as I raced by. "You," she said, extending her long, knobby finger toward me.

"Um." I tried to shield the mess in my hands. "I'll be with you in just a minute." I dropped the remains into a pot—they didn't fill it even halfway—and dusted my palms over the top. I wanted to linger in the closet, to stress and mope and brainstorm. But I had another disaster waiting for me.

Valerie was holding her door open, so I followed her into the room. "You left me this note, is that right?" she said.

I nodded and then hung my head, feeling exhausted and beaten down.

"Is it sarcastic?"

"No!" My head rose up on its own, to show her. I tried to push the image of those empty pots aside and let my general integrity shine through.

"You're far too wound up, my dear," she said at last. "Don't give that old shell another thought. You could break the whole thing, for all I care. In fact, it would probably be best. No shell is preferable to a broken shell, wouldn't you agree?" She hoisted up the box and tilted it toward me like a platter of hors d'oeuvres. "Go ahead. It'll be good for you. Cathartic."

She urged me on with a bob of her head, inching it closer. I searched for a hint of wickedness in her face but found nothing conclusive. The box looked massive and unwieldy in her arms. I imagined the sound Roula would make when she found her pots in the morning, how she might put a hand over her mouth to trap it. I gulped down the sting in my throat. Finally, there was nothing to do but make a fist and strike it down onto the chipped gold shell—but gently, only very gently, to avoid knocking Valerie over.

"That won't do," she said. "Here, my wrists are shaky. Set it down." I took the box and placed it on the rug. "Good. Now you can use your foot," she said.

Again I gawked at her, waiting for some revelation. Then I decided what the heck, what was one more act of vandalism on a day like this, and plunged the heel of my sneaker into the shell. There was a pleasant crunch as it shattered, and I released a long, satisfying breath. But then, as I stared at the gold fragments—I'd really done it, desecrated the property of one of our guests—fear came creeping back. Perhaps I'd let myself fall for a mean and mysterious trick.

"Aha! Much better. Didn't that feel good?" She brushed the pieces off the lid with her foot, scattering them into the carpet. "I suppose we'll let the maid clean that up." She grinned.

"You really don't care that it's ruined?"

"The valuable stuff is *in*side." Valerie floated toward the dresser and turned busy, sifting through papers. "I haven't read the news in days," she said.

"I should probably clean this up now. Those tiny pieces are a hazard."

"True."

In the closet, I averted my eyes from the three pots. At least I hadn't smashed them, I thought—but no, that was a desperate reach, since here was another case where the valuable stuff was *in*side. I peered into them for a moment, as if I might find one sprout still alive. Then I squeezed my eyes shut and stood immobilized, full of anger at myself, with no way to exercise it. I might've cried had I not had a job to do. I snatched up my gloves and a plastic bag and the cordless hand vacuum, determined not to keep Valerie waiting.

She was already on her way out. "Well, I'm headed down for dinner," she said, holding the door to her room open for me. "Cook is making his famous lobster salad sushi. Have you tried it?"

"Not yet."

I stood in the doorway with my equipment, listening as she descended the stairs. There was so much more I wanted to say, to ask her. I had a sense we were connected, and I wondered if she felt the same, seeing as she'd forgiven me and invited me in, allowed me to break her shell, even insisted upon it. I wanted her company, her approval; I felt she could teach me important things. She had abandoned me here with the mess she'd forced me to make, but while I might've resented that with someone else, I trusted her implicitly.

As I raked the carpet clean, I thought of a morning when I was fourteen years old and we awoke to find a kitchen window smashed and my mother's purse, the keys, and the family car missing. Also a bottle of cranberry juice from the fridge, which amused my brother to no end. We discovered a single black glove on the front

steps and tried hard to laugh at that because it was so cli-
ché and obvious, it had to be a prank. The police arrived
and informed us that there'd been a string of similar
break-ins in our middle-class neighborhood, though my
mother balked at that. "But *ours*?" We had a comfortable
house, but the smallest and least impressive on the street.
When they showed us a blurry photograph of the man
they believed to be responsible, my mother gasped. She
claimed the face belonged to a student she'd had in social
studies class a few years earlier, though she couldn't re-
call his name. With that, the crime turned personal. She
was convinced it had been a targeted attack, never mind
all the other houses that had been robbed. She put on a
big show for the police, saying "There must be some
mistake" and repeating over and over how the boy had
seemed perfectly normal, really blending in at school, as
though afraid they might trace the blame back to her for
not having set him on the right path. Once she'd made up
her mind about something, especially if it involved an injustice against her, it became vitally, irrefutably true, and
anyone who attempted to persuade her otherwise was a
traitor, out to make her look bad.

A week later she and I were waiting in line at the phar-
macy when a detective called to say they'd found our car
abandoned two hundred miles away with my mother's
wallet intact, though empty. "See," she said to me after she
hung up. "See."

"See what?"

She abandoned the line in a huff. I followed her out to the rental car. On the way, I tripped over a package of sour candies that must have fallen from somebody's bag and picked it up. She turned the car on and sat staring through the windshield while I inspected the seal on the package. "Ten years as a teacher, and that is the thanks I get," she said.

"You were only a teacher for five years."

"Why do you have to make everything so difficult?"

I ripped the package open and gnawed on a handful of candies, suddenly very hungry.

She reversed out of the spot without glancing in the mirror, and a car beeped behind us. She hit the brake. "That's disgusting," she said, eyeing my full mouth. "Give me one." She sighed aggressively as she chewed—she did some of her best communicating through sighs. Our family learned to pick up on their subtle distinctions, and we'd practice imitating them, which would either delight or irritate her, depending on her mood. There was a day after she was gone when we were together, my brother, father, and I, eating bowls of soup. Out of nowhere my brother did one of her sighs. Somehow it evolved from there, my father offering up various contexts—you're emptying the dishwasher, you're stuck in traffic, you've just woken up from a nap on the couch—while my brother performed. He was so dead-on that the three of us broke into uncontrollable laughter. My first real laugh, and all I could think about was how it would end, how eventually we would have no choice but to catch our breath and move our spoons around in our soup and somehow, every day, go on.

I'd finished gathering the shell fragments and vacuuming the carpet fibers, and Valerie still hadn't returned. I couldn't stall any longer. I sat on the edge of her bed, feeling a stab of anger toward my mother for not having been more like Valerie and for never growing old, because maybe she could have become more like Valerie in her old age. It was childish, I knew, and despicable. I took the chipped gold piece out of my pocket. It was my only memento, the last link between Valerie and me. Then I dropped it to the floor and vacuumed that up too.

Valerie checked out the next day without leaving a message or clue of any kind, not that I expected it—guests weren't even allowed to leave tips, all clubhouse expenses were added directly to a member's account. I'd left home early, didn't even stop by the raspberry bushes on Magnolia Drive, but Roula had still beaten me there and her empty pots had disappeared from the closet. She kept her distance, which only agitated me more—every footfall or turning doorknob was her charging in to tell me I was a nasty, spiteful little brat who had been fired, effective immediately. And what did it mean for my future if I got myself fired from a job in sanitation, one of the most important factors in the spreading of disease? I might as well give up on Phase III before it even began.

I stuck to Roula's commands, attacking the rooms, in and out, never straying from the checklist or turning on the television or radio or even practicing a scene size-up. It was sad and quiet in my head, and I kept bashing my elbows into drawers and bed frames and slipping on my own rags, and once I accidentally sneezed into the microfiber cloth I kept for clearing lint off delicate surfaces. When I began to despair, I'd touch the certification card in my pocket and remind myself that very soon the summer would end and this job would no longer matter. It would be a distant memory, resurfacing only if I crossed the scent of a particular laundry detergent or furniture polish, and then I'd simply give thanks for the fortifying experience, but mostly for all the progress I'd made since.

I told myself that if this hour ended without a confrontation, no confrontation would ever come, and the same for the next hour, and the next. When the last hour finally passed, I wondered if all my worrying had been unfounded. Maybe Roula hadn't cared that much about her plants after all; maybe she'd pitched the empty pots into the trash without a second thought. On the other hand, that might be just what she wanted me to think.

Gary had a date that night with Irina, an online video chat, but we were still having dinner, just one hour late. Yes, it would be one hour late, but we were having dinner, Gary and I—this was a fact and I cherished it. We didn't have to discuss anything about Roula or Valerie, simply sharing a meal would be more than enough. I spent the extra hour tiptoeing around my apartment, wishing their conversation would somehow find its way to me, through an air duct or a fracture in the wall. Before the hour was up, I heard a knock. I saw Gary through the peephole and threw open the door. "Sorry," I said. "Did I get mixed up? I thought it was seven tonight."

"I think I need the night off." I noticed a set of keys in his hand. "Too much on my mind. All the stuff I need to do before Irina comes. I was thinking I should use the time to go shopping instead, get some of that done. Sorry to go changing plans last minute."

"Oh. That's all right."

"You wouldn't want to come along, would you? I was thinking, since you helped me with the kitchen table and all that . . . I could really use your opinion. And it might be kind of fun. But no pressure. We can stop on the way if you're hungry."

"Sure, I'll come along."

My arm wobbled as I tugged on the passenger-side door. I'd never been inside his car, or any other place with him besides the living room and kitchen. The car seemed expensive and newish, except for the center console, overflowing with balled-up napkins and receipts and wrinkly straw wrappers. He tried to stuff it down with his fist. "Sometimes I eat lunch in here. Bad habit, I know."

I thought of saying something about Irina, how she

might appreciate him tidying up, but I was getting tired of revolving my life around someone else. I got enough of that at work with Roula.

He pinned his phone into a dock suctioned to the inside of the windshield and tapped it to play music. I squirmed to see the screen: "They Say I'm Different" by Betty Davis.

"So are you? Hungry?"

"Not really," I said.

"Me neither."

We were in Gary's car, and we were going shopping. We were no longer friends who just ate dinner together, we were friends who drove together and shopped together, which meant we could do almost anything else together and it wouldn't be strange or uncomfortable or even out of the ordinary. We hurtled through town, music filling the car. The road rippled under us and disappeared behind, and all that swift forward momentum became a symbol: we were never turning back.

We parked outside a tremendous home goods store. As the automatic doors slid open and we stepped into the cold processed air, I felt invigorated. Gary, on the other hand, appeared to wilt. Once we were inside, something shifted, and the trip turned into a grave and dreary business in which there seemed no chance for a bit of fun. He stalked up and down the aisles, seeming antagonized by the very existence of bed skirts and mixing bowls and compulsively blotting his head with an old tissue.

"You don't need to get everything tonight," I said as he fondled a woven doormat that read HOME, with a heart for the O.

"No. Just so it's good enough." He dropped his hand. "But what if it's not?"

"Remember what I taught you for when you have those thoughts? You visualize. You turn each one into a banana and then pile them all up."

"Right, I know. And then the monkey comes along, and he's hungry. Et cetera." He closed his eyes. "Come on, Gary," he whispered, pressing his forehead. "I don't have any patience today. I'm sorry." He leaned against the side of the cart, and it took all my strength to keep it from skating away.

"Did something happen when you talked to Irina?"

"Something always happens."

"Do you think she might be a little . . . demanding or something? I mean, maybe that could be why you're feeling so stressed out?"

"She has certain expectations, sure. She likes things a certain way. But a lot of women can be like that. It's just, she always dreamed of coming to the US, like she always had this idea in her head of how great it would be, and I really want it to live up to that. Make it even better if I can. I'd just hate if she ended up disappointed by the real thing. It would kill me."

Over the past few years, I'd grown used to being with only me. I'd learned how to talk to myself, and apart from the occasional breakdown, I was generally receptive to my ideas and at ease in my company. But with Gary, I didn't have as much history and couldn't predict how he would react. It seemed safer to veer away from the topic altogether. "They say the best way to cure a toothache is to walk by a dentist's office," I said.

Gary skimmed his hand along a row of single-serve coffee makers. "I'm not sure I get it."

"It means we make problems worse in our head." I cornered him with the cart. "Now, what we need to do here is prioritize."

"Good. Yes. Prioritize." He folded his arms, thinking. "Well, what do you think is most important?"

"How about we start with curtains. Right over here. Then you can get rid of that old sheet thing you've been using. It will change the whole atmosphere of the living room."

He flipped through panels of fabric hanging from a bar. "Why do they have to have so many options?"

"This would be nice," I said, stretching a gauzy white fabric to the light. "It'll let in the sun."

"Might not give us much privacy, though."

I winced at the word. Here was an opportunity for a smart paraphrase of Florence Nightingale: "Sunlight not only improves a person's mood but has real, tangible effects on the body."

Gary shrugged and loaded a box of the gauzy white

curtains into the cart. "You always have the answer. I'd have stood there all night. What next?"

We passed dining room sets, and with the word *privacy* still banging around in my head, I found the guts to say, "It might be a good time to get another chair or two for the kitchen table." Immediately I wished I could take it back, it was such a transparent and pathetic kind of move.

But Gary, my merciful and true friend Gary, chose to protect my ego and not exploit the opportunity. "Why not," he said. We found a chair that looked like it belonged to the same family as the other two, and he scooted the box onto the shelf under the cart. I strode ahead now, pointing out various products and offering commentary while he relaxed, slumped over the handle of the cart, wheeling it along slowly.

At one point I turned, and he was gone. I found him standing at the foot of an extravagant canopy bed, complete with ornate engravings, a ruffle skirt, and four lacy veils gathered at each corner with large satin bows. "It's very glamorous," I said.

He flipped the placard over to read the price and gagged. "Well. Like you said, smart investments aren't always the most romantic. And I suppose it works the other way too. Sometimes the most romantic investments just aren't smart." His hand brushed behind me, leaving a trace of heat on my shoulder blade.

As we resumed shopping, his face had a faraway expression that made me think he was salivating over the idea of sharing a bed with Irina, any bed, glamorous or not. After a few awkward minutes, he seemed to snap out of it. "The best way to cure a toothache is to walk by a dentist's office," he said. "I'm going to borrow that." He chuckled and swung his head. "I'm normally a pretty laid-back guy, if you can believe it. Man. You must think I'm crazy. But like they say, nothing worth having comes easy, right? If it's a struggle, that's how you know it will be worth it in the end."

I wanted to argue that that didn't apply to every case, but I could tell he wasn't in the right frame of mind for a discourse. We came across a game at the foot of the next aisle, guns loaded with foam balls that you could shoot into two bears' mouths, and I seized the opportunity to distract him. He turned enthusiastic as soon as he pulled the trigger yelling "Oh yeah!" and "Take that!" The balls plunked one by one into the glass stomachs and then rolled forward so you could reload. We threw ourselves into the competition, losing all sense of time and becoming so rowdy that an employee in khaki pants came over and made a motion with his hand. We looked at each other and laughed, then started the game up again, hushing each other with aggressive whispers.

Gary's chest pumped from the physical exertion. "Thank you," he whispered. His breath had a touch of sourness, but I let it wash over me anyway.

We'd worked up an appetite, so we lugged our purchases to the car and walked to the pizza place at the
other end of the shopping center. Gary insisted on paying for his two slices and my single slice, plus two large
sodas that we filled from the machine. Before our pizza
was out of the oven, he'd already finished his soda and
was staring into the empty cup, one hand over his mouth
to shield a burp. "Excuse me."

"Let me," I said, and went to get him a refill.

"You didn't have to do that."

"It's only fair, seeing as you're always the one waiting
on me."

"Hey, I guess that's true." After a long swallow, he
smacked his lips. "Ahh! Everything tastes better when
it's been served to you." He swirled the ice around. "So
maybe tonight we should switch places. *You* spend the
whole time complaining about . . . well, whatever you
want, your choice. And serve my dinner. And I'll sit here
and listen patiently, just like you always have to. And
then I'll give you advice and tell you what I think of the
food."

The pimply cashier called out our order. "I got off
easy," I said, setting down our paper plates. "Compared
with all the work you put into a meal. Plus you paid.
Doesn't seem like a very fair trade."

"Well, you had to put up with shopping with me, so
you deserve a lot more than a slice of pizza." He folded a
slice in half and drove it into his mouth. "Anyway, you're

not getting out of it. I want to hear your best complaining. No holds barred."

"Hmm." I took a bite, the cheese stretching like a rubber band through my teeth, and washed it down with ginger ale.

"Come on. There's gotta be *some*thing."

I pushed a finger through a bubble in my crust. My grievances against Roula, which had lain dormant all evening, now snapped back to life and began clamoring to get out. Why not divulge them to Gary? He would understand, and it might be therapeutic to have him listen and console me, it might be just what I needed. But I had to select the right words, to avoid coming across as too strange or odious.

"See," he said. "That's what's so amazing about you. You really *can't* complain. Probably the only person in the world. They should study you or something. Make a documentary."

If only he could have peered inside my brain and recognized me for the vile person I was! He might find out eventually, like if Roula showed the empty pots to Doug and Doug called Gary, thinking he should be made aware of the kind of immature, vindictive behavior I was capable of, seeing as he'd recommended me for the job. Still, I didn't pipe up. I let him go on believing I was this saintly person when in fact I was the opposite, even worse now for sitting by as he praised me, yes, I was lower than low.

"You've got to teach me your ways," he said. "Although I might be a hopeless case. You might have to use some kind of conditioning thing. Like every time I complain, you punch me in the arm, or I have to give you a dollar or something."

I ate more pizza and drank more ginger ale, trying to push forward, reengage in the present conversation. "If only we could put you in your own Skinner box," I said.

"Skinner whatta?"

"B. F. Skinner. He was like the father of operant conditioning."

"Oh, right."

"Actually he didn't like that term. It should be 'operant conditioning chamber.' Basically a cage that no light or sound can penetrate, so you can control all the stimuli."

"That's just what I need. A coffin, basically. Ha." He wiped the grease from his mouth and gazed off, mulling things over. "Then again, if you can't complain, what's there to even talk about?"

"I think that counts," I said, and held up a fist as though threatening to punch him.

He tipped his cup, like touché. "Damn. Maybe we should start tomorrow. What's the saying? Never put off till tomorrow, what you can put off until the day after tomorrow." He smirked.

"Very wise."

He laughed, and the warm, simmery sound reminded

me of the evening we'd spent with his mother, how easy-going he'd been then. "Let's practice. How about you try to tell me a story that involves zero complaining," I said.

"I'm boring, through and through."

"What about something from growing up? Or about your mom?"

His face brightened. "Actually, okay. Remember that joke you asked me about, about the gravy lady? That one's kind of a good story, definitely one of the most exciting things that ever happened to us." He sat up straighter, pushed aside his empty plate and dirty napkins. "So I was in high school, and she was working at this random office, my mom, as the receptionist or whatever. And a guy got shot right outside her building. It was pretty crazy since it wasn't like it was a bad part of town or anything. Drug-related, I assume. But anyway, she was there when it happened and she ran out and called nine-one-one. The local news came, since it was such an unusual thing around there. And one of them interviewed her about what happened, so she told them she heard the shot and ran outside and saw blood coming out of his bullet hole. She said it just like that: blood coming out of his bullet hole. So then the next morning she was driving me to school and we were listening to one of those stupid morning shows on the radio, you know, where they pull stupid pranks on people and have people call in and stuff like that. She always liked those shows for some reason. And anyway, they played the clip of her interview and the radio hosts were cracking up over it, like it was the funniest thing they ever heard. One of them goes: 'What did you think would be coming out his bullet hole, lady? *Gravy?*'" He caught his breath. "Huh. So anyway, that's how it started. Probably not as good secondhand."

"No, it's a great story. I can't believe that really happened."

"I guess you'll be the one showing up to nine-one-one calls like that pretty soon. You'll have all kinds of stories. And you better remember the good ones, so you can tell me."

"Definitely, I will."

As we bumped back into our driveway, I noticed Gary's mailbox for the first time in months. I felt shy and sentimental, as though seeing an old friend I'd neglected. It looked lonesome but accepting, like it was proud of me for outgrowing the need for it.

"Back to reality." Gary sighed as he popped the trunk.

"I can help," I said, trying to grab the handle of a bag.

"I've got it." He sounded tired.

"Are you sure? I don't mind."

"That's all right, Amy." He hauled the bags up the steps and then eased them down to fish for his keys. I stood on the walkway behind him. "Good night," he said.

I watched him wrestle the bags inside and close the

door. I was still standing there when he switched off the porch light. The word *reality* crackled in my head, and that other word, *privacy*, came back to join it. Of course life would change when Irina arrived—I wasn't that naive—but how exactly? If things went smoothly, he would have me to thank for it, but then he also wouldn't need me anymore. Would we still be the kind of friends who could eat dinner or go shopping without it being strange or uncomfortable or out of the ordinary? Would it still be okay if, say, I knocked one evening to use the printer, or would they close the new curtains I'd helped him pick out and pretend not to be home?

I rapped lightly on the door. Like a gift, it opened. Gary didn't smile or say anything.

"Um. Did I drop my keys in one of the bags?"

"They're right there. In your hand."

A honking laugh flew out of my mouth and was carried off by the air. "I must be more tired than I thought," I said. "Oh, also, I just remembered. I don't think I can come for dinner tomorrow like we usually do. Could you do Friday instead?" I held my breath.

"Sure, okay. See you Friday," he said, and closed the door again.

I entered my apartment feeling relieved. There was no reason I couldn't come for dinner the next day, but now I had proof that Gary wasn't the only one who could change plans at the last minute; in fact, he was happy to accommodate me, even on a Friday night, which was much more significant than a Thursday, without demanding any explanation. So it followed that even if one day he no longer needed me, he would still want me around; he would never close his new curtains and pretend not to be home. If it ever did work out and Irina actually showed up here—and I was beginning to doubt she would—they would quickly realize that they were better with a third party.

At the refrigerator, I read my letter slowly—*congratulations, congratulations, congratulations*—swallowing each word and letting it absorb into my bloodstream. I couldn't be bothered to open my exam book or track the status of my package for Phase III. I'd already made extensive progress, I was more confident than ever before, and after such a full day, it felt wonderful to let exhaustion rise up and consume me. I slept in my clothes without worries or visions.

SEVEN

At the clubhouse, I continued to obey Roula's instructions, still flinching at every sound and checking for her over my shoulder, but with less urgency now that a day had gone by peacefully. Again she showed no interest in me, so I determined to show no interest in her, not to give her that satisfaction, in case she was in fact paying attention. By lunchtime, I'd built up a reserve of optimism and a small appetite. As I went to retrieve my trail mix from the closet, Roula stepped out from the shadows. "Look," she hissed, thrusting something into my face.

She'd started wearing beige compression socks with her shorts, and I glared at the sheen of the nylon, tight as a tourniquet around her calves, and at the flesh of her knees, how it puffed over the top of the elastic, because I didn't need to look up, I knew exactly what she was holding.

"Someone destroyed them," she said. "I came in the other morning, and this was all that was left." She jostled the loose dirt around. "It was when that old woman was staying in room one. I always thought she had something off about her. Some people think they can treat us however they want, just because of our job. I've seen it before. I grew them from seeds, since when I first started here." She paused, waiting for me to react. "You don't know anything about it, do you?"

I shook my head. "Maybe it was an accident."

Roula blinked. "Maybe," she said.

I fled into room 3, locked the door, and stood trembling. It wasn't the real me who'd wrecked those plants. I'd been in a state of temporary insanity, which Roula had driven me to. The things we do during a difficult time don't define us, that's what Peter had said. But that didn't mean those things couldn't still change the course of your life, like getting you fired, or kicked out of school and sentenced to five hundred hours of community service. Peter had tried to prevent it back then. That was why he'd slid my exam aside and set his elbow on it—though I could see the number at the top, 48%, even worse than the last, despite my studying harder than ever, staying up most nights. "You know," he'd said. "These tests, sitting around trying to remember Jung's theory about this or that—it can all feel pretty meaningless in the scheme of things."

I was possessed by the number at the top of the page, bewildered by it, but also energized. It didn't reflect all the work I'd done, but that just meant I'd have to work even harder, and I liked the idea of that.

"We both know you're more than capable and you're willing to put in the time, there's no issue there. But we, all of us, need to take care of ourselves first." He paused. "Amy, I don't want to overstep, but have you put any thought into taking the rest of the semester off? You could take next semester too, if that felt right. The school is very accommodating when it comes to situations like this."

Situations like this—I turned the words over a few times in my mind, and then I knew. Nnenna. She must have told him about my mother. She'd come to the funeral and brought some other people too, but the moment she saw me, she'd left them all behind, even her boyfriend, Nick, because she understood that I needed her to sweep me away and into the bathroom where we could be alone. "I'm in shock. I had no idea she was that sick," she'd whispered into my hair. "Me neither," I said, and only then did I realize how much of a lie that truly was. Nnenna, generous and always clean-smelling, made you want to melt into her arms, and that's what I did. It was the only time I broke down all day, and I did so with abandon because she made me believe we'd stepped outside time and space into a temporary void where nothing counted. But apparently it *had* counted.

"I don't need a semester off." I'd already had to beg my father to take me back to school to make up the work I'd missed, and now I was finally up to speed, had even read ahead for all my classes. With a little more time, I'd get my grades back up, maybe even better than before.

"What about someone to talk to, a professional, have you looked into that at all?"

"Like you?"

"Right, someone with a similar background, but not me of course, since I'm your teacher. And I'm just a research wonk these days. But there are a ton of great people out there. The Mental Health Services Center has an excellent staff. And they have counseling groups for students who have suffered similar losses."

"Thanks, I'll think about it," I said, but my mind was only on Nnenna now.

I found her at her desk in our room. She looked up when I slammed the door. "So he suggested I take the rest of the semester off, the rest of the year even—is that what you wanted?"

"What?"

"It's exactly what you wanted, isn't it? Get rid of me, and have Nick move in. You probably have him packing right now." I had the sense I was moving and speaking at double speed, and I didn't want to slow down.

"Don't you think taking a little time off would be good for you?" The tremble in her voice made me want to knock her to the floor, stomp on her throat. "It doesn't have to be a big deal. You can just come back whenever you're ready."

"No, actually. I happen to think it's the worst possible thing I could do. But apparently my opinion doesn't matter." Though the words were my own, it felt like I was acting out a scene, my voice and my movements overly exaggerated, theatrical. I found it liberating. "No, wait, I'm sorry, you're right. This is definitely something *you* should decide, behind my back. How silly of me."

She stood so abruptly that her chair rolled backward, and she had to catch it with one hand. "Look, I didn't know what else to do." I could always tell when she felt overwhelmed because her hands would vibrate in the air as she spoke, her fingers all hyperextended. "It's impossible to talk to you. And I know you really like Peter, so you might actually listen to him. And he'd be a lot better at dealing with something like this than me. I don't know. But you can't go on like this forever, just studying twenty-four seven. It just won't work. It's not healthy."

"It never bothered you before."

"You know it's not like before. Come on, Amy. You've been acting like—I don't know. But this has nothing to do with Nick. I don't know why you even brought him up."

"Ha. As if you're not the most transparent person in the world. If anyone here needs an intervention, it's you. He obviously has you brainwashed, that's the only possible explanation." I smiled, impressed by my own performance. "You're literally the only person on the planet who would date him, you do realize that, right? It's actually kind of hilarious. Everyone thinks so."

"What, you can't be a bitch to your mom anymore, so now you have to be a bitch to me?"

This seemed to shock her even more than it did me. She turned and stood looking out the window with one hand around her neck. I stared at her numbly. "I'm going to get food," she said at last. She had trouble getting her arms into her jacket. "Look, um. I'm sorry I said that. I don't know why you're trying to hurt me, of all people, but I won't hold it against you because I know you're in pain, even if you don't want to admit it. I guess you just need to take it out on someone. I'll be the mature one here, as usual."

That would be the last time I saw her—she didn't even show up to court, just had them read a statement on her behalf.

As I listened to her footsteps echo down the hallway, my arms began to itch. I looked down and discovered red splotches all over them. I scratched and paced. I had never felt so free of emotion and in need of action. I lost all awareness of where I was, until I stopped moving and looked up at the wall. One of the paintings we'd made together was a tropical garden, full of hidden objects. Random, meaningless things: an airplane, a basketball. And in the middle, a giant human head sprouting out of a flower stem. She'd called it a self-portrait. I needed it to disappear. But when I closed my eyes, the image only multiplied. I wanted to scream, I did scream, without opening my jaw, freakish, strained noises trapped in the back of my throat. I drifted to Nnenna's side of the room. She kept candles on her dresser, even though they weren't allowed in the dorm. I'd never seen them lit, though they had been, probably when Nick was over and they knew I'd be out all night at the library. I picked up her lighter. The flame was my twin, wild and hot and ready to make something happen. I brought it to the wall, to the curled edge of the garden. It ignited and then burned out. I took the delicious wisps of smoke into my lungs. The smell invigorated me.

I tore the painting down, and the rest of them too. I piled them on her bed along with her clothes and notebooks, her candles, her towels, her photographs. I flicked the lighter again and watched the flame spring back to life, just as wild and ready as before. I didn't care what it would mean. There were so many things in life that I couldn't do, couldn't undo—not an hour had gone by since my mother passed that I didn't think of them—and now I finally had the chance to do something, I held the power right here in my hand, and so I had to, I just did, I just had to.

■

I fixed my face in the mirror of room 3. This situation with Roula was not the same, I was not the same, and I would not let myself be banished from the clubhouse like I had been from school. If anyone should have to go in front of a judge, it was Roula. She was the pathological one here, lying in wait, biding her time until the moment I'd finally regained some morale—it was no coincidence. She'd been playing with me this whole time. And she'd purposefully muddied the details, knowing how that would torment me. Of all the guests who came and went, why had Roula singled out Valerie? Could Valerie have witnessed what I'd done and acted as Roula's informant; could the two of them possibly be working together, orchestrating some scheme against me?

Once my hands had steadied, I splashed water on my face and skulked down to the second floor. Doug's laughter resounded from the kitchen, where he was probably bugging the cook to add more sugar to his dish. I inched toward his office. The door was ajar; it creaked when I pushed it. I moved quickly. I skimmed through his filing cabinet, past financial reports and employee records. Finally I found a file with new member information and, behind that, a folder with a handful of member directories, each spiral-bound with a photograph of the clubhouse on the cover. He would never miss one. I scrambled out, gently hinging the door back to its original position.

Roula would be gone for exactly thirty minutes. She refused to forfeit even a millisecond of her lunch break, whereas I would eat in big gulps standing up, keeping my muscles limber. I thumbed through the Cs until I found Valerie Calvano. If I used the phone in the housekeeping closet, she would recognize the number of the clubhouse and be sure to pick up. Then I could confront her about her role in all this, diplomatically at first, getting tougher if I had to. Roula had put her empty pots back on the table, and though I turned away, I could feel them behind me as I dialed, nosy, disapproving.

The ringing droned on and on, until an automated voice broke through to tell me the mailbox had not been set up, please try again later. I tried the number again, and this time someone picked up—a woman, but much too hoarse to be Valerie. "Good afternoon," I said. "I'm looking for Valerie Calvano."

"Why, is she trying to ruin your life too?"

I lifted the phone from my ear and gawked at it. "I'm not sure," I said.

"This is her daughter."

"Really?" She didn't sound like a person who could be related to Valerie. She was rough, with a smoker's voice. A television played noisily in the background.

"Well, we've never taken a test. That's not a bad idea, now that I think of it."

"Will Valerie be in tonight? I could try to reach her then."

"She doesn't live here anymore. Moved to one of her summer houses. She was generous enough to leave this place for me." She made a snorting noise, between a laugh and a cough. "What's this about?"

I considered hanging up, but then what? "I work at the yacht club, she's a member here. She recently stayed in one of our rooms."

"You the manager?"

"Assistant manager." She hadn't made any effort to adjust the volume on the television. "Is that *The Price Is Right*?"

"An old one, from the eighties. It was better back then."

"I think so too."

"But the outfits!"

I felt annoyed at myself for indulging her. "So you see, one of our guests left behind a beautiful pot of twenty-four-karat gold butter. That's a kind of exfoliator for your skin. I'm trying to make sure it gets back to its rightful owner. It could be Valerie's."

"Where does a person get off putting gold on their face?"

"Do you have her new number, or is there someone else there I could speak with?"

"Just me, myself, and I. She made sure of that," she said, her voice full of venom. She coughed again. "For solid oak? You've got to go higher than that. Come on, lady."

For some reason, my impatience gave way to an overwhelming curiosity to hear whatever this psychotic woman had to say. "What do you mean, she made sure of it?"

"She wants me to die alone. That's what gets her up in the morning. My husband—*ex*-husband—he had a problem with pills. He didn't want to feel anything, and I can't blame him for that. But his heart was pure. I don't give up on people, it's not in my nature. Thank god *that*'s not genetic. She wouldn't help me out unless I did it, the divorce. I'm sure she doesn't talk about *that* at the club. She goes around like nothing ever happened. It's easy for her."

"Valerie?"

"I'm not even supposed to have contact with him. But she can't control everything, despite what she thinks. I have a second cell phone she'll never know about. Bob Barker is just torturing this girl. Show her the damn card already! If I could go back, I wouldn't do it. Jason had his problems, but I don't give up on people. All I ever wanted was to get the hell out of this place and, what do you know, I'm right back where I started."

I was baffled, but not unmoved. I could understand how it felt to have Bob Barker be the most prominent figure in your life. "Sometimes out of suffering comes the cure," I offered.

"Says who?"

"For example, there's this type of treatment, for cancer. It's pretty promising. They extract cancerous cells from the tumor and alter them in a lab, then inject them back into you."

"I wouldn't let them try that on me. It was doctors who got Jason addicted in the first place. He used to say a doctor's just a dealer dressed up in a white coat. I'm going to sell this house and take the money, and then we're going to move to Spain or Italy or California."

Now I realized that I'd been duped, sucked into her warped little universe with a half-baked story. Somehow she'd known from the tone of my voice that the fraught-mother angle would work on me, get me to lose track of my common sense and my purpose for calling in the first place. "Congratulations," I said. "You're a supreme idiot. I lied before. I don't work for any club, I work for Valerie. I'm her representative, and everything you've said has been recorded. You can expect to hear from her tomorrow. I wouldn't get too ahead of myself with those plans if I were you."

I crashed the phone down, out of breath. I hated her, whoever she was, but I hated myself more. This had been a disastrous waste of time, and I should've known better, there was no way Valerie and Roula would have formed an alliance against me. They were as far apart as two people could be. I was stuck somewhere between, and still too far away.

■

I didn't go home when my shift ended. I drifted aimlessly around the parking lot of the clubhouse, watching two gulls peck at the shreds of a Styrofoam cup. A group of members or guests who had been properly introduced congregated near a parked car with a silver mat accordioned across the windshield to block the sun. A man wearing sunglasses on a leash around his neck attempted to rest his butt against the car, then jumped up at the heat of it. I didn't get close enough to hear their conversation, but I caught the words "Thoroughbred" and "Steve Jobs."

Roula emerged from the clubhouse, strutting on her compression-socked legs and cooling herself with a paper fan. As she crossed the parking lot, I followed. I couldn't think of anything else to do. I prowled behind her all the way to the bus stop, where she sat on a bench for twenty minutes under the spotty shade of a tree, obsessively fanning herself. I didn't mean any harm. I only wanted to see whatever I would see. When the bus finally came, I waited for her to plop into a seat in the back, then ducked into a seat up front with my hair spread over the side of my face. I monitored every pull of the stop cord, stealing glances over my shoulder.

The bus had no air conditioning, and as it swerved and jolted, my legs slipped across the seat, leaving dark streaks of sweat. I tried not to get too close to the window, since it had a patch of glue on it, full of stray hair and fuzz. After a rickety hour riding inland, doubt set in—it hadn't occurred to me that Roula's home could be so far away. Did she really spend all this time riding the bus every day? It was getting late, and I still didn't know what I was even doing here. If only I hadn't switched dinner plans with Gary from tonight to tomorrow, if only I'd had a reason to get home! I scanned once more for the top of her head, but they all blended together now, and I couldn't get a better view without exposing myself. At the next stop, I gave up and made a run for it. I didn't slow down until the huffs and screeches of the bus had died away. As I hunched to recover my breath, I saw that I had only myself to blame. I'd accomplished nothing beyond stranding myself in an unknown place, with no clue how to get back home. I tried taking out my certification card—Amy Hanley, Registry No. E4068211—then tucked it away, not in the mood.

I slogged under the heavy sun on two bloated ankles for an hour or more, and just as my faith was nearly depleted, I came upon a cluster of trees. I'd reached the far end of the woods where I used to roam, back before I'd started my summer job. I felt so revived that a verse from Longfellow's poem, written in tribute to Florence Nightingale, came to mind, and I spoke it aloud:

> Lo! in that house of misery
> A lady with a lamp I see
> Pass through the glimmering gloom,
> And flit from room to room.

That house of misery—I knew it well. I'd lived there for years after college, amidst the glimmering gloom. Though I tried changing apartments and zip codes, the four walls around me stayed the same. For some reason, I was stubborn about finding the way out on my own, coming up with endless excuses not to follow the advice Peter had given me on my last day as a student. Then eventually, a day came, a quiet regular day with nothing unique about it, when I just happened to strike the right balance of mental clarity and emotional detachment, and found myself making a phone call.

The psychologist sat in a noisy leather chair and tunneled his finger into his ear and said that everyone grieves in their own way, at their own pace. "Don't worry about what you think you *should* be feeling or doing at any given point. You need to give yourself permission . . ." I had the urge to spit in his face. He'd simply assumed that I was like his other patients, that I'd shown kindness to my mother and now deserved to show kindness to myself. And he was forcing me to go along with it, to sit in the usual spot and respond to the usual questions, all of it so thoroughly civilized, it was grotesque. "Some people find it helpful to talk to the deceased, commune in whatever way makes sense to them," he said. "Nothing shocks me anymore. I had one patient who believed his mother spoke to him through his eBay account, suggesting items to bid on—things that would only have meaning to the two of them. You might laugh, but I love it! I think it's wonderful. Truly." Behind him hung a display of oil-painted portraits in heavy frames, amateur, oversize, and mostly hideous. When he noticed me glaring, he said, "Original Delilah Thorpes," then made a vague gesture toward the nameplate on his desk: Harold J. Thorpe, PhD. He cleared his throat. "My daughter," he said. "She likes to do important women through history." I spent the rest of our time together studying those paintings. Susan B. Anthony wearing what looked like a dead cat around her neck. Harriet Tubman with a deformed mouth. I imagined smashing the frames and holding a lighter to the canvases.

After, I went home, sat on my floor, and waited for nightfall. I analyzed the shadows, tracked every sound. I licked my finger and crawled around trying to detect discrepancies in temperature, which I'd seen on a show about the supernatural. Finally I opened my laptop and typed in "eBay." Then I snapped the laptop shut and kicked it across the floor. I vowed to never return for another appointment, and I didn't. However, I'd gotten something out of that first session after all, the tiny germ that Peter must have known would reveal itself. The only nonhideous painting on Dr. Thorpe's wall had featured a mystical woman in a white bonnet and apron, who I couldn't get out of my mind. She looked almost familiar, a distant relative I couldn't quite place. She held a lantern in her outstretched arm as though casting the light on something vital, something she intended to show me that lay just beyond the frame. I only had to follow her. *Florence Nightingale, Lady with the Lamp, Angel of Crimea, 1820–1910 / "How very little can be done under the spirit of fear."* The next day I went out and bought a book.

But now as I plodded through the woods, with Long-fellow's exaltations still lingering in the air, I felt embarrassed and insecure. How ridiculous to admire Florence Nightingale, to strive to be like her, when in reality you were just a chambermaid who had insulted another chambermaid and then tried to chase her home, you were nobody and had nothing, not even a college degree. Just a bogus certification card sweating in your pocket. Maybe I'd been fooling myself to think this treatment could ever work, but then, what was the alternative? Give up hope, settle for mediocrity, go around feeling sorry for myself?

The narrow stream where I used to sit had developed a green slime along the edges. When I paused at it, a cat emerged from the trees, skinny with a nappy coat. She began sniffing my legs. "Get lost," I said. It looked like she had suffered some cruelty, but I'd already absorbed so much of the world's dust, I couldn't bear to take in any of its cats on top of it. I moved along, aware of the cat padding behind me. "Get lost," I said again, more forceful this time, and kicked my foot in her direction.

When I first moved into Gary's in-law apartment, there had been an orange cat that would climb up the stairs and paw at my door. I called him Sesame Seed because when I plucked one off the side of my bagel, he seemed to like it. He wore a little bell around his neck, so I knew he had a home, probably with a big affectionate family who loved to stroke his ears and feed him sardine-flavored treats and dangle pouches of catnip, and yet he still chose to come and visit me, every day for weeks. He would tuck into my lap and clean himself, and we'd sit at the window, where he'd twitch at every leaf and bird. I began to expect him, and when I heard his bell, I'd open the door and get a little dish of water ready and a pinch of cheese or whatever was in my refrigerator. When I had to go out for work or an errand, I'd race back, worried he might be waiting, and all the way home, I'd picture his little pink nose and whiskers and have to fight the smile from getting too big on my face. Then one day he didn't come. He gave no warning signs. I kept the door open all day and night and into the next day, when I finally went out and hunted around the neighborhood, calling, "Sesame Seed, Sesame Seed," but not too loudly in case someone should question me. For weeks I'd rush outside every time I heard a jingle, only to find a dog on a leash, or a bicycle, or the coins in my own pocket. One of the neighbors put up a wind chime, and the sound would grow roots in my ears, especially when I lay in bed at night. No matter what, I couldn't kill the last tiny bud of hope. But it was like Sesame Seed had dissolved into thin air. And I worked hard not to resent him but to be thankful for the time we'd had.

The scraggly cat purred and rammed her face into my shinbone until I conceded. I combed my fingers through her coat, the least I could do. She just kept purring and rubbing against me, and I couldn't deny that it felt nice. I'd let her follow me a while.

By the time we reached the edge of the woods, her fur had fluffed up a bit and didn't look quite so mangy. She let out a heartbreaking cry, and I got an idea. I gathered her up in my arms. She curled her tail and fit nicely there, and we trekked on toward home. Her little heart beat furiously. Florence Nightingale first heard her calling after saving the life of a sheepdog with a wounded leg when she was seventeen. Years later, she rescued a baby owl who became her beloved pet, Athena.

The cat bristled when we passed a man spraying his window boxes. To soothe her, I rubbed the pads of her toes and told her how the largest artery inside the body, the aorta, was approximately the size of a garden hose. When we came to 8 Magnolia Drive, I let her paw the raspberry bushes while I popped one in my mouth, overwhelmed by how sublime it tasted and how thirsty and hungry I was. When we finally made it home, I knocked on Gary's door, worn out but trying to stay strong for her, scratching her neck and whispering "Look cute" into her soft ear.

He lifted a corner of his new white curtains before opening the door. "Amy," he said. "And . . . a cat."

"I know I canceled for tonight. But then I had a great idea. To help with everything you've been going through. You know how you've been really stressed out? Well, a lot of studies have shown that pets can be a great stress reliever. It's physiological, even just a few minutes can bring your blood pressure down. When I was in college, they used to bring dogs to campus at finals time, to help the students relax. But cats are a lot less of a commitment. They basically take care of themselves. Plus, isn't she cute?" I made her paw wave.

"Huh. A cat. Jeez, I don't know." As he leaned in to scrutinize her, she let out a wild meow, making him jump and laugh. He gradually brought one finger toward her nose and she licked the end of it. "That's nice." He patted her head.

"Hear that? She's purring."

"I guess it *could* be good, for when Irina gets here. It'll be a stressful time for her too. And she'll probably be home alone a lot, especially at first. She might get lonely. Maybe it's not a bad idea."

The cat leapt out of my arms and scooted through Gary's legs, right into his house. "Look at that," he said. She trotted through his living room toward the kitchen.

"Looks like she made the decision for you," I said, relieved by her enthusiasm.

We watched her for a moment in silence, and then he cleared his throat. "If you want, I was about to have dessert. You could come in and have some."

"Okay." I got the impression he wasn't really in the mood for company, that he was doing me a favor, so I promised myself I'd leave immediately after dessert.

Gary prepared brownie sundaes with caramel sauce crisscrossed over the top, then he poured the melted ice cream from the bottom of the carton into a shallow bowl and set it on the floor. The cat lapped it up. "I'll have to get some cat food tomorrow," he said.

"And a litter box." The caramel sauce tasted sickly sweet, but I gobbled it up anyway. We sat in the two original chairs that had come with the kitchen table, while the third one we'd purchased stayed in its box, propped against the wall.

"How's the brownie? I made them. Just from a box."

"Perfect," I said. "I like the walnuts."

As we ate, the cat snaked around our feet and nuzzled the legs of our chairs. When she got sick of that, she sank her nails into the notches of the screen door then plucked them out, one paw at a time, so the door rumbled and shook. She became fixated on the motion, repeating it again and again, and the noise called attention to the comfortable silence that had settled between us. I felt astounded by my luck, to have a friend to be silent with. But then the cat would not quit. The noise became oppressive and our happy silence regressed into its more familiar form, an obstacle that had to be surmounted. "Maybe we should let her out into the yard for a few minutes," I said.

"I was thinking she should be an indoor cat."

"Why?"

"I just thought, if Irina's stuck at home while the cat goes out, she might feel . . . I don't know." He stabbed his spoon into his bowl, mashing everything together. "I guess it just seems safer, all around."

I had envisioned us sharing custody—the cat coming for regular visits, padding freely from his house up to my apartment and back again—but I didn't feel right suggesting that now. Anyway, that kind of arrangement might just develop naturally over time. "Then you won't have to worry about her getting hit by a car or anything like that," I said.

"Exactly." As he took a bite, I caught a flash of his impeccable front teeth, not one speck of brownie. "It was nice of you to think of me, with the cat. Sorry if I seem a little out of it. I had this email from Irina and, well, you know how it can be. It just gets harder the longer we're apart. But hopefully she'll get here soon, then you won't have to put up with my craziness anymore."

He meant it to be kind, but I felt a bit deflated. The cat continued her scratching. "She certainly has stamina," Gary said.

"We should give her a name. I like Athena. But that's just one idea."

He brought our dishes to the sink, nearly tripping over the bowl he'd set down for the cat. "I think I'll wait and let Irina decide." He turned on the faucet.

"Yeah," I said over the rush of water. "I guess we should wait and let Irina decide."

My front door jammed as I pushed it open. Something thick had been dropped through the mail slot—a magazine. The cover had a staged photograph of two medical professionals kneeling by a patient, one performing chest compressions while the other attached an automated external defibrillator. "EMS Monthly" was printed across the top in block letters, and under it: "Highlighting News, Stories, and Innovations from the Field of Emergency Medical Services." *EMS Monthly*? I must have gotten up one night, half dreaming, and ordered it online, maybe with the idea of incorporating it into the third phase of my treatment. I had never done anything half dreaming before, but perhaps it was evidence that my obecalp had soaked into my subconscious as hoped. I peeled open the plastic sleeve, and a white slip of paper fell out.

You've been gifted a year subscription!

TO: Amy
FROM: Proud Dad

MESSAGE: Thought this might be useful for an up-and-coming EMT like yourself! We love you & we're so proud. Hope to see you soon.

I had the urge to press the paper to my cheek and hold it there. When I brought it down, I checked to make sure the words were still there as I remembered them. I walked to the refrigerator with the paper out in front of me, making it wave like a flag. I hung it next to my congratulations letter and read them both aloud once, twice, three times. *FROM: Proud Dad.*

I sat in bed with the magazine, gliding my finger over the pages. This was real, all of it. An up-and-coming EMT like myself. Just like everyone else opening this magazine, flipping through these same articles. I read about hazmat disasters, pediatric seizures, prehospital blood transfusions. When I couldn't keep my eyes open anymore, I rolled it up and slept with it in the crook of my arm like a teddy bear.

EIGHT

The regatta began the same day my package for Phase III was scheduled to arrive. I'd spent $95.43 before tax, the biggest purchase I'd made in months aside from rent, enough to qualify for free shipping and to represent the kind of significant investment needed for a successful obecalp treatment: $55.49 for dark blue pants featuring cargo pockets with multiple compartments and straps, double-faced knees, and a stain-release fabric finish; $34.99 for a khaki button-down shirt with chest pockets, a mesh ventilation panel, and reflective trim; and just $4.95 for a regulation Massachusetts EMT patch, no questions asked. It was amazing what you could find for sale online with just a quick search. I'd been tracking the package as it made its way from Oregon, jumping to a new state every day.

The weather report predicted this would be the hottest day of the summer so far, but the early hour still had a hint of crispness, and as I hustled to work, the birds were active and the houses had a soft glow. Doug had hired a private company to help with the event. They'd set up white tents on the lawn outside the clubhouse, and inside them a team of employees with tucked-in shirts were busy dressing tables in thick white cloths and unloading goods from a van parked on the grass. The parking lot was filling up with shiny cars, and groups of wealthy, boat-loving people socialized on the clubhouse deck, drinking coffee and wearing pale-colored clothes. Valerie didn't appear to be among them. Passing the kitchen, I could feel the dizzy motion of the cooks inside as they stirred and baked and iced.

"Amy!" Doug called. He'd wheeled his chair to the door of his office. He removed a toothpick from between his teeth and pointed it at me. I'd been avoiding him since rummaging through his office for the member directory, and now my heartbeat quickened. He pedaled himself backward and tapped the toothpick on his desk. "I have a mission for you, should you choose to accept. We've got a flower order waiting. All paid for, but Kurt forgot to request delivery. Today of all days! You've got a car, right?"

He had selected *me* for this mission, which meant he

still considered me just as worthy and dependable as ever, and I felt so relieved that I forgot to say no, I didn't have a car, and he interpreted my silence as an answer.

"You're a lifesaver." He handed over a receipt with the shop's information and the order number. "Remember, if you're swarmed by mosquitoes, swat to kill." He was still laughing about that as I ducked out of his office.

Somehow in the course of those few minutes, the temperature had skyrocketed, as had the number of people in the parking lot. I wove through them, happy to leave the pandemonium behind, though I couldn't escape the humidity pressing in from all sides. The flower shop was only a mile away, and if I hurried, Doug would never suspect anything. He would be occupied with other preparations for the regatta, and I could always say there had been a long line or a minor issue with the order. But I hated to lie! If the order was too bulky or heavy to carry, I'd have to weigh my options: I could make several trips, running all the way back to the shop, or I could take only what I was able to carry and blame the discrepancy on the florist, although that was a slimy thing to do, and he might call and demand a refund. I focused on maintaining a brisk pace and trying to stay optimistic.

The order was waiting on the floor, a tag on it that read "Salters Cove Yacht Club." I wanted to cheer—it was a large crate, but I would easily be able to fit my arms around it, and I basked in my good fortune as I presented the receipt to the cashier. When she asked if I wanted a hand getting it to my car, I declined firmly, then squatted to hug the crate. It had more weight than expected. I braced myself and doubled my efforts, trying not to distort my face since I could feel her eyes on me, judging whether to intervene, in which case I'd have to lead her out to some stranger's car and pretend to search my pockets for the keys. "Have a nice day!" I called.

I stumbled out of view of the shop and adjusted the crate against my hip. If I put it down, there was a chance I wouldn't be able to lift it again, so I kept moving, inching my feet forward, my hands turning slippery with sweat. I recited my congratulations letter by heart, just in my head so as not to sacrifice the breath. I was Amy Hanley, nationally certified emergency medical technician, Registry No. E4068211. I could handle anything. When it isn't feasible to carry a patient, EMTs use an emergency drag, and perhaps I could apply that here. But the shoulder and ankle drags would only work if the crate had limbs, and the blanket drag required a strip of fabric. During training, I used to long for the chance to execute a real-life firefighter carry: to drape a patient's body over my shoulder and experience, in the most tangible way, the gravity of my role in the world. Now, with my knees wavering and the sun throbbing on my head, I ridiculed myself for being so foolish.

My breath ricocheted off the side of the crate and splashed, hot, back at me. I tried to focus only on that, on each breath, and to imagine the crate was a growth, an irregular mass comprised of my own tissue, and if I could only convince myself it was benign, it would be. Eventually I felt the hump of the curb under my shoes: I'd made it to the end of the street. I crossed to the next without attempting to look for traffic. For all I knew there was a parade of cars already watching, waiting for me to fall. Soon after, my hands became too slippery and I was forced to wiggle the crate to the ground. I took inventory of my aches, checked circulation, sensation, and movement of each limb, tested for capillary refill in the tips of my fingers. All this because I couldn't simply say "No, I don't have a car!" Then again, wouldn't Doug have a hunch that I, the chambermaid, did not in fact own a car, and couldn't this be some elaborate form of punishment? If so, Roula would be behind it. I spun around, as though I might find a clue out there on the sidewalk. Besides passing cars, the only noise came from a pub with its door wedged open, muffled voices and laughter. The air inside looked cool, dark. All at once my dry mouth began to open and close like a fish, and I tasted the shot of rum Doug had shared with me, it flooded my greedy tongue, and then I found myself hauling up the crate and carrying it through the door.

Inside, two ceiling fans chopped the air, making me tingle all over. I thudded the crate to the ground beside a stool and ordered a rum and Coke with extra ice. Sweat drooled down my legs and into my sneakers. The instant the bartender slid the drink toward me, ice clacking, I guzzled it down and requested another.

The television—how I'd missed it these past weeks!— played a familiar reality show: two strangers dropped onto a deserted island with no clothes and only one tool apiece had to prove their survival skills. At the other end of the bar, a couple discussed the show, projecting their voices for the benefit of the bartender and me and the one other customer, an old bearded man slouched over his drink. "You laugh now, but just you wait," the woman was saying. "When everything's gone to hell and there's no more running water or electricity or grocery stores, then all those people living in huts in Africa will have the advantage." She moved her plastic straw aside and sucked right from the glass. "*You* certainly couldn't hack it, anyway. He wouldn't survive one day without beer and a TV."

"What would be the point! Right, Jim?"

The bartender nodded without looking up.

I only wanted to savor my fresh cold drink and follow the closed captions, but the slouchy old man turned out to be even more burdensome than the loud couple. He kept burping, sending puff after puff of foul breath into the air, making no attempt to cover his mouth.

"God. Do you mind?" I said, flapping the air. "That's disgusting."

He burped once in my direction. I could hear gas circulating in his gut, and his burps began to detonate even faster, more like hiccups.

The couple had paused to listen. The woman said, "You tell him, hon!"

"You probably have heartburn," I said. "Alcohol can be a trigger." When he refused to acknowledge me, I said, "I once read about a man who had the hiccups for two and a half years. He thought it was heartburn, but it turned out he was wrong. It was a brain tumor."

The man huffed off his seat and into a booth in the back.

"Is that true, or did you make it up?" the woman asked.

"I'm an EMT," I said, and held my card up.

"I once had the hiccups for an entire week, remember that? I tried everything, even had Dale try to scare them out of me—as if it's not scary enough just looking at him."

"It wasn't a *week*," he said. "It was like a day." He stood and told the bartender they needed to head out, they'd be back as soon as humanly possible. An alarm sounded in my head—how much time had I let pass? I rushed to put money on the counter and heave the crate into my arms.

The couple held the door for me, and as I passed through, a plan began to materialize. I followed the sound of their footsteps, groaning and panting to advertise my struggle. It was a shameful ploy, and normally I wouldn't have the nerve, but I was desperate and emboldened by the rum and those two strangers on the deserted island.

"She can't carry that," I heard her say from somewhere on the other side of the crate. "Honestly, Dale. When's the last time we did our good deed? We're low on karma."

There was a sigh, a pause, some whispering. I let my groans intensify. Finally the man peeked his head around the crate. "Just where do you think you're headed with that monstrosity?" he asked.

"Just down to the Salters Cove Yacht Club. It's not too far."

"A yacht club! I thought you were an EMT."

"It's just a summer job."

"Come on," she said. "We'll drop you off."

Reclining in the back seat, one hand securing the crate beside me and the air conditioner on full blast, I felt triumphant. "I liked how you said that, 'Do you mind?'" the woman said. "It's disgusting to go around burping, in a public place like that." She held her hands over the air-conditioning vents. "It's way too hot for you to be carrying that all this way. You could've passed out! They're lucky we helped."

They didn't know the way, so I told them where to turn and pull over. They squirmed to get a better look at the clubhouse, swarming with even more people now. "This kind of thing makes me sick," the man said.

"Well, thanks very much," I said. "I really appreciate it."

The woman twisted to face me. "You make sure you

tell them what I said. It's too dangerous in this heat. You could've passed out."

"This place can't afford delivery?" he said.

I grunted my way through the mob and dropped the crate under the first white tent, hoping it was the right place; I couldn't make it one more step. Two employees with tucked-in shirts swooped in. One of them said, "Finally." They separated the layers of the crate and began pulling out the contents, peach and yellow bouquets arranged in crystal vases. Some water had spilled out and collected at the bottom. No wonder it had been so heavy. I lingered, in case one of them felt inclined to thank me or include me somehow.

"So, what's on the menu?" I asked, to remind them I was still there.

No one answered. Not that I blamed them. They already had a whole team, each with his own designated role and a white tucked-in shirt with a stiff collar, and meanwhile I wore a ratty old T-shirt, now drenched in so much sweat it had changed color. They would never guess that I had my own professional uniform, arriving tonight by 8:00 p.m.—the secret made me feel giggly, untouchable. As I walked back to the clubhouse, the damp shirt slapped against my skin, making a sound like applause.

I found the package waiting outside my door. Though tired and sore, I made a ceremony of it, scrubbing my hands clean before running a knife along the seams of the box. I methodically inspected the pants and then the shirt, taking note of each thoughtfully planned detail and tugging on the material to demonstrate its durability. I saved the patch for last. I closed my eyes and passed my finger over the embroidery as though reading braille: the NREMT symbol, the letters in "Commonwealth of Massachusetts" and "Emergency Medical Technician," the coat of arms in the state seal. With a sewing needle and thread, I fastened the patch to the shirt sleeve with painstaking care. Then I got dressed, topping it off with my black treaded boots and a ponytail.

I observed myself in the mirror from every angle, taking it all in. I opened my laptop and set a ten-second countdown on the webcam. I stood back, my sleeve to the camera and my hands on my hips, looking over my shoulder. I smiled, waiting for 0. It looked good, except you could see the mess in the background, so I positioned myself in front of the front door and tried again. I typed an email to my father, thanking him so much for the magazine subscription. "P.S. Here I am in my new uniform!" I wrote at the bottom, and added my brother to the cc line.

In science, there is a preference for simplicity. The principle of Occam's razor says that the simplest explanation tends to be true, and as I looked over the photo one last time before pressing send, that principle worked in my favor. It was much easier to believe that the person in front of me was an EMT than to believe she'd gone through all the trouble of creating a three-phase treatment to placebo herself into passing an exam.

NINE

"Seared salmon and panzanella. With corn, shishito peppers, and Thai basil," Gary said as I took a seat at his kitchen table. "Whatever all that means." He dropped our plates right on top of a layer of envelopes and newspapers. I hadn't been over for a few days, and it seemed he'd spent that time accumulating as much trash as possible, crusty bowls and pans and takeout cartons with food fossilizing inside. I, on the other hand, had been making the most of our off nights, getting used to the feel of the uniform against my skin and the sight of the patch on my arm in the mirror. One night I'd even ventured outside with it after the neighborhood had gone to bed, just one quick trip around the block, running at top speed as though responding to a cardiac emergency.

"Panzanella?" I asked.

"Some Italian thing—well, obviously. Like a salad but with bread instead of lettuce. I guess a salad made of bread should be right up my alley, ha." His face was visibly damp, and a little scrap of onion skin was stuck to his forehead. "Oh, I almost forgot . . ." He touched his head and discovered the onion skin there, snorting when he saw what it was and crumbling it between his fingers. "These shisisto peppers, or whatever they're called—apparently they're supposed to be sweet, but then every so often one happens to turn out spicy. Don't ask me why people would even bother with them, if that's the case. But just so you know. Of course, that would be just my luck."

I ate slowly, not because of the peppers but because I was still distracted, taking in the state of the kitchen. He'd converted the third kitchen chair into a combination recycling bin, trash can, and laundry basket. I spotted the glass vase by the sink, full of dirty silverware. "So," I said. "How have things been? Is everything okay with you?"

We heard a meow, and the cat came striding in. She gave my ankles their customary greeting and meowed again, more forcefully. "She doesn't like anyone eating without her," he said, standing. She bounded over to take a handful of treats from his palm, and it gave me a clash of bittersweet feelings, seeing how familiar and exclusive they'd already become.

Gary watched her wander back to the living room

and wiped his palm on his pant leg. "When I have the AC on, she likes to sleep right here." He raised his elbow, circled the space under his armpit. "I wasn't sure if I should let her sleep in the bed, you know, in case Irina didn't like that. But at this rate, it looks like a cat's the only thing I'm going to be sleeping with. Might as well get used to it. Is your salmon rubbery?"

"Not at all. I'm practically inhaling it." I tipped my plate toward him. "So, *is* everything okay? You seem a little, I don't know, down."

"To be honest, things are kind of rough right now. A little up in the air, I guess you could say. We had a fight. Me and Irina. I mean, not that we haven't had fights before—that's normal with any relationship. But this was, I don't know. Different."

"What was it about?"

"Well . . . you, sort of." The blood drained from my face and neck. "I mean, not really, not like it's your fault or anything." He cast his eyes down and prodded the slab of fish on his plate. "It's her friends, really. They keep putting ideas in her head about how I need to get her a bigger ring and a new house, because they think it's weird, someone else living here. Especially another woman."

"But it's a separate apartment."

"That's what I told her! She has no idea how expensive things are here, what the housing market's like—it's just not feasible. I never thought someone that beautiful would get so jealous. I know she's just nervous, that's why she gets so hung up on every detail. But I can only take so much, you know? It's always all about her, all the time. What Irina wants, how Irina feels."

I discovered a half-dissolved tomato on my tongue—I'd forgotten to chew. But now I saw it was my turn to talk, to respond somehow, and I fought to swallow it down. "That doesn't sound very fair," I said. "It's a lot of pressure to put on you."

"Well, so the big news was she finally got her interview scheduled at the embassy. But now she's saying she's not going to show up. She doesn't want to come anymore. It's over, that's what she said. And she's going to mail the ring back. So dramatic." He stabbed a cucumber with his fork and narrowed his eyes. "I always hated cucumbers."

"Do you think she meant it?" My voice came out quivery. It took me by surprise, how much I hoped he would say yes, she'd meant it, it was over, for good. With time he'd recover from the disappointment, and I would be there to help every step of the way, we would take care of each other.

"Who knows. Honestly, it would be a relief at this point." He lowered his plate and made a kissing sound, and the cat reappeared. It wasn't like him to leave food behind.

"If you feel relieved, maybe that's a sign. You guys do seem to have a lot of issues. Maybe you're just not that compatible."

"To top it all off, I'm supposed to go to a wedding, of

all things. And I can't back out—it's for the head of my division. It's like the universe gets a kick out of making me suffer." He shuffled through the heap of mail on the table and unearthed an invitation, which I recognized instantly. Once upon a time I had pried it open with a butter knife after steaming it over the stove. Coming face to face with it again, without any of the haste or secrecy this time, I almost broke out laughing.

"I thought once I was engaged, I wouldn't hate weddings as much," Gary said.

"I've only been to one, that I can remember. My cousin's. And that was a pretty long time ago."

He scraped the edge of the invitation across the tablecloth, collecting crumbs. "To tell you the truth, I was actually married before."

I felt my head jerk forward, as if I had no control over my own neck. "You were married?"

"I like to pretend it was just a bad dream. I hardly ever talk about it. Irina doesn't even know." He raised his eyebrows, seeming almost amused by the idea of breaking that news to her. "It only lasted a couple months. She was cheating pretty much the whole time. So yeah, that was—" He scrunched his nose.

"That's awful."

"Yeah." He'd amassed a pile of crumbs, and now he used the invitation to cut it into smaller piles. "That's partly why the ninety-day thing makes me so crazy. I can't make another mistake, it almost killed me the first time. I promised myself I wouldn't rush into things again. But the way the visa works, they don't leave you any choice. But I guess none of that matters now anyway. All this worrying for nothing, if it really is over. She might never even talk to me again. So anyway."

"I could go to the wedding with you, if you wanted. To keep you company. Maybe if you had a friend there, you wouldn't hate it as much."

"You'd do that?"

"Sure."

"It's on the Cape, a week from Saturday. I was planning to just drive back late, avoid the Sunday traffic."

"It could be fun."

"The food should be good at least—he's making his famous southern barbecue. And it'll be really laid-back, more like just a backyard party than a regular wedding, so you don't have to worry about dressing up. Hank's a good guy. I only met her once or twice. She's got a couple kids from a previous marriage. But—I don't know. What do you think Irina will say? She'd probably never forgive me."

"I thought it was over."

"Maybe."

"Well, if she really cares about you, she wouldn't want you to go and be miserable, when you could bring a friend. It can't always be all about her, if it's really going to work. She needs to consider your feelings too. Give and take. She should be happy that you're happy." I felt queasy as it came out of my mouth. Give and take, that much was true, but from what I knew about Irina, there was no way she would understand, let alone be happy. Here I was, his most trusted adviser, setting him up for failure. But on the other hand, appeasing Irina clearly wasn't in his best interest, and maybe my role as his friend demanded that I act in his best interest even when, or especially when, he was unable or unwilling to do so himself. The doomed look on his face, the disorder in his kitchen, the relentless scraping of the invitation across the table, collecting more and more crumbs—all this conveyed a clear message that his mouth wasn't yet ready to articulate: he wanted a way out and needed me to guide him toward it.

"It *would* be nice to have the company," he said. "You're right, that shouldn't be too much to ask. You're sure you don't mind, though?"

"Positive. We can just relax, make the most of it. You'll forget about all this stuff." I finished my meal and leaned back, placing a hand on the knot of my full, satisfied stomach. "Hey, none of our peppers turned out to be the spicy kind. The universe isn't completely against you."

He smiled, a meager, fleeting smile, but a smile nonetheless. "I'm sure lucky I've had you around this summer," he said. "I mean, I feel bad, you probably feel like you're in a soap opera or you're my therapist or something. But I don't know what I would've done." He reached across and patted the table near my hand.

It wasn't until I was back up in my apartment, reading my congratulations letter one last time before bed, that the dreadful, intractable, excruciating problem presented itself. I'd just finished luxuriating in a long, cool bath during which I'd strategized about all I needed to do before the following weekend: get my hair cut and purchase a dress that would be special but still casual, an airy style that would let me float by Gary's side, self-assured and even-tempered, the polar opposite of Irina. He would watch me in my new dress with my new bouncy hair and discover how simple and easy things could be, and then a song comes on that he doesn't hate—a classic, maybe Ray Charles or Frank Sinatra—and we glide onto the dance floor together, enjoying the experience without taking ourselves too seriously, and it occurs to him that he already has everything he needs. When my fingertips had shriveled up, I drained the tub and stepped into my uniform. Just as I reached the refrigerator and began "Dear Amy," it hit me, the one detail my brain had blocked out. A week from Saturday, that would be—August 25. But no, that couldn't be right. I opened my laptop and checked the calendar, running my finger over the days. I found the email confirming my registration for the exam. The numbers appeared on the screen, the 2 and the 5, in obnoxious bold text. Still, I couldn't help refreshing the page as though it might somehow change. Even after

I stopped hoping and wasn't even looking at the numbers anymore, just glaring straight ahead with hot unblinking eyes, my finger continued to press the button, refreshing the page over and over and over again.

I flopped facedown in bed, knowing I would wrinkle my uniform but too dejected to care. I felt disappointed for myself, but even worse, I had finally made a friend and now I had to disappoint him too. Right now Gary was in bed feeling relieved, trusting that he could rely on his closest friend to be at his side, the one bright spot in a time of darkness and heartache. He had been married before! Just when I thought he was no longer capable of surprising me. For him, this wedding was not a joyous occasion but a dangerous one, conjuring up painful memories, especially now, as his relationship with Irina imploded, and I knew as well as anybody how ruthless memories could be in their pursuit of you. I needed to go back down and deliver the bad news, before he had time to solidify it all in his mind. But I couldn't. My legs wouldn't go. I would have to stop by in the morning before work; that would give me some time to come to terms with the situation. And if by chance I found he'd left early or wasn't available for some reason, I would leave a note that he would be sure to see the instant he returned home. Tomorrow, I would face it all tomorrow.

The morning came, and I left for work without knocking or writing a note. It didn't feel so much like a decision, more like my body was doing things and not doing other things, and I had no choice but to cooperate. Still, nothing was permanent yet, and I could be more pragmatic and levelheaded in the light of morning. Technically it was not impossible to cancel the date of an exam up to twenty-four hours in advance, though I hadn't wanted to admit that at first. The idea of putting it off even one extra minute, after all my laboring and strategizing and outright lying, felt almost as crushing as failure. The letter on my fridge, the uniform in my closet, the card in my pocket—I felt a sense of responsibility to them. They had to be official and irreversible, they relied on it. And I'd carefully crafted them to build up to a single end point, August 25. I pictured my father searching online for a gift and coming across *EMS Monthly*, eagerly entering his credit card information. I pictured Gary at the bakery, requesting a custom cake. Lying had only been okay when I knew that, on August 25, it would transform into the truth. How could I go turning my back on them and on my future self, after she'd put her faith in me? I traced the shape of my certification card against my leg—Amy Hanley, Registry No. E4068211. *FROM: Proud Dad. Congratulations, congratulations, congratulations.*

But on the other hand, the wedding was a onetime affair. There would be no do-overs, no way to make it up to Gary. I was the only thing standing between him and a pit of misery, and he was counting on me, as he had been all summer, and I hadn't let him down yet. If the roles were reversed, I wouldn't want him to jeopardize his future in any crucial way, but I would also be touched by his willingness to sacrifice for me, and what was a friend, if not someone willing to make sacrifices in your time of need? I had a chance to prove to Gary and to myself that, unlike Irina, some people were willing to put the needs and feelings of others above their own. And by refusing to be indifferent to his suffering, by not ignoring or minimizing it, wouldn't I actually embody what it means to be an EMT more than I would by getting a passing grade on some exam?

Postponing didn't have to feel like giving up, if I didn't let it. If I edited the date on the letter, it could simply mean an adjustment to the treatment plan, a common practice with any patient. Plus, the additional time should only make the treatment more potent, enabling me to pass the exam with even more confidence and ease. By the time I navigated through the crowd arriving for day two of the regatta, I'd settled it, and soon I was up in room 8, dusting the nightstand with the calm determination that comes with knowing you're doing the right thing.

Two small boys were staying in room 8 with their mother, and they'd transformed the nightstand into a police headquarters. The officers smelled like graham crackers and stuffy noses, and, as I swabbed around them, careful not to intervene, my lower back spasmed, still tender from carrying the box the day before. It reminded me once more how lucky I am that my organs and tissues and cells have been assembled in the right way, not only so that I might do hard work and every day strive to do better but also so that I might take full advantage of my time off, like the following weekend, when I would accompany Gary to a wedding on Cape Cod. It was really happening. "It's really happening!" I announced to the tiny policemen in room 8, because I had to tell someone.

That weekend I set out to take care of my wedding preparations. Though it felt strange to leave the house without reading my letter or pocketing my card, I'd decided to put my treatment on hold until after the wedding so I wouldn't be distracted or tempted to change my mind. After, I would be recharged and refocused, ready to select the best available date, amend my letter, and resume my treatment plan, maybe even add to it somehow, a Phase IV.

I stopped by the beach on my way. The ocean was crammed with swimmers, their belongings left behind to cook in the sand, umbrellas and towels the colors of ripe summer fruit. They flounced their heads and arms up and down in the water like cookies dunking themselves in milk. It must have made me smile because when

I turned away, a homeless-looking man sitting with his hands roofed over his eyes made a comment. "A radio-active smile," he said. It surprised me, partly because I'd never seen a homeless person here before, and partly because I wasn't accustomed to drawing such attention from strangers. I swiveled my head and saw no one else, so he had meant me, my smile.

An ice cream truck had parked nearby, and spontaneously I joined the line behind a group of teenage girls with tan lines that mapped all the different styles of bathing suits they'd worn that summer. They'd drawn on their ankles and calves with black permanent marker; one had incorporated her mosquito bites into the shapes of flowers. She was lifting her hair in front of her face, to simulate how bangs would look. "Don't do it," her friend said. "Syd can pull them off, because obviously, it's Syd. But have you seen Madison's? Her skin's way too oily. It looks like they're glued to her forehead. But she'll do whatever Syd does."

"I thought you liked Madison."

"I like her in the sense that . . . she has a car." They squawked with laughter. The sound brought me back to the days when I was one of them, flitting here and there, never caring too deeply or trying too hard, never needing to. Last summer, standing in line behind girls like these would've plunged me into depression. I might've even tapped one on the shoulder and tried to warn her that life wouldn't always be this way, so effortless and so abundant. But now I had no reason to meddle in anyone else's business because I had my own to attend to, a wedding next weekend and important errands like getting a haircut and finding the perfect dress.

The ice cream man pointed to the Cash Only sign and the girls made a fuss, whining and pleading, though half-heartedly, until one, the leader, gave up. "Come on," she said. "Let's pretend like we're blind, deaf, and dumb," and they stampeded off behind her, flip-flops clapping like mad. I ordered an ice cream sandwich and carried it to where the homeless man sat. I knew better than to laugh or feel sorry for him, but I could still extend a little goodwill by offering up the ice cream. After everything the universe had blessed me with lately, I felt an almost superstitious duty to pay it forward, or else.

The man took the sandwich and squinted at it with uncertainty or even disgust. I felt him on the verge of saying or doing something hurtful, something that could cut me down from my lofty place, so I sped away and didn't look back.

I headed for downtown, full of a growing appreciation for myself and the place I called home. A sprinkler whipped in staccato circles, throwing out water in long silver ropes. Two dogs pulled at their leashes to greet each other, their tails going like windshield wipers. A woman in a wide-brimmed hat pulled a boy and his toys in a red thing behind her, and I couldn't summon the word for what that red thing was called. I felt delighted by such an odd, inexplicable lapse. Only once they'd rolled by did it finally come to me: *wagon.* Wagon!

A car blared its horn. The sudden noise spooked me so that I snagged my foot on a knob in the pavement and nearly fell. It honked again. I hid my face, walking faster and clutching the material of my shorts. Once on this same street, a truck had barreled by me and a boy had lunged out the window and yelled "It's his birthday!" I'd had to watch them disappear, off to have a good time, while I was left alone on the sidewalk with no one to help get that voice out of my head. I'd tried talking to myself, even singing, but all I could hear was *It's his birthday, It's his birthday, It's his birthday.*

But then I heard a shout that sounded almost like my name. I turned and saw Gary. He had pulled to the side of the road and was leaning out of his car to flag me down. I approached his window, a pit opening in my stomach. There had to be a reason he'd found me here, and most likely it was a bad one, like to tell me he and Irina had made up and our plans for the wedding were off. My own words—*It's really happening, It's really happening*—rang through my head just as they had through room 8, only this time with a mocking tone.

"Man, you must've been lost in *some* daydream," he said. "These people think I'm some raving lunatic. Probably taking down my plate number as we speak." He looked disheveled and wet, with his T-shirt suctioned to his skin and the seat belt pulled tight, restricting his movement.

"Did something happen?" I said.

"I went and jumped in the ocean, just like that. First time in years I've gone in. I got the urge this morning, so I just got up and did it. Right off the pier. It's like I'm a new man, see. Free!" He spread his arms. "I haven't heard from Irina at all, but I'm actually okay with it. I'm actually feeling pretty good about things. Even starting to look forward to next weekend." He reached behind him, trying to pull some slack into his seat belt. "Unless, you . . . changed your mind?"

"I didn't change my mind." And thank god I hadn't.

"Great. I was just on my way to get the car washed, but then I saw you walking. Thought you might want a lift. Where you headed?"

"Just downtown, to do some errands." I wanted to protect the details, in case he tried to interfere with my good intentions, insisting I not trouble myself or waste any money. "But I really don't mind walking."

"No, no, I insist. Your chariot awaits. I can drop you on my way."

I marveled at how his passenger seat felt familiar to me now, just like his kitchen table. He'd emptied the trash from the center console. "That's okay," I said, buckling in. "I actually like the car wash."

The rush from the open window cleared my face and

flung back my hair. I closed my eyes and imagined I was being tugged by the current of a river: I was a hardy stone surrounded by other hardy stones with no concept of the past or future, content to inhabit this one little pocket of Earth forever.

When the rush ceased and I opened my eyes, we were outside the dark tunnel of the car wash and Gary had his top half hoisted out the window so he could push buttons on a machine. The vibrations of the idling car had a sedating effect on me. As we moved through the phases of the wash, he made comments like "Isn't it funny how you want to duck. Your instincts" and "These things always reminded me of giant linguine." He was feeling jovial and chatty, and I appreciated that without making any effort to match it, for I was a content little stone and simply wanted to let the glorious current tug me along.

Gary dropped me by the drugstore, where I flipped through fashion magazines, searching for an inspiration photo and anticipating the cherished occasion of a haircut, which meant a visit from another person's hands, massaging your scalp, adjusting the angle of your head. According to this magazine, you had to choose the right style for your face shape—mine fell somewhere between a heart and an inverted triangle—and consider hair type, body type, age, occupation, even personality. This was a lot to take into account, and I stood at the rack, growing dizzy from the perfumed pages, until finally I landed on a style that seemed flattering enough, with the hair resting an inch above the shoulders and shorter layers around the face. I paid for the magazine and carried it under my arm to Radiance Salon and Spa. I'd passed this salon many times. It looked fancy, with a bubbling fountain out front and painted rocks lining the path to the door. Now was the time to splurge.

Inside, it smelled fruity and chemically. The customers looked like planets under their round black smocks, with the hairdressers moving in orbits around them to snip and prune, and everyone laughing and chatting, watching their reflections in the giant mirror and waiting for the new, improved version of themselves to be revealed. I couldn't wait to join in. At the front desk I found a bowl of pastel candies and a jug of hand lotion with "Tester" written on the front, but no receptionist, and no bell either. I waited, peeking around the corner every so often at the row of damp heads. One of them was bound to notice me. I tried waving. I didn't want to interrupt and wasn't sure of the protocol; maybe you were supposed to have an appointment just to step inside. I scolded myself—someone about to attend a wedding on Cape Cod should've thought to call ahead.

A blow dryer wailed. I pumped the tester lotion into my palm but couldn't get it all rubbed in and had to blot the excess on my shirt. There was a cluster of sleek white armchairs and I contemplated sitting in one, but I didn't know if that was a good idea or how much longer to wait. My neck was getting hot, and the magazine had gone limp under my arm. I wished I hadn't brought it—they had a whole stack of them here anyway, fanned across a sleek white table at the center of the sleek white chairs. At last I let the magazine flop to the floor and walked out, the door chiming behind me in an awful, merry way.

Out on the sidewalk, I took measured breaths and tried to regroup. I gave myself a pep talk about not letting some stuck-up salon with a tacky fountain demoralize me when I had important plans and no time to sit and sulk. I entered the clothing boutique next door, where the attendant greeted me right away, asking how I was. "Sick of people," I said.

"Preaching to the choir." She pushed her cat's-eye glasses up into her hair, a short pixie cut that complemented the oval shape of her head expertly. "Just give a shout if you need anything."

I browsed through a rack of bland dresses, giving them a once-over and then pushing them down the line. My patience waning, I grabbed a fistful of hangers. In the narrow fitting room, surrounded on all sides by my reflection, I quickly grew exasperated by all the zippers and buttons and hooks. I'd never liked shopping. My mother used to insist on taking me to the mall for back-to-school sales every year, no matter how much I protested. She'd strap on her pocketbook each August, optimistic that this time she would say or do something irresistible, and for just an instant, she would catch me enjoying myself. Once she'd detoured us to a kiosk selling the most flamboyant, hideous hats. "Let's pretend we're in a movie montage. It's so fun when they do that, try on a million hats or something." She picked up the two most revolting ones, plonked one on my head, one on hers. "We have to take a picture. Would you mind?" she said to the man working the kiosk, already thrusting her camera into his hands. "We don't have *any* pictures just the two of us." Right before he pressed the button, I pulled the hat down so it covered my face. "Oh," she said when she realized.

We'd given each other the silent treatment on the drive home. Except for one thing. She said it softly, maybe not even meaning to say it aloud. She said, "I always used to imagine having a daughter . . ." Then she trailed off. It wasn't like her to hold back, and it haunted me more than any sentence she finished.

But what I would've given to have her here with me now. To step out in a dress and find her waiting there. The two of us together in the next stage of life, the one where we could be friends, sharing the details of our adult lives and laughing about those angst-filled years that seemed so ridiculous and hilarious now. I would ask her opinion, listen to what she said, finally let her see my excitement, let her share in it. She would know exactly what looked best, she always had. And when we had found *it*, I'd ask a stranger to take our photo, me in the new outfit she'd picked out and her at my side, my arm hugging her tight, my head resting on her shoulder.

But I would settle for so much less than that. Just hear-

ing her voice—just for a moment, saying anything to anyone, even far off in the distance, barely intelligible. Or no
voice at all. Just to crouch down and see her feet on the
other side of the door. For that I would've given up my
plans with Gary and any other plans I might ever have
again, any good thing that might have come to me in the
future. The wish burned in my chest until I was doubled
over. All she'd wanted back then was to bond with me
over something superficial and fun, and I refused her just
as I'd refused her so many times before, and after. I shuddered with disgust for myself. I still couldn't understand
why it had been so difficult, so utterly impossible, for me
to humor her even once.

None of the dresses was exactly right, exactly worthy,
but I'd been in the fitting room so long and no other customers had come in, so I felt compelled to make a purchase. I chose the cheapest one, a light blue sleeveless
dress on sale for $29.99. As the attendant beeped the tag,
she said, "This will be a nice color on you," in a patron-
izing tone that made me regret the decision. If instead I'd
flung the merchandise into a corner of the fitting room
and stalked out, *she* would have been the one left feeling
pathetic.

"Actually, it's for a friend," I said. "Can I get it gift-
wrapped? It's her birthday. She's throwing a big party."

"I have the perfect paper." She pulled her glasses down
her nose, not in a suspicious way but a way that showed
she was getting down to business. The wrapping paper

had a pattern of wildflowers in an earthy color palette that managed to be both sophisticated and whimsical at the same time. She was right, it was perfect. She nestled the dress in a bed of cream-colored tissue and then folded the paper around the box, meticulous in her creases and her application of tape, which she drew from a dispenser shaped like a high-heeled shoe. She topped it off with a ribbon, crimping the ends so they fell in glossy ringlets across the top. When she handed it over with a gift receipt and a small complimentary card, I felt sorry for misunderstanding her before. I carried the gift proudly in front of me as I walked home, quickening my pace whenever a car passed, as though I was running late and the birthday party was just up ahead.

I drenched my hair in the kitchen sink, then combed through the snarls and hacked six inches off, snip snip snip, without hesitation. It came out decently, especially considering that I couldn't get a great view of the back and had only my memory of the magazine photo to use as inspiration.

As it dried, I opened the complimentary card from the dress shop, tapping my pen against my chin as I contemplated the blank space. *Congratulations* came to mind first—*congratulations, congratulations, congratulations*—because this refrain had become a reflex, as automatic as a muscle contraction after the tendon gets hit. While that was a promising sign in terms of my obecalp treatment, it wasn't the reflex I wanted to activate now. Instead, I wrote "Dear Amy, Good luck at the wedding," and the words from Gary's mail all those months ago came back to me—*Be selfish, have fun, don't walk away with any regrets*—so I wrote those down too, then sat on my bed and presented the gift to myself. I admired the wrapping paper one last time before tearing through it and throwing off the lid. The dress was more impressive than I'd remembered, the fabric buttery between my fingers. More important, it was a true gift, the kind that inherently warrants gratitude, because it was generous and compassionate how I'd cheered myself up, refusing to let an unfortunate experience at Radiance Salon and Spa send me into a tailspin. I lifted the dress to my heart. It smelled clean and unmistakably new.

TEN

Thirty minutes in, we hit traffic—heavy traffic. Every once in a while it would break, revealing a glorious stripe of asphalt before us, but then a half mile later, I would blink and it would be back, even worse than before and seeming rather pleased with itself. Neither Gary nor I acknowledged it aloud, as though we might jinx it. I kept busy aiming my pits at the air-conditioning vents and experimenting with the weightlessness of my new hair, freshly washed and fluffed, by flicking my head. The traffic didn't carry any ominous meaning, I told myself, it was a typical part of a weekend trip, a nuisance anyone who takes weekend trips could relate to—and this was also what I planned to tell Gary when his good mood inevitably turned sour. He'd created a playlist specially for this drive, our drive, titled "Cape Cod Cruisin'." The fact that we'd done little to no cruising so far hadn't seemed to faze him yet. At one point he began pounding the wheel, and I thought, Here we go, but it turned out just to be his way of punctuating part of a song, which I leaned in and took note of: "Sweet Jane" by the Velvet Underground. Still, each time he lowered his foot back on the brake, I braced myself, hoping to get it over with.

My exam would've been halfway over by now. Every minute that ticked by on the dashboard clock made the decision more tangible, more absolute. But I breathed through it, surprised by own composure. Soon I stopped thinking about the time in terms of the exam and instead in terms of the ceremony, which was set to begin at four. With three o'clock approaching and still nothing from Gary, no nervous tic or angry muttering, I couldn't contain it any longer. "Three," I said, pointing to the clock. "Did you see? It's almost three."

"Indeed."

"So do you think we'll make it in time?"

"Not by four, no way. But that's probably better. I'm betting they start late. Now we won't be stuck making small talk."

I eyed the side of his face, waiting. A rusty car with a duct-taped window cut into our lane, forcing him to slam on the brakes so hard that we were launched forward and then knocked back against our seats, and all he said was: "This poor guy. His wife's at the hospital right now, about to go into labor. Godspeed, my friend!"

Although I was impressed by his self-control and grateful that Irina's effect seemed to be fading, I also wondered about my complete lack of effect. He hardly seemed to register my presence beside him. Was it better to have a negative effect than no effect at all? "How's the cat doing?" I asked, before the chatter could get too loud in my head.

"You mean A—What was it you wanted to call her again? Figure we might as well give her a name already."

"I'm not attached to anything. We could come up with one together."

"Good idea. Let's brainstorm. Hmm. Hmm. Maybe we need some inspiration." He lowered the volume and wheeled his head around the car and out the windows, left side then right. "Braintree," he said, pointing to a sign for Exit 17. "Braintree? No. That's not it. That would imply that she's smart. I think she's more average." He found this so amusing that he decided to entertain himself this way for the rest of the sluggish drive: "Here's Abington. Could be Abby for short? Eh, but that doesn't sound much like a cat." "Hingham, Weymouth. Man, those don't exactly roll off the tongue." "Look, there's Marshfield. Marsha for short? 'Marsha Marsha Marsha.' Too *Brady Bunch*." "Kingston? Too manly. That'd be a good name for a dog, though. Don't you think?" He eventually found the answer on a sign that read "Sandwich/Mashpee." "Mashpee! Now that's cute. Little Mashpee. It's perfect. Don't you think?"

"Perfect," I agreed, though without much feeling. I'd been worried about being late, but now that we were getting close, a new, opposing set of my nerves revved up. I found myself praying for the traffic to somehow get worse and, when that failed, for the steering to go haywire or a tire to fall off. Gary mapped the end of the route on his phone, and while at one time I may have delighted in the bizarre companionship of the robotic voice, now it only added to my anxiety. When it announced the final turn toward our destination, sending us up a steep hill, Gary glanced over and said something charitable: "I won't really know anyone either, except for a few work people. And it's not like we're close. I don't care about mingling. And we can always leave early." It showed he was attuned to my feelings and didn't find them unreasonable, yet all I could do in response was stare out the window at the trees crowding the pavement, everything blindingly sunny and green.

We came to a line of cars parked half on the road and half on the grass, and Gary pulled up behind the last one. "Probably as close as we're gonna get," he said. My hand was clammy on the door handle. "Hold on a sec." He reached into the pocket on his door and then held out his palm. Inside was a lighter and a small glass pipe. "Helps take the edge off," he said, and lit the top, blowing the smoke into the back seat. He offered it to me. "It's good quality, medical grade. Pretty mild." I looked at it. I picked it up and breathed in a steady stream, my throat burning raw. Afterward, he helped himself again and pushed his finger around in the charred bits. "I had a little before we left. Just to make sure I'd be relaxed."

"Isn't that dangerous? Like, if you're driving?"

"It was only a tiny bit."

"I didn't know you smoked."

"Every once in a while. Special occasions. What about you?"

"Sure, special occasions."

I took another inhale, and then he finished it off and returned it to its hiding place. "Shall we?"

My feet were jelly when they hit the ground. With every step I managed to take, the hill seemed to stretch longer and steeper ahead. The sun poked its tentacles at us through the trees, and insects dive-bombed my face and my armpits stung where I'd shaved that morning and the lingering smell of marijuana curdled in my nostrils until I thought I was going to get sick—all this, just to get sick! But at last we reached a clearing with a grand house on a large plot of grass and the endorphins kicked in and a sea breeze whipped through, so cool and refreshing that I was cured.

Gary had been right, because by the time we edged our way into the yard, we were almost an hour late and yet a handful of guests were still working, without any urgency, to arrange folding chairs in front of an arch, most holding cans of beer in one hand and popping open chairs with the other. "Beer," Gary said. "Just what we need." We skirted through clusters of people to find the row of coolers and consumed our beers quickly and silently. The cold can fit like a key in my hand, the drops of condensation rolling in heavenly wet tracks down my arm. We started on two more. I could see Gary eavesdropping on a nearby conversation that, from what I could gather, concerned the horrendous traffic conditions. When a man said "I took my bike," Gary swung around and said "You *biked* all the way up that hill?" "Motorcycle," the man said. This cracked Gary up, which in turn cracked me up, and we kept on cracking up until I had a cramp in my side.

Everyone migrated to the folding chairs, drinks in tow, and a lady in the back brought a violin to her chin. She didn't play the usual bridal procession but something much more lovely, almost melancholy, that gave me a pang of nostalgia for some vague, unknowable time. The head of Gary's division strode up the aisle, accompanied by a teenage boy with a lopsided tower of hair that suggested he was a kindred spirit, a person who understood how difficult it could be to enter a salon and boldly stand your ground. They wore shorts and flip-flops, and when one of the groom's toes snagged in the grass, he did a giant skip on one foot and wiped his nose—some snot had dripped out—and I nearly clapped, I was so exuberant: I did love weddings, especially today, now, this.

Next came the flower girl, wearing yellow overalls and carrying a basket of petals, and then finally the bride, in a loose white dress that wrapped around and tied at the waist like a bathrobe and a smile so big and full of spectacularly crooked teeth that I had to reach out and squeeze the flesh on Gary's upper arm. Then I stopped, remembering that I'd never even met these people before. The marijuana must have messed with my equilibrium, and I had to get ahold of myself before Gary wondered if I was unhinged.

The ceremony lasted only ten minutes or so, and then the couple romped down the aisle hand in hand and everyone set their cans and plastic cups on the grass in order to stand and cheer. And I joined them, whooping along in earnest, with an overflowing heart, cheering for these two dear souls who had found each other at last, and for hope and love and sacred promises, for myself and Gary and all of us, here and everywhere. In the midst of it, an image of Florence Nightingale entered my mind. Not the tireless hero ferrying her lamp from soldier to soldier, but the feeble woman at the end of her life who, having rejected every suitor, found herself isolated and bedridden and surrounded by Persian cats that she claimed would lick the tears from her eyes. I wanted to weep for her and all she had missed out on, underestimated. When they reached the end of the aisle, the groom turned back and said, "Now, we barbecue!" and everyone cheered again.

Gary and I collapsed into our chairs. He leaned over clumsily and said, "I feel great."

"It didn't upset you?" In my manic state, I'd completely forgotten to check on him.

"Not at all. In fact, I don't feel anything." He poured the last drops of beer into his mouth. "Except hungry. *So* hungry. I can't *wait* for barbecue." He peeked into his empty can. "I should probably slow down."

"I got all emotional, for some reason."

"You did?"

"I know, it's embarrassing. I don't even know them! I guess there's just something about weddings."

"Don't be embarrassed."

"Gary." A man clapped him on the shoulder. "How's it going? Good to see you, out of the office."

"Good to be out."

"You've met my wife, Carly? And Lyla's somewhere under here. She can sleep through anything, so long as it's Mom holding her."

"This is my date, Amy," Gary said. The words activated every muscle in my body. I yearned to check the expression on his face but didn't dare move my eyes.

"Andy," the man said. I shook his hand and made an awkward gesture to the woman, since her arms were full with the baby, hidden under a hat. We all said nice to meet you, then the woman said, "We didn't meet before, did we? At the holiday party? I had the worst case of pregnancy brain back then."

"No," I said. "I didn't really know Gary then."

"Oh, I envy that! Just getting to know each other. All the excitement. The butterflies." She gave her husband a look. "Not to say this stage doesn't have its benefits. You certainly get comfortable."

"We're pretty comfortable already," Gary said. Again my muscles activated. So much chaos erupted inside the walls of my chest that it seemed a miracle no one put a hand to my head and asked if I needed to lie down. So Gary believed we'd fast-forwarded through the first stage, the one marked by excitement and butterflies but also uncertainty and anguish—it was the only stage he'd ever made it to with Irina, even though they'd been engaged, and yet he and I were already past it, already on to something steady, important, mature. I hadn't considered it this way before, but now it struck me as so obviously, so magnificently, true.

"Well, don't rush it. That's my unsolicited advice. I was one of those girls who swore I'd never let my husband watch me in the delivery room." She leaned in as though to confide in me, but didn't adjust the volume of her voice. "Like I'd rather *die* than have him witness all that blood and gore down there. Then the next thing you know, I'm spread-eagled, like, *Blah!* I'm, like, That's your problem—you're the one who's going to be stuck with those images in your head. Sorry, way too much information. I have zero filter these days."

"She doesn't get out much anymore," Andy said.

"It's true," she said, smiling.

"So have you checked out the house yet?" Andy asked Gary. "It's pretty neat to see how he adapted to the landscape, with the breezeway there between the two wings, each at a slight angle. They're connected below grade, but you can only tell from the ocean side. Anyway, you should have him give you a quick tour, or at least go explore on your own." Gary said he would, and then we entered a lull, so Andy said they'd better get Lyla in the shade. "This is the longest we've had her out of the house, and I'm going to have a heart attack before we even get to eat."

"He's a maniac," his wife said over her shoulder as they started to walk away. "I really am worried about his health!"

"Well, if your chest starts to hurt, find Amy! She's an EMT," Gary said.

Despite the countless times I'd thought or said those words myself, they caught me off guard, as though I couldn't begin to fathom where he'd come up with them. "Not exactly," I said quietly at the same time as she said, "Oh, good to know!" so mine went unnoticed.

The smell of charcoal smoke billowed toward us. Gary gazed at the grill, its heat wrinkling the air, the platters of raw meat and veggies waiting to be seared. "Oh *man*," he said, eyes shining.

"Is there anyone else you need to say hi to?" There was so much to learn from what Gary said to these people! And who knew, some of them might become more than just colleagues: we might start meeting for game nights on the weekends and organizing a Yankee swap at the holidays and even splitting a vacation rental on a lake up north.

"No. This is perfect, just sitting here. This is all I want to do. Is that okay?"

"Sure," I said, though my feet hopped around in the grass, restless.

"I hope it's okay that I said that, 'date.' Just makes things easier."

"Of course, no problem." My eyes wandered in every direction except Gary's. The flower girl came running toward us with an inflatable bat and bonked our knees, laughing. "This is my mom's wedding," she announced. "She's the bride."

"It's a very nice wedding," I said. "Did you help her with it?"

"That's my mom over there, with Hank. He's better than my real dad, except he has a bald spot right here. It used to have hair, but then one day it didn't grow anymore. It could happen to my brother one day too, except it probably won't, since my real dad doesn't have a bald spot. My brother's inside, being on his own. His name's Jonas. I'm Denali."

"Denali? That's a unique name," Gary said.

"That's because I'm named after a mountain in Alaska. It's also called Mount McKinley, but my mom said she'd never name me that. Because of the president. Who was a *Republican*." She dropped the bat on the grass and fidgeted in her overalls, yanking on the straps. "I hate when it's hot out. That's why I'm going to live in Alaska one day, with the Eskimos. I love Eskimos. Winter's in my bones."

"Alaska, huh?" Gary said. "But you know, it stays dark there for half the year—the sun just doesn't come up. Though personally I think that sounds kind of nice. Perfect for hibernating. Maybe I was a polar bear in a past life. What do you think?"

"Polar bears don't hibernate."

"Is that right? Well, maybe it was a penguin. Kids *did* use to say that I waddle." He stood and tottered from one leg to the other with his shoulders hiked up and his arms held stiff at his sides like two flippers. He seemed to lose control of his own motion and then finally hopped on one foot and crashed back down into his chair.

Denali cocked her head. "You're weird."

"Me? No way."

She tugged her headband down to her neck and rubbed the skin on her forehead where it had left an impression, tiny grid lines. "Feels like a waffle," she said.

Gary leaned in to inspect. "Hmm. It kind of looks like one too. Like a delicious waffle. Now I'm *really* hungry."

"Yuck!" She shrieked and darted away, one eye checking back over her shoulder, hoping for some kind of action.

Gary didn't disappoint. He rose to his feet, bellowing, "Fee-fi-fo-fum, I smell the blood of an Englishman!" and thudded after her with giant monster footsteps. I didn't mind being left on the sidelines; in fact, I was magnetized. I could've watched them go on like that all day. When Denali finally decided to be caught, he picked her up sideways and pretended to munch the meat on her forearm like it was corn on the cob.

Denali sat with us while we gorged on barbecue. Gary attacked ribs and pork butt and soft-shell crab with a fanaticism that brought him repeatedly to the verge of choking, and I was not much better, raking a bone with my teeth to pick up every last tidbit, my hands soggy with oil and barbecue sauce. Denali observed, pressing her thumb into a buttermilk biscuit. "Wow," she said, shifting her eyes from Gary to me. "Would he really have eaten me?"

"Oh, no." I wiped my mouth and gave her a serious nod. "He only eats kids when he's *really* desperate. And only for dessert. He says they're too sweet for a main course." Gary gestured in agreement, his mouth full.

"We have cake for dessert!" Denali said. "And there's two kinds, chocolate for me and coconut with the shreds on top for my mom. Plus grilled peaches, 'cause that's what Hank likes."

"Phew," I said. "Then you shouldn't have anything to worry about."

The three of us had formed a happy little triangle, and then a woman coasted by, pulling all our eyes toward her and dismantling it, just like that. She was impossible to ignore. She wore a skimpy dress that exposed her slender shoulders and the plank of her back, firm and suntanned beneath a wild flow of long, sun-dappled hair. When a breeze came, throwing the ends of her hair out in a miraculous, iridescent display, it sucked the dress tight against her body, and sucked the breath from the three of us as well, for we could now see the precise contour of her round butt and athletic thighs. It seemed to me that such a being could not be made up of organs made up of tissues made up of cells, at least not the same organs and tissues and cells that made up the rest of us.

"She looks like a mermaid," Denali breathed.

"She does," Gary replied.

I'd come across plenty of attractive women in my life and could recognize them as such without any further reflection—I knew my standing, and it was decent enough, I didn't care to work to improve it or resent others who did. But the existence of this particular woman felt like a direct challenge to my own, and rather than put up a defense, I wanted to join her and revolt against myself. Why had I decided to cut my hair, anyway? Why hadn't

I let it grow long and lush and golden while I lounged in a bikini, letting the sun polish my dull complexion?

Spellbound, Denali hopped to her feet and followed the woman without even a wave goodbye. Gary and I sat in our chairs, doing our best to appear oblivious. He finished eating. I let ants crawl onto my plate. Around us, guests launched ceramic balls, beanbags, and horseshoes at their corresponding targets and screamed in triumph and defeat. "We could play," Gary said. "Yeah," I agreed, but neither of us made a move.

"You're good with kids," I said after some time.

"Well, she was fun. You are too."

"Fun?"

"Good with kids. But, yeah, fun too."

We went and served ourselves large blocks of cake. By the time I'd whittled mine to the last bite, the woman had graciously moved out of sight and I'd recovered somewhat. The fact of her existence no longer seemed so catastrophic. I felt mortified and petty. I'd turned her into a villain to justify my own villainous impulses. It was possible Gary had hardly even noticed her and that Denali would've left at that moment regardless of who had passed by—it wasn't like she was going to stay with us for the rest of the evening.

At dusk, they turned on Christmas lights and passed around bottles of mosquito repellent. The teenage boy unraveled a long extension cord and set up a turntable in the far corner of the yard, creating a little station for himself. Music erupted as he hovered over the equipment, his body rocking, his face hidden by that tower of hair, even more lopsided now thanks to a giant pair of headphones. The music—an electronic style with an unrelenting beat and erratic computerized vocals—didn't exactly fit the occasion. It made me both proud and apprehensive, because here he was making a contribution that required tremendous bravery, but you could never be sure how that would be received. To my surprise, people didn't hesitate. They gravitated to the grass around him and began gyrating.

Denali discovered us again, her lips and teeth now stained with icing. "That's my brother," she said. "He has anger problems. That's why my mom bought him that stuff. He wants to be a DJ."

Her mother appeared behind her, and I couldn't help thinking, Here she is, the bride, it's really her. There was a flutter in my stomach, as though I'd come face to face with a celebrity. She gathered Denali's hair in her hands. "Nali, don't you think you've bothered enough people for one night?" She tipped Denali's head back and they stuck their tongues out at each other. "Hi, it's Gary, right? Been a while. So glad you could make it, though. Sorry if she's been a pest." She turned to me and extended her hand. "I'm Samantha."

"Amy. Thank you so much for having us. This is a beautiful wedding."

"Oh, thanks." She rolled her eyes and blew hair out of

her face. "You stop caring about all the superficial things the second time around. But you guys are having a good time?"

"A great time," Gary said. "Congratulations to both of you."

"You two have got to get out there. At least to humor my son. He's been planning for this for months. But don't tell him I said that. He'd kill me. Right, Nali? Come, my pumpkin pie. Come dance with me." They locked hands and sailed away.

Gary stood transfixed, watching them sink into the crowd with an expression of bewilderment. "I hate dancing." He sighed. "I'm terrible. And this? Music to have a stroke to." He sounded increasingly agitated, but I could tell it came from a vulnerable place, as though he took their dancing as a personal attack, meant to expose his shortcomings. "Seriously, why wouldn't they just ask him to play something else? *Any*thing else. Even the crap my mom listens to—that'd be like a godsend right now."

"It's nice, though. They're showing how much they support him. He probably feels empowered."

Gary's face softened. He turned to me with an odd smile that first gave me the sensation that a body part had come exposed, and then that my feet had left the ground. "Where have you been?" he said. He watched the dancers for another few beats and then took hold of my hand. "I'm terrible, I'm warning you, the worst there is."

"No one cares about that."

"Yeah, right. Dance like no one's watching."

Now that I saw that the teenage boy had plenty of other supporters, I didn't care much whether we danced or not, but I got the impression that maybe Gary wanted to be coaxed. "We can make it fun," I said, leading the way. "We can make anything fun."

At the edge of the stomping crowd, we swayed and bounced. Gary always kept himself tethered to me in one way or another, but I didn't mind being his anchor, or the spray of his sweat, or how he moved in clipped steps that reminded me of his penguin impression. My body went rigid when the mermaid woman twirled past, but he didn't appear the least bit interested, so I too lost interest, even closed my eyes to focus on forgetting her and being me, gliding my fingers through my new hair, the fresh ends. When I opened my eyes again, his face was close to mine, and he was saying something. "What?" I said. "What? I can't hear you."

"I said, am I embarrassing you?" His hot breath tickled the hairs in my ear.

I shook my head in an emphatic no. Then to prove it, I hurled my body into the most disjointed, over-the-top moves I could come up with, every part of me convulsing and my feet stomping the grass to a pulp, one foot nearly tripping the other. He keeled over with laughter, then drew me into a hug so I was swallowed up in his arms, my nose squished against his neck. I inhaled the spiced scent of a product melting off his skin, deodorant or soap or cologne, and his body odor seeping through, which I didn't hate. As he released his arms, his lips skimmed mine. The contact was so fleeting it had to be an accident, the result of so much haphazard movement. I kept dancing. But he plunged toward me again, with more conviction this time, so that it couldn't be mistaken: we were kissing, Gary and I, the two of us, kissing like we were any other couple enjoying ourselves at a wedding on Cape Cod. When we finally stepped back, I was lightheaded and out of breath. The only thing to do, the only way to keep from exploding, was to dance, so I danced, and Gary danced too, we danced together, closer now, his hands finding my waist—until he said "Come on," and hooked my wrist.

The house was split into two halves, their roofs extending above the gap between them, and this was where he steered us. "Phew," he said. We touched our throbbing ears and let the breeze fly sweetly into our faces. From here we had a view of the glossy black ocean below, though in the dark, it was more of an absence than a presence. As my sweat evaporated into the night, I felt chilled, purified, and slightly disoriented. If not for the taste of his saliva in my mouth, I might have convinced myself it had all been a vivid hallucination.

"This is the breezeway Andy was talking about," Gary said. "Helps with ventilation."

I lifted my arms to the air. "I *love* breezeways." I tried to pin the remaining drops of his saliva to the roof of my mouth with my tongue.

"Let's go explore," he said.

The right wing opened into a gigantic living room with a soaring ceiling and one wall made entirely of windows that framed the ocean. At the far end a staircase spiraled up around a pillar and disappeared into a doorway cut into the top of the wall, just below the ceiling. "Neat," Gary said. "This is like his own twist on a widow's walk. Usually they're on the outside, on the roof." He led us up the staircase, knocking on a step as we went and saying "Oak." At the top we discovered Hank's office, which had another wall of windows, a desk with two computer screens, and a third screen mounted on the wall.

In the basement, we found the passageway that connected the two halves of the house. It was softly lit by bulbs in iron cages, and the walls had built-in shelves displaying rows and rows of books, arranged by color to produce a rainbow effect. As we made our way toward the cracked door at the other end of the passageway, we heard sucking sounds, and then muffled, breathy voices. "Shh," Gary whispered, his eyes alive with curiosity. We flattened ourselves against the books on the wall.

"We should, you know, meet up," a deep voice said. "You're not that far. Just a straight shot on 1A."

"Mmm," someone said, a woman. "Don't you think we should see how the rest of tonight goes first?"

"Ah. I thought tonight was just a dry run."

"Well, hopefully not *dry*." She let out a warbling laugh, then a yelp as the sucking resumed, louder this time.

Gary and I exchanged goofy looks, our eyebrows up and nostrils flared. "Sounds like someone else had the same idea," he whispered. I wasn't sure whether he meant the idea to take a tour or to use a tour as an excuse for a private rendezvous, and that made me uneasy. "Guess we'll have to cut this expedition short."

"Guess so," I agreed, and we giggled quietly.

"You know what," he said, cupping his ear. "That kind of sounds like Donny. Thought I saw him around earlier. An accounts guy."

"Maybe we shouldn't listen?" It was intriguing, sure, the type of thing I would've killed to stumble across when I was so desperate for other voices that I was even willing to steal Gary's mail. But now we didn't need them, just like we didn't need Irina, or anyone else: we had our own story, and it was just as compelling as any other.

The air stiffened as though the hallway itself, the floor and the walls and the shelves and every single book, even the pages huddled together inside them, was waiting in anticipation, and I waited too, waited to see what this night would mean, until at last Gary had mercy on us. He hinged down and kissed me, which meant we were doing this, we were kissing each other, not only at a dance party but in a house that was empty apart from the voices that began to recede as we took over the stage, demoting them to audience, perhaps straining to hear *our* noises now. In all this time, I hadn't forgotten how to kiss. After the initial shock, it came naturally. He moved his hands to my shoulders, and something scratchy, a hangnail or split cuticle, grazed my skin. The intimacy of that amazed me, even more than his tongue in my mouth. His hands flitted from my arms to my waist to my lower back, too timid to land in one place for long, and this left me pleasantly dizzy, rocked by the bright spark of each new touch and the reverberations it left behind.

We paused for a breath and I said, "Do you still feel high at all?" Only after it came out did I realize that a corner of my brain had been hard at work, trying to eliminate all potential factors.

"No. Wore off hours ago." He stepped back and adjusted the bulk around his belt. "But I did do some cocaine in the bathroom. Just a couple of lines. To get me in a dancing mood." His hands still on his belt, he kicked his legs out into a brief, fumbling jig.

"Ha, ha," I said. But when he stopped moving, his face went deadpan. It had a tinge to it, like he had nothing to be ashamed of but now I did, because I'd revealed myself to be naive and uptight, and there was no way to play it off now.

Finally a twinkle flared in his eye, and his expression cracked. "I'm *kid*ding," he chimed. "You're too easy." He clasped my shoulders and jostled me a little, trying to get me in on the fun, and I was happy to concede because this was the kind of toothless needling that came out of Gary when he was feeling uninhibited and affectionate, and it was kind of fun being tricked, the prickle of uncertainty and the hot rush when the truth was revealed, I could get used to it and even play some games of my own.

"Maybe we should go somewhere more private," he said, backpedaling to a door at the beginning of the passageway. Before he even turned the knob, I could tell from the mood and the smell that this was where the teenage boy slept. While he groped around the wall for the light switch, I turned my head, for I felt an allegiance to the boy and didn't want to betray it by snooping in his private room, let alone sprawling on his unmade bed with Gary, plus I didn't know exactly what Gary expected to happen once we were inside—we'd already come so far today, astonishingly far, and now we could slow down, get our bearings, enjoy it.

Luckily, Gary was having trouble finding the light. "He should've thought to put in clap-on lights," I said. "Or a motion sensor."

"We'll have to remember that when we're building *our* house. Mansion, that is. Maybe in Hawaii?"

I rocked my head, pretending to weigh the pros and cons. "Hawaii could work."

"We'll need a special wing for Mashpee. With a screened-in porch, so she can attack it from all angles."

"She'd love that."

"And what else?"

"A breezeway, definitely. And maybe a widow's walk like he has, with a special room at the top just for me."

"Now you're just copying Hank. You've got to be more creative than that."

"Well, I don't know anything about houses! You have to teach me."

"Okay, I'll show you some really unique ones. Get your creative juices flowing."

"Maybe we should keep going with the tour," I suggested. "We could go back upstairs. Use the front door. I know you wanted to see it."

"All right. But first . . ." He looked back down the passageway, toward the door with the voices. "Should we try to get a quick peek? See if it's Donny?" He began tiptoeing back while I tagged behind, clutching the corner of his shirt. We heard a purr roll up a throat and "You smell so good." Gary was pumped up, eyes blazing. It occurred to me that on the other side of the door could be the mermaid woman, naked from head to foot. Although it was only a slim possibility, I wasn't sure I could survive it.

As Gary's head nudged forward, I felt along the shelf behind me, the spine of the last book and then the smooth marble bookend holding it up, and suddenly, almost without my own knowledge, I shouted, "Police! Open up!" With a jerk of the wrist, I sent the bookend to the floor and the books behind fell domino-style in a thunderous cascade. Gary jumped and grabbed my hand, and we careened down the passageway then up the stairs, out the door, and behind some bushes, giggling as we made it to safety.

"You're dangerous," Gary said, breathless. He was stooped with his hands on his knees, looking up at me.

"Maybe," I said, drawing out both syllables to sound coy. "Did you see who it was?"

"I couldn't see anything. What a rush. Maybe I should've been a detective. Although you'd make a terrible partner. You'd definitely get us killed."

"But at least I'd keep things interesting." We smiled at each other, and I could see that despite his joke, he already considered me to be his partner, and not a terrible one in the least. We were in harmony more than ever before, thanks to everything we'd shared that day and over the course of the summer, and we were ready to take on anything together, the brightest days and the blackest nights.

He caught his breath and stood admiring the house. "I've got to say, I do like what he's done, just the whole feel of it." He draped an arm across my shoulders. "Yeah, they've got a little piece of heaven up here."

I followed Gary's gaze upward. A house had never seemed so precious or consequential, and everything that went on inside it, even the most embittered exchanges or tedious chores, seemed precious and consequential as well. The four of them up here together, working through life— wasn't that all the heaven a person could ever hope for?

"A family, and a nice big house for the kids to grow

up in, with an office and a yard—all the details planned out just the way they like," he said. "It's really all I've ever wanted."

"I know what you mean. Family is what's most important, in the end. But I've sort of been putting that off to the side. I figured I probably wouldn't have kids."

"I think that'd be a shame. Honestly, I do."

I bit my cheek, envisioning it: a porch with a swing, a green lawn, bread rising in the oven, Gary bursting in from work to start up some horseplay with the kids, and always, one child or another calling for me or tugging on my leg and their friends coming for playdates and neighbors popping in, a warm home full of rollicking chaos where moments of solitude would be so rare that they would be treasured and even sought out. It was the most generic scene, and yet it appeared in my head like a divine revelation.

"What about your family? Like, growing up?" he said. "I don't know anything about them. Except you have a brother."

He wanted to know me, everything there was to know, and for once it didn't seem impossible to talk about it. "My mother died. Six years ago." I swallowed. I'd never said it aloud like that before. "I guess it's kind of like you with being married—I don't like talking about it much. But you told me, so I should be open too."

"I'm so sorry." The words sounded sincere, and I found their lack of originality comforting—I didn't want to feel original. My throat filled. Even if I'd been able to speak, I knew there were no words that could communicate just how undeserving of sympathy I truly was.

"I'm glad you told me, though," he said. And then he understood, either from my face or from instinct, not to say more. It felt like I'd weathered a storm and just discovered all my belongings still intact: I'd somehow managed to hold on to myself. I wanted to squeeze every inch of Gary's body but settled for his hand. He interlocked his with mine, filling the gaps between my fingers so we formed a solid block and I could no longer sense which parts belonged to me.

Our conversation had swept the sound of the music away, and in this interlude, it came flooding back with even more intensity, a rhythmic thumping and a lyric set on repeat: *There's no limit, no, no, no limit.* Gary winced. "I think I've had enough synthesizer for one night. I'm pretty exhausted. But I had a great time. I can't tell you how glad I am that you came."

"Me too."

"So should we head back?"

A cynical part of me cried out, telling me to stall, to cling to this place and this day for longer, for forever if possible, but that was a vestige of my old life. I had every reason to feel confident and strong. "Yeah," I said. "Let's head back."

On the highway, Gary put his hand on my knee and let it rest there, a declaration. In the seclusion of the car, our new togetherness felt more significant and more nerve-racking. But his hand on my leg proved that it was durable, not only meant for a dance party and a stranger's basement but also for a future beyond.

The "future beyond"—those words sent my mind into a hyperactive state, spurred on by the music he played at low volume, the ideal soundtrack for private fantasy. Soon I was overflowing with inspiration, all the plans we could make, how easily we could weave our lives together. I could help him find a renter to take my place so we'd have the extra income when I moved downstairs. I'd do the cooking so he wouldn't have to stress anymore, and watch cooking shows for tips and recipes until I could really impress him. We'd go shopping for more furniture and decor, this time with just the two of us in mind, then invite his mother over for a big housewarming dinner during which she'd take me aside to say she had a feeling when she met me that we'd end up together, and she's so happy she was right. I'd bring him to meet my father at a restaurant, and when Gary snuck off to preemptively pay the bill, he'd take my hand and say he'd worried I'd never get out of my rut, but now he saw I'd come through it and found a kind, good man to settle down with, and he was beyond ecstatic that we could finally start a fresh chapter as a family. For Thanksgiving, we could host everybody at our house potluck style, with my brother on video chat so he wouldn't feel left out. Or, if Gary and his mother had their own tradition, we could switch off every other holiday between his family and mine.

"You know," I said, trying not to sound too frenzied, "I just can't believe how much time I've spent worrying about becoming an EMT and having some important career, when maybe I don't even need any of that to be happy. Maybe it was just something I had to go through, like to get me here. And now I can leave all that behind. It's weird, but it's also kind of freeing in a way."

"Really? But your EMT stuff, that's like who you are. I couldn't imagine you without it."

"It's just a job."

"I thought you said it was a calling. Like that woman you like. With the bird's name."

"Florence Nightingale."

"Yeah, Florence Nightingale. In any case, might as well give it a shot for a while, right? See how it goes. I mean, you've already done all the work to get certified."

"Well, not exactly—" I hardly got the words out before I burst out laughing. The whole matter had lost its hold on me, and I felt unbelievably light and giddy, as though I'd just recalled some ridiculous antic from my youth. "Actually, I skipped my exam. It was supposed to be today."

"Huh? I thought you already finished all that, like a month ago."

"I lied. Just a little," I said impishly, waiting for him

to get in on the fun. He didn't respond, so I added, "Not to you. I mean, I did lie to you, but it wasn't on purpose, like to trick you. It was to trick myself."

He squinted at the road. "I don't follow."

"It's just that I'd been having trouble passing the exam. I'd already tried twice."

"I didn't know that."

"I knew all the material, I just needed to get out of my head. You know, like, just relax, believe in myself. So, if I convinced myself I already *had* passed, then I *would* pass. That was the idea anyway."

"Huh."

"Do you get it? It probably sounds a little nuts. But like, you've heard of the placebo effect? Doctors will use a little deception to help convince the patient they're getting better, and then they really do get better."

"I guess so."

"Never mind. It was a stupid idea anyway, I see that now. More of an experiment than anything else."

He was quiet, seeming to mull that over. I thought about adding further explanation, but it all sounded lame in my head.

"So everything then . . . ," he said. "And when I got you that cake—"

"I know, I felt terrible about that, really. I'm sorry. I wanted to tell you the truth, but then it would defeat the whole purpose. My intentions were good. It was the whole 'ends justify the means' kind of thing, you know?"

I wished we were sitting across from each other so I could see more of his face. "I've never lied to you about anything else, I promise. And I'll never do it again. I hope you aren't mad."

"Well, honesty is a big thing for me. Probably the biggest thing, given my past. You should understand that." His voice had an edge that startled me. I hadn't really expected him to be mad. I thought he might call me weird or crazy, have a laugh at my expense, roll his eyes, but this sounded like real anger. I felt moved by how much he cared, by my capacity to injure him. It seemed to validate everything and guarantee that with a little time he would forgive me and we would look back on this and laugh. "But wait, so, the test was really supposed to be *today*?" he said.

"It doesn't matter now. I decided to go with you instead, and I'm really glad I did. I knew how important it was to you."

"It was just a dumb wedding! I could've gone alone. I would've survived. If I'd known, I— I just wish you'd told me all this before. Because now I'm feeling guilty, like it's partly my fault."

"Please, don't feel guilty. Really. It was my choice. And it's not like I won't have another chance to take it, if I want. But to be honest, now I'm not even sure I want to."

"I thought it's what you always wanted, to be out there saving lives, helping people."

"You don't need to be an EMT to help people. Having

a family, that's all about helping other people. And you get to bring new life into the world." I loosened my seat belt so I could shift my body to face him. "Just picture it. You could design the perfect house, with everything we want put together in one, all the details exactly how you like them. And I could have a garden and grow fresh vegetables. You wouldn't have to worry about cooking anymore, I could do all that. And take care of the family. I mean, eventually, down the road. It could be really nice, don't you think?" I pinched his leg, the visions playing one after another like a spectacular movie in my head.

"Oh. That's— I mean, we were just kidding around before. I don't want you to go making any decisions based on me, if that's what you were thinking. We still don't even know each other that well—obviously. That's really clear to me now."

"Of course. I only meant it's fun to imagine things like that, just daydream really. It's not like I'm planning our wedding or anything." I tried to laugh, but it had a fraudulent sound that I couldn't reel in, as though my own voice was determined to incriminate me. "We can just take it one day at a time," I said as firmly and soberly as possible. "Get to know each other better."

"I don't know, Amy." The way he said "Amy," I almost didn't recognize it as my name. He leaned his elbow against the car door and breathed audibly. His eyes stayed locked straight ahead on the road. "It's been a crazy week, and this is kind of a lot to take in right now." He paused, but I could see his jaw still working in his cheek, his teeth grinding together. "Not to mention, things with Irina are still kind of up in the air. I'm not in the right place to go jumping into anything. This is my fault, I shouldn't have let things go so far today. The whole thing was a bad idea. Can we just take a step back?"

"Back?"

"Yeah, like back to being friends. That seems like the best thing for right now. Don't you think?" He swerved around a car, mumbling "Delinquents" under his breath. We were tearing down the dark highway with a velocity that made my breath catch, as though he wanted to demonstrate just how desperate he was to be rid of me, to put an end to this day and all the promise it once held.

My voice came out shrunken and creaky, almost not at all. "Should I still plan to come for dinner this week?"

"I was just going to cancel my meal subscription. The whole point of it was for Irina. I'm perfectly happy heating up frozen dinners. Save a lot of money too."

He pretended to be interested in a song and turned up the music, bopping his head along to make it seem convincing.

I felt stunned and confused, and slightly hostile too, like someone had just snuck up behind me and whacked me in the head. I struggled to replay everything that had been said since we'd entered the car, to isolate each moment and find some logic in the progression. I compulsively touched my temple, as though it might help my mind function better. But the whole situation was just preposterous, beyond reason, against the laws of nature even. I gave up trying to understand and instead scrolled through every possible thing I could say now that might redeem me, even minorly. Finally I gave up on that too, deciding I couldn't trust my judgment.

My fingers crept toward the space between our seats, the emergency brake. I could pull it, take charge, prevent us from going on this way any longer, but then what? It would only stop the car and not Gary, who had already retreated as far as he possibly could while still stuck in the seat beside me. We streaked past a sign for Duxbury, and I thought of the cat-naming game. It seemed like a memory from a previous lifetime, as unreachable as the quarter-moon I knew was out there but couldn't currently see.

"So what were you printing then?" Gary said. "That night. When you said you passed your exam."

"It was . . . nothing. Just something I had to get printed." If there had been an emergency brake to stop the mechanisms inside my body, I would have pulled it then, but the world is not that humane. My body held me hostage while it carried on: my lungs extracting oxygen, my pituitary gland secreting hormones, my gallbladder collecting bile.

A couple miles later, Gary stirred, and I sat up, confident that he'd come around and was ready to make amends. "What did you say?"

"I yawned," he said.

Despite my infuriating good health, I was like an invalid there, trapped in tight quarters with nothing to do except stare at the window, which the night had converted into a mirror. No matter how I scrunched my eyes, trying to force my vision to the outside, my own reflection bled through: my right eye blinking back at me with its 6 million cones and 125 million rods, the pupil dilated into a big black hole. A student group on campus once hosted a debate between a scientist and an evangelical, and the evangelical said that the complexity of the human eye was proof of God's existence. God!

At some point I said, "You've had to do a lot of driving today. We could pull over and switch. I haven't driven in a while, but my license is still good."

"No. It's fine. I want to."

I must have dozed off after that, because the next thing was my head colliding with the window as Gary made a sharp turn, and then I realized we were back home, in the driveway. I closed my eyes again and pretended to be asleep in the hope that somehow it might disarm him, like when I was a child and wanted my parents to have to carry me inside. He poked my shoulder with all the warmth you'd use to flick a bug off your food and said, "We're here."

ELEVEN

I wiped the bedposts in room 9, my rag going up and down and up again, losing track of which post I'd started with and whether I'd already completed all four posts and, if so, how many times. Despite having slept through Sunday and as many hours as possible on Monday and Tuesday, I was in a heavy fog and planned to stay that way, depriving my brain of even the mildest pleasure or stimulation. I wished I could tear open my skull and flush it out with bleach and felt it was an injustice that I couldn't—why shouldn't people be allowed some say over what goes on in their own skulls? The room went dim. I figured it was my imagination acting up, trying to get a rise out of me. Then I looked out the window and discovered the sun missing. Fat clouds had trundled in, and the ocean was churning. Wind began to blow raw against the glass. I watched waves hack at the sides of the boats and people dart in and out of the tiny house at the tip of the T-shaped dock. The room fell quiet and still. There was a rumble of thunder, and when a splintering noise followed, the earth blinked and I felt a release. A storm—it was so perfectly fitting I felt I must have manifested it, just by the force of my own violent mood.

Doug's voice came booming in from the hallway. He was singing to the tune of an old hot-dog commercial:

Oh, I wish I were an internal auditor
That is what I truly wish to be
'Cause if I were an internal auditor
Everyone would be in love with me
Oh, everyone would be in love with me.

He was constantly coming up with new versions of this song. He didn't often come up on the hotel floor, and his singing grew louder and louder, and then the door to room 9 swung open. "Time to batten down the hatches, eh? Just making sure we're all sealed up." He knocked twice on the door frame.

Thunder cracked, louder this time, drawing us both toward the shuddering window. We stood side by side, watching. The anticipation made me feel off-kilter. A rod of lightning skewered the clouds and finally the rain fell, thin and distinct at first, in bullets that burst when they hit the surface of the ocean. Then came a surge like a giant exhale and the rain crashed down, blending the sky and the ocean into one big gray stew. "And we like to think *we're* the ones in control," he whispered. "Kind of puts it all into perspective, doesn't it?"

I murmured in agreement. I felt exposed, imagining that all my vengeful urges and inconsolable thoughts had escaped from inside me to set this storm in motion, and any moment now he would recognize my role in it.

"A good storm always gets me thinking about the old days," Doug said. "Can you imagine? A bunch of guys stranded out there on a ship, running around like mad while the captain barks orders. Not knowing what the hell is going on or how long it will last. Just that some god is mighty angry."

"Yeah, they used to think everything came from the gods. Even diseases," I said, discovering how glad I was for conversation (how long had it been? days, not since the ride with Gary) and how ridiculous I'd been: attributing a storm to my own mood was even more absurd than attributing it to a god—how egotistical I could be! "Hippocrates was the first one to challenge it."

"Nowadays we've got radar and satellites, you can track all of it, wind, moisture, pressure. Sure, you can still get caught unawares, but it's not the same. Call me crazy, but sometimes I want to know how it felt—out in the middle of the Atlantic, no radio, no Coast Guard. Just you and your brothers fighting to stay one step ahead."

Wind lashed the flags down on the flagpole. Lightning spiked, and we both flinched. "I can see what you mean," I said. "But probably most of them died. People were always dying of things that could easily have been prevented. Like scurvy. Thousands, millions, of sailors died from scurvy before they finally figured out it was just a simple vitamin C deficiency."

"How'd they find out?"

"A controlled trial. A doctor divided all the sailors with scurvy into groups. One was assigned to eat oranges and lemons. And they were lucky, because the others were assigned vinegar or seawater or even vitriol, which is what they used to call sulfuric acid. He published the results, but people ignored it at first, like a lot of important discoveries."

I could feel Doug studying the side of my face. "Your parents must've done something right," he said. "I don't get it. My kids won't even pick up a book. They're only interested in whatever it is they've got on their phones. My daughter's the worst."

For a moment I was flushed with the warm, pleasant sensation that comes with flattery. Then I remembered my life. The conscionable thing would be to tell Doug not to worry, his kids were better off, and not to waste his admiration, because this was the extent of me, the only answers I had and they'd brought me nothing and taken me nowhere, I couldn't even make it through a simple trip to Cape Cod.

"Anyway, I should be thanking the gods that the cruise isn't set to leave today." He hitched his pants and headed for the door. "This should mean an end to the heat, I hope. Now I can get back on my exercise routine. Ha." He palmed the swell of his stomach and dipped out of the room. He started singing again, a new version this time—"Oh, I wish I were an iPhone app-li-cation, That is what I truly wish to be"—his voice accompanied by the gusts and cracks outside, the relentless volley of rain.

When I'd finished for the day, I posted myself at a window in a vacant room. I wanted to avoid Roula, and everyone, to move invisibly from here to somewhere else, somewhere far, far away, where I could sleep away the hours. What I would have given to have plans with Gary tonight! To know that at this moment he was in his kitchen counting out tablespoons or preheating the oven in anticipation of my arrival. But we didn't have plans; we might never have plans again. How could I have been so reckless? Letting my foolish reveries endanger everything we'd built. For this recklessness I deserved to be punished, yes, but not permanently. Even though Gary had acted brutally in the heat of the moment, he was a reasonable person, or could be, when he had me to guide him, but even without me, if given enough time, reason should eventually prevail. In the meantime, I would make it like I didn't exist. If I could continue to avoid him, he wouldn't have a chance to double down on the things he'd said, and I wouldn't have to witness the way my presence grated on him. And then, after a week or two of not seeing me, of suffering through dreary, flavorless Hungry Man dinners during which a pleasant memory of me would naturally arise, he might soften a bit, start to forget what a maniac I'd turned out to be, and even miss me a little. It might be a long shot, but it was all I had.

The rain slackened and the clouds began to wither, letting spots of muddy light filter through. From the window I saw Roula emerge then disappear under the bowl of an umbrella. I waited for the umbrella to cross the parking lot, my jaw tight, before retrieving my things from the closet. Just as I'd begun my wearisome descent down the stairs, I heard "Hey" behind me—it shot like a blade into the back of my neck. My legs went stiff. I couldn't handle one more thing, especially the pigeon-toed waiter.

He was drying his hands on the front of his apron. "You're on your way out, sorry." His skin looked mildly irritated, as though he'd just blown his nose. "I wasn't sure it was you at first—did you cut your hair? Looks nice. Anyway, I just thought I'd see if you wanted to come to a party. Tonight, at my house. My parents are away all week."

"Your parents?"

"We have a pool, too bad the weather's crap. Looks like it's starting to clear up, though. It'll be a bunch of people from here and from school. It'll be a good time."

"I'm probably ten years older than you."

"Age is just a number," he said, smirking.

"Look, if you need someone to buy alcohol for you, you can just ask."

"No, no, that's all taken care of. I'd really like you to come. I think you'd have fun. But if you already have plans or something, no big deal. Here, let me give you my address, in case." He patted his apron and back pockets. "I must've left my pad in the kitchen." He looked back at the kitchen door. "Here, I can just write it on your hand," he said, uncapping a pen. He stepped closer and used his other hand to keep mine steady while he wrote. I was too depleted to resist. He smelled like seafood and steam from the dishwasher. "My name's Jeremy, by the way. I'm not sure if you ever knew that. You're Amy, I remember." Our eyes met briefly before I turned to go. "Any time after eight!" he called out behind me.

■

The lightning was just a scribble in the distance now. I made no effort to rush or cover my head; I enjoyed the cool taps of rain, particularly when they surprised me in the eye. The tide was out, the exposed beach dirty and deserted but for one lone figure tracking the sand with a metal detector. There were no people on the street, no sounds but the weather and the slow march of my feet. The sidewalk appeared to be moving, twitching in response to every needle of rain. It was littered with debris that had shaken loose from the trees. When I reached for a berry on Magnolia Drive, my foot slipped on a pine cone and it spun off, jeering at me. I cornered it with my shoe, cracked its ribs.

Through the gray drizzle I noticed him, the same homeless man from before. He was sitting outside an orthodontist's office, a soggy cardboard sign propped on his chest. I paused in front of him. "Adapt or die," I read. "Do you really think it's that simple?" I figured a free ice cream had earned me at least a shred of civility.

"You smell like chemicals," he snarled. "You work for the government. Don't try to lie." I bolted away while he shouted, "Watch out! She's radioactive. Don't let her lie!"

Once I'd turned the corner, I stopped under a tree and sniffed my shirt and hands. The chemical fumes of cleaning products did linger there, but only faintly. I turned my hand over. Jeremy's message was smudged but still readable: "21 Sargent St." I knew that house; it had a particularly grand fence. Under that he'd drawn a stupid little smiley face with an extra line so it looked like its tongue was sticking out. Age is just a number—how original!

I'd been meandering for a good hour or more when I came upon the supermarket where the deli workers used to know my name. I dodged inside and paced the perimeter of the deli, trying to scout who was behind the counter. It was her—the woman with the mustache who had once been my favorite before she'd insulted me. She yawned into her hand. When she turned to get something behind her, I saw she had sprouted a belly—in fact, she was extremely pregnant. She rocked on her feet, flaunting the ugly eggish shape of it, her apron straining to hold it in. The sight of it turned me bitter and spiteful. I gave up hiding and strutted right by, close enough to feel the puff of air blowing from the vent at the bottom of the display case.

"Oh," she said. "Did you want to hear the specials? We've got a nice hot Spanish salami today, and a slow-roasted pork—"

My hand in the air signaled her to stop. "Actually, I'm on my way to a party. Thanks anyway." I didn't look back to see her reaction, but my own words kept chirping in my ears, making my face hot—what did she care about me and whether or not I was going to a party? And a high school party at that!

I entered the liquor store next door. I perused the rum selection, then thought better of it—they were young, and rum might be more than they could handle; I didn't want to be responsible for any accidents. I waded through rows of wine bottles wearing stylish, mysterious labels and came to the refrigerator section, finally tugging a cheap bottle of champagne out by the neck.

"Celebrating something special?" the clerk asked as she beeped the sticker.

"I just passed the EMT exam," I said, partly out of habit and partly as a trial—to see how it would feel, whether anything could be salvaged. It felt as arbitrary as if I'd claimed to have passed the bar or a kidney stone.

"Oh, congrats. My sister's a CNA. She's constantly telling me to switch my shift so I can take night classes like she did. She's always got the answer, even when you didn't ask the question. *Especially* then."

"I hope she respects her calling. Not everyone is suited for it."

"Me, I get squeamish around blood."

■

The storm had boiled the heat off, and I wished for a light jacket or at least a change of clothes and a shower. I passed a lonesome bench and considered abandoning my sad pilgrimage so I could warm its lap and enjoy the bottle in peace. But I'd only end up terrorizing myself, replaying what had happened on the car ride home and envisioning all the nightmarish things that could still happen, and then I might be tempted to seek out Gary before he'd had proper time to stew. So why not go to the party and distract myself, what did I have left to lose?

He'd taped a note to the front door with tiny letters that said "Come around back." At the towering fence, I heard voices and got the urge to bulldoze right through and melt into the crowd, take on the form of them. Jeremy's parents had dressed the outside of the fence in old fishing rope and strung up an assortment of buoys the shape and color of Popsicles, reds and yellows and blues. The latch on the gate was loose. Soft light winked through the crack, and I put my eye to it. Kids—they were kids—pumped beer from a keg and arced Ping-Pong balls toward pyramids of disposable cups. A girl pranced by in a bikini.

After all that, I couldn't bring myself to do it. What had I expected anyway, to stroll in and strike up a conversation about college applications? It was impossible, and depressing. I trudged on to the next house, slumped to the curb, and rocketed the cork off the champagne. I chugged until my throat fizzed and my eyes watered. The pavement felt damp, and I stuffed the plastic bag under my butt and chugged more. Everything began to shimmy.

A gang of boys burst through the gate, howling and climbing over one another like mice. One broke from the group and came toward me. "Amy?" Jeremy said, curving his hand over his eyes as if the sun were shining. "What are you doing sitting out here? We were just going on a quick beer run. Hey, you guys go on without me!" he called back. One of them said something in a goofy voice, and they laughed and piled into a rusty car, the engine growling. "Don't mind them," he said, a bit unsteady on his feet. "Come, come in."

The gate tremored behind us, announcing my passage to the other side, not that anyone took notice. Kids flowed in and out of the house and congregated on a patio and in the grass. "Is that actor guy here?" I asked, scanning their faces.

"Shell? No. He got fired. Finally. What an asshole, right?" I followed him through the yard, dimly lit by a row of bamboo poles spiked into the ground. "They're just LEDs," Jeremy said, tapping his nail against one. "They make them flicker so it looks like a real flame. My parents love fake crap like that. That too." He stopped short, nearly losing his balance, to point out a table made from a wooden crate, with webbing around the base and a sheet of blue glass on top. "Supposed to look like a lobster trap."

We dropped into lounge chairs in the grass. Two girls in bikinis vaulted themselves into the pool, spritzing my ankles with water. "There's Liza and Bridget—from work," he said.

"Seems a little cold for swimming."

"Not if you just killed a bottle of Smirnoff! It's flavored like marshmallows. They go crazy for it."

"Alcohol actually lowers core body temperature. You might *feel* warmer, at first, since it increases blood flow to the skin. But really it's diverting blood away from your vital organs. That's why being drunk is a big risk factor in cold climates. It can lead to hypothermia."

"Ooh, champagne. Classy," he said. "Can I have a sip?" His lips were so dehydrated that they made a peeling sound as they opened. The top lip snagged on his

front teeth and he had to use his tongue to unstick it.
He paused just before the bottle reached his mouth. "But
what are we toasting to?"

"Your parents being away."

"To you coming out tonight!" He put his lips where
mine had been and triumphantly sucked some down.
"I'm glad you decided to come." He'd changed out of his
waiter clothes and into a red T-shirt printed to look like
the label on a bottle of sriracha, with the rooster in the
middle and words like SHAKE WELL and NET WT. 17 OZ.
The red of the shirt accentuated the reddish tip of his
nose. "I want you to know, I'm not like what you think
of as a typical guy my age." Mercifully, he returned the
bottle to me. I wasn't nearly drunk enough yet. A while
ago I'd stopped keeping alcohol in the house—it wasn't
like Florence Nightingale went around getting wasted.
During the Crimean War, she'd even created a transfer
system to encourage soldiers to send their money home
rather than spend it on alcohol. But what did she have
to do with me anymore? The boys came roaring back
through the gate, two of them lugging a keg. "All right!"
Jeremy cheered, to no response.

One of the boys careened toward us, flanked by two
others. "So who's your friend?" he said. "No need to
hide over here." He came behind and gripped Jeremy's
shoulders. "My brother Jeremy here, he's a stand-up guy.
Hardly ever *talks* to a girl. He's holding out for someone
special. Are you someone special?"

"You're such an asshole," Jeremy said.

"I'm just trying to help." He turned to his friends and they agreed, he was just trying to help. "Okay, okay. We'll leave you to it." He gave me a long look, and the three of them staggered away, laughing.

Jeremy exhaled. "That's word for you. Blaa"—he made a noise almost like gagging, with his tongue extended. "I mean *Ward*, like the name. Not *word*." He touched his forehead as if to measure his level of intoxication. "Man, I started early." He checked my expression, and I suspected he was trying to judge whether to play his drinking up or down, which would earn a better reaction from me. But I couldn't have cared less. I wasn't sure if it was the alcohol or the companion or both, but having zero stakes in a conversation made me feel almost euphoric. "Don't know why my parents had to give him such a stupid name anyway."

"That's really your brother?" They seemed to belong to two different species, let alone families.

"Three more days till he goes back to college. See, he's like the perfect example of the typical douchey guy. In a fraternity and everything."

"Boys in my high school, they used to rank all the girls based on looks. They did it every year. The Hot One Hundred. They had a whole complicated system with different brackets and they'd all vote online and certain girls would move to the next round depending on their percentage. It took a month at least, and they wouldn't tell the girls anything until the very end. Then they'd have a conclusive list of the top one hundred girls in order, best looking to worst."

"See, I'm not like that," he said. His fingers had migrated to the arm of my chair, wriggling near my elbow. "That's disgusting."

"I thought it was sort of impressive, in a way. At least they were rigorous about how they collected their data. I mean, people can't help but be attracted to certain people and *not* other people. There's no need to pretend."

"You're interesting." He turned his head to swallow a burp, faced me again, and swallowed a few more times. "I want to figure you out."

"I'm not a math problem."

"Ha. I know that. I'm not, like, trying to find the square root, like carry the one—" He broke off into a fit of laughter. "I just mean . . . I want to get to know you. All the girls at school are exactly the same, like they're too scared to be themselves. You can't even tell them apart. But you seem different."

Different. It wasn't a word I felt like hearing. "I'm not," I said. "I'm the same as them."

"Liar." He smiled like this was a flirtatious game we were playing, then suddenly held his chest and grimaced. "I've got to run inside real quick." He stumbled to his feet. "Did you want a sweatshirt or something? You look cold."

"Okay."

"Be right back. Don't go anywhere."

I closed my eyes and reclined, taking long swigs of champagne. The sweet taste had turned nauseating, but the effect was just right.

"So are you really into him or what?"

My eyes flicked open. It was like my vision was on a delay, like I had to fit the puzzle pieces together to make it work. A figure stood above me, blotting out the light from the fake tiki torch. Finally I registered who it was: Ward, the typical douchey guy, at least according to Jeremy.

"Don't be ridiculous." I took another, more dramatic swig.

He was pleased by this answer—I'd played my part well—and he swept his hair back and settled into Jeremy's chair, scooting it closer. "How do you know my adorable little brother anyway?"

"I don't really." I liked how the champagne warped my voice, made it echo in my head. "He's just always trying to hit on me at work."

Ward was good-looking in a way that had unanimous appeal, moody eyes and two well-punctuated dimples, and he knew exactly what type of effect this had on people. He reminded me of a boy from my high school, Brady Caldwell—he usually dated the girl who had been ranked number one.

"Oh, Jeremy," he said. "He watches way too many movies."

"I guess someone needs to teach him about the real world."

"Just what I was thinking." Ward grinned. He glanced back at the rowdy house and his buddies lagging in the doorway, half surveilling him and half playing a game that involved tossing quarters toward an empty can.

He grinned again, hollowing those dimples, and strapped one hand to the back of my head. As he leaned in, I felt giddy with anticipation: here was my chance to thrust him away and make a fool of him, he would be shocked, he was so used to having everything go his way and come so easily, his life had required no effort at all. He made a gradual approach, probably out of courtesy to me, so I could behold the kingliness of his bone structure up close—his face the exact opposite of Gary's, which was made of mush—and I breathed in the scent of cologne and cheap beer and spearmint gum from the hot cave of his mouth and then, before I could make my move, his lips had collided with mine. He went all out, plunging his tongue in and swirling it around. Before long it felt less like a dream and more like my life, like I had unlocked a door hidden inside me, and I started to surrender and even enjoy the experience, the simplicity, the meaninglessness, even the audience. Gary had said he couldn't imagine who I'd be without my EMT stuff, but that just proved he didn't know me at all, since a person's identity wasn't the same as her job, especially if she didn't technically even have that job and now most likely never would. And maybe *this* was who I truly was—impulsive, adventurous, superficial, fun—and if these were the people who brought that out in me, who appreciated and accepted me and invited me to parties and even competed for my attention, perhaps I shouldn't fight it, regardless of how old they were. Age *was* just a number, after all.

Ward looked coy as he pulled away, with a subtle bite of his bottom lip. I took the pose as a challenge, daring me to one-up him and to one-up Gary, who actually thought he was something special and irreplaceable in my life, that he and his mush-face were the object of my desire.

"How old are you?" I asked.

"Nineteen, almost twenty. Why, how old are you?"

"How old do you want me to be?" I felt fierce and drunk and my singular wish was to feel even fiercer and drunker, until I could no longer recognize myself. This is a pop song, I thought, and you're the star: a fearless, tantalizing force of nature. "So," I said. "Want to go somewhere?"

He didn't flinch except for the slightest flare of his nostrils, almost imperceptible. He had the same stoicism as Brady Caldwell, the kind that resembles maturity but is actually manipulation, leading you to believe, for example, that a smile from him means infinitely more than a smile from anyone else and to work harder as a result. "My room." He stood, smoothing his hair back with both hands.

I hadn't made a fool of him and no longer wanted to—we were connected now—but I could still shock him, force him to doubt for the first time in his life that he had it all figured out, including me. "Or how about over there?" I pointed to the bushes along the side of the house.

His eyes darted from the bushes to his friends, and back to me.

"It's dark enough," I said. "And doesn't being outside make you feel more . . . alive?"

"Sure, yeah. Whatever you're into." He sounded the tiniest bit apprehensive, and I relished that.

We edged around to the side of the house where a narrow strip of lawn ran between the bushes and the fence, and I put my hands on his chest and pushed him down to the ground. "Whoa," he said. He palmed the grass. "It's still pretty wet."

"Even better." I mounted him and started to suck his neck.

"Damn, you're kind of a freak. I like that," he said as I unzipped his fly and stuffed my hand inside. "You do this kind of thing a lot?"

"No more talking."

I hadn't had sex in a long time—the closest thing had been Gary's hands on me in the basement. But this seemed to be an asset more than a hindrance, as I had no comparison to distract me or routine to fall into. I followed only my instincts. We wrestled on the hard wet ground, unable to decide who was the aggressor. I enjoyed the feel of my bare skin against the grass and the champagne whirring in my head. While he sucked on my nipple, I laughed aloud at how strange and joyful life could be. His touch reminded me of the rain that had fallen earlier that day: each drop distinct and remarkable at first, then becoming so numerous that they flowed together into one great pool and I was bathing inside it, buzzing from head to foot.

His penis seemed to glow from within. I immediately wanted to take it and absorb it inside me. I hurried to pull my underwear down. "I actually like a bush," he said.

"Go," I urged, opening my legs and bracing my heels in the grass.

I loved the filled-up feeling so much that I was disappointed when he had to withdraw slightly in order to begin thrusting. But soon the rhythm itself became pleasing, and I kind of forgot about the rest of him, that he was a person and we were in the world. I focused only on the part inside me. Each time it drove in, I clenched as tightly as I could, as though I might be able to trap it there forever. I growled with the effort, and my growls took on a life of their own. I felt no need to tame them; in fact, I wanted to sing.

Was this the meaning of life? I had been feigning asexuality for so long. It had become easy, even natural. A nonissue. Now as I locked my ankles behind Ward's back, I saw how wrong that had been, how tragic, how totally insane . . .

But then, while it was still only just beginning, Ward seized up, grunted a long, drawn-out "God," and shuddered to the ground. It took a second for me to realize he had just ejaculated on my thigh. "Holy shit," he said, rubbing his face. "That was unreal." He'd lost his stoicism, and although I was disappointed that things had cut off so abruptly and in such a mediocre fashion, I also felt powerful, as though I were the god he'd called out to.

The space inside me seemed cavernous now, so I stuffed my fingers in, trying to fill back up. "Oh, shit," he said. "Let me finish you." He moved my hand out of the way, slid his fingers in, and wiggled them as though gesturing for me to come closer. After a few minutes of that, he brought his tongue down. It occasionally felt good, especially the warm puff of his breath, but it didn't give me that complete feeling. It mostly tickled. I considered faking an orgasm, not for his sake but because it might be kind of fun. So I quickened my breath and made increasingly high-pitched noises and thrashed around. It *was* pretty fun, and even seemed to enhance the physical sensation. But when the theatrics were over and Ward emerged, saying, "The alphabet always does it," the space felt even more cavernous than before. I questioned if I *had* actually done it for his sake and kicked myself for being so spineless and unimaginative.

He rolled to his side, perching on his elbow to look at me. "So," he said. "Don't you want to know anything about me?" He smiled and plucked a blade of grass.

"Not really." It sounded harsh, but inside I felt grateful for his vain attempt at flirty conversation. I began to relax again. I lay my head back in the grass to observe the twinkle of a passing plane.

"Actually, I do have a question." I rolled to my side and mirrored his position. "What would you think of a guy who goes on a trip to Ukraine to find a wife? Like he buys a special tour through a company called Sincere Romance that helps you meet single women and sends you all this advice about how to get them to marry you."

"That sounds pretty fucked up. You know someone who did that?"

"You're right. It *is* fucked up."

"That'll probably be Jeremy someday."

"Yeah, probably."

He sat up and appeared to be listening—a siren sounded in the distance. It grew fainter and disappeared. He relaxed again. "People think if you're an athlete, they let you get away with anything, but it's the exact opposite. They're ten times harder on us. They suspended half our team last season, complete bullshit."

I walked my fingers up and down the rack of muscle in his abdomen. "I'll bet you have under fifteen percent body fat."

"Soccer and lacrosse."

"What about video games?"

"You mean do I like them? Not really. Seems like a waste of time."

"So what do you want to do? Like after you graduate."

"Make *money*, you know. I'm not going to be one of those guys who moves back and just hangs around here." A commotion erupted in the yard, a chorus of voices yelling "Oh!" like a game had just ended in a shocking upset. "You think they could hear us before?" he said.

"Sounds like they're pretty occupied. Who cares if they did."

"I've never done it outside before. In a car, but not full-on dirt and grass and shit. It's sexy as hell." A glob of semen began to slide down my leg, and I reached down to touch it. "Shit," he said. "Here, use this." He handed me his T-shirt and I balled it up and used it like toilet paper—it struck me as a pure and tender offering, the perfect closure to our evening. I put my shirt back on and shook out my shorts.

"Are you going to give me your number?" he said. "I don't even know your name."

"Let's keep it that way."

"You're hooking up with someone?"

"Let's just say, it's been a crazy week. I'm not in the right place to go jumping into anything."

"Seriously?"

"It was fun, though. I had a good time." I tried to make

my face convey that I didn't mean to be cruel, I was just an impulsive, adventurous, superficial, fun person who had a whole host of other impulsive, adventurous, superficial, fun times ahead of her.

"I would've lasted longer if I hadn't been drinking so much."

"I know."

"All right. So that's it, then?" When I didn't answer, he said, "Okay, if that's what you want."

We rounded the corner back to the yard, Ward still naked from the waist up, carrying his shirt in a sticky ball. The crowd seemed to have swelled. As we emerged side by side, everyone tittered and stared. A girl in the pool stopped paddling and said "Oh my *god*." Ward whispered into my hair, "Guess we're on our own now," and swaggered off. Halfway across the yard, he paused, and that's when I noticed Jeremy standing there, apart from the crowd. Ward touched his shoulder as he passed, on his way to rejoin his buddies, who laughed and whooped and sealed him inside their circle, which slowly wheeled itself into the house.

I didn't move. Jeremy stood there, facing me, a sweatshirt crumpled in his arm—the sweatshirt he'd retrieved for me, because he'd thought I looked cold. He was the only person who'd noticed I'd cut my hair. In the dark, it was difficult to see the expression on his face—I was thankful for that. Finally he put his hand on his gut, waddled toward his house in his pigeon-toed gait, and vanished.

I found the champagne bottle in the grass. Just the dregs were left, but I sucked them down anyway and walked to the edge of the pool. One of the girls at the other end said "What's she *doing*?" They both laughed. The surface of the water had a sheen to it. I considered jumping in. One of those girls would have been willing to hold me under, would have welcomed the opportunity, no doubt. A few moments passed. Then I pushed the empty bottle into the water like a toy boat and left it floating there.

◾

Jogging home, I felt heavy and bloated. My breath whooshed in and out, and my feet slapped the pavement hard. The contents of my stomach reeled, sending up the sour fizz of gastric acid, and before long I was doubled over, spewing it all out onto a stranger's front lawn. When there was nothing left, I mopped my chin with my shirt and again propelled myself homeward. I wished the storm would come bursting back to crack open the sky and wash me away.

At the corner of my street, I slowed to a trot. My body was clean and empty now, purged, and if not for the throbbing in my temple, I might've felt free. I hugged myself to calm the goose bumps. Most of the houses were dead—it was probably midnight or later—but the porch light was on at my house. When I spotted a shape on the front steps, I figured my eyes were lying. But as I got closer, I saw it was him, undoubtedly him. "Gary?"

"I was waiting for you," he said. "It's so late. I wasn't sure you were coming home."

I was waiting for you. I felt full of a godlike power for the second time that night. So he didn't need any more space after all; he'd already forgiven me and found himself longing for my company and regretting his callousness, and so he'd planted himself here to wait for me, waiting all this time, probably for hours—the thought of it made me nearly collapse. I was overwhelmed, but not exactly shocked. Rather, I had the sense of having been shot into the air and falling back to Earth, coming to rest in my rightful place. Yes, *this* was my rightful place, I felt that clearly now. My despair had tried to persuade me otherwise, but I wouldn't let that happen again.

"Wait there," he said, and disappeared into the driveway. I held my breath. He came back pushing a handsome beach cruiser bicycle with broad handlebars and a chipped coat of paint. "I wanted to get you a little something," he said. "And I figured it might be useful. Since you don't have a car or anything. It could save you some time." He stood with the bicycle thrust forward and his face hanging back in the shadows, unsure. "It's not the fanciest model obviously. I bought it from a guy at work.

Used to be his daughter's. He assured me everything's working—no rust or anything. To brake, you just pedal backward." He lifted the back end and spun the tire to demonstrate. "But I can always return it to him, if you don't think you'll use it."

"I love it," I said, hugging my fingers around a handlebar. It was the truest of true gifts, a symbol to show he was sorry for overreacting, for making terrible and impulsive threats like "Maybe we should take a step back." In exchange, I forgave him for the hurt he'd caused and let go of any animosity I had been carrying around. We were going to be okay, Gary and I, more than okay, possibly the most important people in each other's lives. And I should've known that all along, should've had more faith in our bond, which would be even stronger now that we'd overcome our first adversity. He transferred the weight of the bike to me, and I was so keyed up that I threw my leg over and took off pedaling. "It might be too dark!" he called after me.

I made a dizzy, zigzagging lap of the street. There was nothing bad in the world. There was only the night with its golden streetlights and friendly crickets and the mosquito that flew straight into my open mouth— welcome!—and the endless coursing of my legs as they pumped round and round. At the end of the street, the bicycle spurred me onward, and I had to coax it back the other way.

I fumbled the dismount—it had been a while since I'd

ridden, and I wasn't used to this method of braking—but I landed on my feet and stabilized the bike. Gary had returned to his position on the steps. I chopped the kickstand down, letting the handlebars nod to one side. The trip had left me delightfully woozy, teetering from one leg to the other.

"You like it?"

"It's perfect," I said, sitting down beside him.

A rustle came from the bushes, and Gary stood to investigate. "She hated to stay cooped up inside," he said.

"The cat?"

"I tried. But I felt like a monster, doing that."

"Maybe she just needs a little adventure. I bet she'll come back in the morning." I let my leg drift toward his.

"Looks like you got run over or something," he said, gesturing to my lap. I looked down at the dirt on my shorts and knees, and my heart sank. While Gary had been searching for the perfect true gift and waiting patiently, all night, to present it to me, I'd been rolling around with a fraternity brother at a pool party. I felt ill. Had I betrayed Gary? And if the answer was yes, as I suspected it was, did I need to confess what I'd done, so that we could have a fresh start, marked by honesty and trust, especially given how important honesty was to him? It was the last thing I wanted to do right then—and maybe not necessary. The night was just a fluke, after all, completely out of character, and seeing as he already had doubts about my character, this would only confuse

him further. And what would be the point of that, beyond alleviating my own sense of guilt?

"Just a little dirt," I said, folding my arms across the
front of my clothes. "Thank you for the gift. You really
didn't have to do that."

"Well, I wanted to give you something, to say thanks
after all you've done for me this summer. I was feeling
kind of bad about how things went, you know."

"Me too. But it's okay, it's all okay. Just a misunderstanding. And now we can move on, like it never happened. I just wish I'd known you were waiting. I would've
come back sooner." I shivered and tried to snuggle up
against him, but his muscles tensed.

"There's no way I'm getting any sleep tonight anyway." He laughed, shaking his head and looking at his
hands as though he'd never seen them before. "You're
not going to believe it, what's been going on. These past
couple of days . . ." He began rubbing his hands together,
palm to palm, with accelerating speed. Then he clapped
and said, "She ended up going, to the interview. Irina.
And she got it. She got the visa. She's coming. She's actually coming."

"What do you mean, she's coming?"

"I know, can you believe it? All this time waiting
and then suddenly it's like it's happening so fast. I sent
her the money and she bought the first ticket available. In fact"—he lit up his phone to see the time—"she
should have already taken off. And then she'll be here,

tomorrow. Or today, actually. Like, eleven hours from now. Feels like I'm in a dream, or some alternate universe." He turned to study my face. I couldn't fathom what he saw there. It was like he'd been speaking another language and I was still working to translate the words, slowly and with immense effort. "I thought it might be kind of weird, telling you, after everything, but I knew you'd be happy for me too, since we've been friends. And you've done so much to help me—us. Am I a hundred percent sure it's the right thing? No. But it's a risk I've got to take. You get that, right?"

"But I thought you broke up."

"I guess we both just needed a little time to ourselves. Finally I called her and we had a long conversation, hashed everything out."

"But you were happy you broke up. You said you were better off, remember?"

"That's just what I was trying to tell myself. We love each other, that's what it comes down to. And we've already come this far, put so much into it. We owe it to ourselves to at least try."

"Maybe you just feel obligated to follow through now, after all the time and effort you put in. You don't want to disappoint her, I can understand that. But, I mean, take a step back and think for a second. All she's done these past few months is make you miserable. You said yourself it's always all about her, she's selfish and demanding, and couldn't care less about your feelings. And if she's like that now, just imagine how she'll be after you're actually married."

"Come on, Amy."

"I'm serious. It's not too late to change your mind. You could just not show up, or you could show up and hand her a ticket for the next flight back."

He hoisted himself up to the top stair, knees angled toward my face. He closed his eyes and pinched the bridge of his nose as though he'd suddenly come down with a migraine. "Look, I get why you would say that. And it's my fault, I know. I should never have brought you to the wedding, it wasn't a fair thing to do. And I'm sorry for that. Irina was right, all along. I should've listened to her. I shouldn't have let us spend so much time together. Yes, I vent sometimes, but I love her, I really do, and she actually wants to be with *me*. This is a once-in-a-lifetime chance. Maybe it doesn't make sense to you because you've never been in love like this, but one day it will."

I turned my head, physically repulsed. I'd never realized how unbelievably vain and obtuse he could be. "It's not about any of that. I'm only trying to look out for your best interest. To keep you from making a huge mistake." When he didn't respond, I knew I had to recalibrate. I needed to put my feelings aside and get strategic, before it was too late. "But no, you're right, I shouldn't have said that. I'm sorry. I guess I'm just in shock a little. But you know your relationship best. And if you've made up your mind, I'll support you. I'll help however I can. I'm actually excited to meet her, despite—everything. We can just start fresh, clean slate. I'm sure I'll like her, once I actually get to know her. Maybe I can stop by after work. Or next week maybe, if you want a few days by yourselves."

"Well, that's the other thing I wanted to talk to you about." He adjusted his position on the stair, adjusted it again. "I was thinking it would probably be better if you didn't come by. It would probably be a good idea if you started looking for another apartment. I don't want to leave you homeless or anything, just whenever you're able to find one. We already have a lot stacked against us as it is, and you know how jealous she can be. It will just be one less issue we have to deal with. You can understand that, right?"

"You don't have to worry about me saying anything. I can forget the wedding ever happened. It's already forgotten, out of my mind, *woosht*." I flicked my hand as if casting off the memory. "We're just friends, I get that. That's all I want too, honestly. Once we all hang out together, she'll see there's no reason to be jealous."

He stroked the back of his head. I could see a damp spot on the armpit of his shirt. "It's not that I don't trust you, but sometimes, I don't know. The way your mind works and stuff, it's just different from mine. So I'd just feel better this way—"

His words embedded themselves in my chest and

pulsed like a second heart. I stared out at the dark street, praying the bicycle would blow itself up.

"I'm not trying to hurt your feelings, it's just that you know she's already been giving me a hard time about you, and the whole living situation. If she ever found out about the wedding, she'd freak out. She'd never forgive me."

"I thought honesty was so important to you."

He sighed into his hand. If he wanted to marry Irina, I could deal with that—I'd never truly wanted to take her place anyway, I didn't love Gary, I wasn't even attracted to him. But to abandon me outright, to relegate me back to a stranger and force me to move to some terrifying new place where I knew no one and had to start all over, when *he* was the one who had invited *me* in, asked for *my* help, brought *me* to the wedding, kissed *me*—that idea made me wild. "Maybe I *will* tell her, then. She deserves to know."

"You know that's not your place." He put his hands on his thighs and stood up. "This wasn't exactly how I wanted to spend my night, getting threatened. I've got a million things I need to be doing right now, but I took time out of that to talk to you, out of respect." He went to his front door. "So I'm hoping that once you cool off, you'll decide to show me the same respect."

I jumped to my feet, my whole body shaking. "She's just using you, can't you see that? She's basically a mail-order bride!"

"Oh my god, is that what you think? I need to get out of here." His hand trembled on the doorknob. "We met on a *dating* site, for your information. Everyone's on them now."

"No, you didn't." My body stiffened. I felt a vicious, evil spirit enter me; I barely recognized my own voice. "You paid Sincere Romance for a ten-day tour, Odessa, Nikolaev, and Kherson." I pleaded with myself to shut up, but I was too far gone now, completely deranged, pain exploding through my body, though with some pleasure mixed in it too—the dumb, delicious look on his face—I wanted to squash him and any good feeling he'd ever had. "And they said 'Don't take her shopping' and 'Don't let her make arrangements for the date' and 'Be selfish, have fun, don't walk away with any regrets.' Now, that's pretty fucked up. Any *normal* person would say that's pretty fucked up."

"What? Where did you get that? I don't believe this." He thudded across the porch and I cringed, afraid he was going to hit me, then wishing he would. It wouldn't matter anyway, everything was lost now, and for good this time. Then he turned and said to himself, "This is insane, right? How do . . . You know what, no. I don't want to know. Don't say another word. I just need you out. Yes, tomorrow, you're out. You and all your stuff. Are you hearing me? Don't let me see you again. I'll call the police if I have to."

Just before he opened the door, there was a peculiar

stillness, and for a moment I thought we might agree to laugh—the whole thing felt rather absurd. Still, I would've begged—I had it in me to try anything then, even something degrading or manipulative—but he saved me the effort by slamming the door and locking me out there alone.

I stood, paralyzed and blank, for I don't know how long. Then I went to the door and pounded with my fists. "It's not like I actually care about you, you know!" I hoped the neighbors would hear, the entire town. "I was having sex with someone else, just an hour ago. Some- one a million times better than you!" I pounded and pounded. It was silent on the other side.

I sat back down on the steps. The roof dripped. The bicycle bowed its head, feigning innocence. I placed two fingers on the tender part of my wrist. With psycho- genic shock, blood pressure can drop so rapidly that you may not be able to detect a pulse. Inside me, capillaries were dilating, blood was draining from my brain, and any moment now I would faint. When Gary discovered me out here unconscious, what would he do? Hack me into pieces and throw them in a junkyard? Or maybe the sight of my helpless body would prompt him to review everything that had happened and to realize that I was actually on his side, as I had always been, I was only try- ing to protect him and to preserve what little was left of his dignity.

The fainting refused to happen. The cat surfaced in

the bushes. Mashpee, that was the name Gary had landed on when we were together in his car, not even a week ago. I got up and started after her, yearning to bury my hand in her warm fur, but she darted out of my reach and disappeared.

Up in my apartment, I hunched over my *EMS Monthly* magazine. I needed to feel my hands physically overpower something, kill its very essence. I mutilated the pages one by one, ripping and slashing with my fingers, even chewing on some of the scraps and swallowing. I hunted for more. My crumpled new dress, where I'd hurled it to the floor Saturday night. When I sank my face into it, I tasted smoke, barbecue sauce, insect repellent, marijuana, and above all, body odor—both mine and his. I tore it along the seams, then tore each piece again and again until there was nothing but tatters.

Nothing but tatters—that would be the state of Gary's life by this time tomorrow. How long would he wait at the airport? It might take four, five hours, even longer, maybe until someone notified the authorities about a suspicious man loitering, for him to finally see that he'd been stood up, to finally toss out his tacky bouquet and hobble back to the garage to discover just how much he owed for parking. Driving home, he would have to face that he'd been robbed and tricked and would never hear from Irina again—at least she'd spare him from having to go on with the charade any longer—and that he had no one, especially me, to offer any condolences. Yet at this moment he was still downstairs, feeling like a hero. He believed he had two women fighting over him—he was even more deluded than the rest of us, and they weren't placebo-type delusions but the destructive, lethal type. Deep down in his gut he knew it too. That was the real reason he'd befriended me and told me things he hadn't told anyone at work. I was the only one cowardly enough to go along with it, not to question him—so cowardly I was even willing to sacrifice my own future and everything I'd worked for. And now I would be homeless on top of it.

To keep from crying, I glared at my face in the bathroom mirror. This was a trick I'd developed as a child, since crying made my face look silly and melodramatic, and when I caught a glimpse of it, I had to laugh, I could no longer take the matter so seriously. But it didn't work this time. Taking a shower was the opposite kind of trick—it fostered self-indulgence and wallowing. I took a shower.

Behind the shelter of the curtain, under the thrumming spray of water, I mourned and wailed and spoke to myself: "You will always be a stranger, that is your destiny." If my own mother couldn't understand me, how could I expect anyone else to?

When I'd worn myself out, I toweled off and tried to will myself to sleep. It made me sick to think that Gary was so close, just on the other side of the wall, and yet so much farther away than when he was only my landlord, before I'd ever started reading his mail. Outside, a car whisked over the wet road, something threatening in the sound of it: it seemed to be rushing right at me. I braced myself for a collision, yielded, even welcomed it, but it never came. Lying in the dark with my arms over my face, I could still detect a hint of bleach and artificial citrus on my freshly washed skin. Over the course of this summer I really had absorbed a portion of the world's dust, and some chemicals must've come along with it. It seemed that this job was intent on sticking with me.

Another car passed on the wet road, and this one sounded like a voice whispering, *Shhh, shhh.* "Shhh, shhh," I whispered back. That was how my mother used to comfort me when I was still small enough to seek it. She would place an electric heating pad on my belly, stroke my hair, saying "Shh, shh" and "There, there." Shh, shh, there, there—as though she'd looked up the word *comfort* in a manual and was following procedure. But now I understood it, because now I had things I wanted to express and didn't always know how. I would've read that manual if it existed. And now I also understood that no matter what she had said or done, it would never have been enough, since there is no comfort another person can offer that is wholly satisfying. "Where shall I find God?" Florence Nightingale once asked herself, and her answer? "In myself." In myself. In myself. Even so, if my mother were still here, I would invite her over and turn off all the lights—that was the only way we could ever have difficult conversations—and then I'd tell her everything I ever wanted to say. I'd stroke her hair and whisper *Shh, shh,* and *There, there* until my fingers went numb and I'd used up all the breath inside me, and even though it wouldn't be perfect or wholly satisfying, it would be something.

TWELVE

At dawn, I looked out the window with some expectation, as though a major catastrophe might have transformed the world while I'd been lying in bed praying for sleep. There was no trace of Gary's car or the bicycle. So I lugged myself back to the clubhouse the same way I always had, one sore foot after the other, and eventually discovered that I'd arrived and was standing over a toilet with my cleaning caddy. I must've turned on the television because the low drone of voices filtered in from the bedroom, though I couldn't make out what they said. I found my backpack next to me on the tile floor, so overstuffed it wouldn't close all the way. I only vaguely remembered packing it. Inside I found my laptop, my toothbrush, my deodorant, a few pairs of socks and underwear, a change of clothes, and the Ziploc bag I kept under my bed with all my personal documents: tax and loan records, bank account information, passport, social security card. Everything I would take if I were never planning to return. But hidden under all that, a layer of useless trash. The blue pants and the shirt with the patch, the pathetic congratulations letter and certification card, the key to an apartment where I was no longer welcome. I picked up the key and squeezed, digging the serrated edge into my palm, then released. It plonked into the water and sank to the bottom of the toilet bowl. I held the letter and card in my hands. Now I could see them for what they were: a couple of flimsy, illegal forgeries. As I pitched them into the toilet, I had a feeling of déjà vu, as though a part of me had always known it was going to end this way. Of course this part of me had known and yet done nothing to prevent it—I was never willing to save myself from a moment of shame.

I flushed. Good, I thought. I'm free. I looked down at the empty bowl, half hoping they would pop back up. But no, this was the way it should be. If a person couldn't manage to hold on to a single friend or a place to live, who could trust her to preserve the finest traditions of her calling? Who would believe she even had a calling in the first place, or that she would ever do anything worthwhile like save a life? Only she would have the idiotic idea to try to placebo herself—ha. You had to laugh.

Then something caught my eye, a flicker of movement at the bottom of the toilet. The corner of the card.
It waved there in the water, taunting me. I grabbed my
toilet brush and thrust it into the bowl, stabbing and
grinding like mad. I needed more. I added a mountain of
powdered bleach, whipped and beat it into a thick paste.
I blindly pulled bottles from my caddy and let the contents flow out, listening for the slosh of toilet water and
then chucking them behind me. A dense, chalky puddle
formed. The way it simmered and frothed, I thought of
a witch's brew. The toilet was my cauldron. I eyed my
uniform on the floor. I wadded up the shirt with the arm
patch at the center, twisted the pants around it as tightly
as I could. I dropped the bundle in. I dumped more and
more cleaning liquids on top, plowing the brush into the
middle and churning it all up. I could sense the potency
building. When I paused and gazed into it, an image ma-
terialized. Florence Nightingale, but with a monstrous
face. She was angling her lantern toward the dark throat
of the toilet, as though beckoning me there.

The room began to blur. I was surrounded by a kind
of fog that stung my eyes. I rubbed their sockets. I was
dizzy, my senses drifting away from me, sight, smell,
touch. "My name is Amy," I said. "I'm here to help you."
I tried to stab the brush into the bowl, my arms weak and
wavering. *Is the water brackish? Did it come from rocky
heights? Administer oxygen by non-rebreather mask. The*

thoracic spine. The pack-strap carry. All of the above. My eyes were on fire and my organs writhed inside me. I staggered into the side of the tub. *Tachycardia, tachypnea. Prehospital blood transfusion. Don't take her shopping. Turn them into, into bananas. Bananas. Then a monkey. Shh, shh. There, there.* I managed to suck in a burst of air, then choked on it, coughing into my hand and shuddering. I looked at my hand and saw blood.

■

When my eyes opened again, I was splayed out in a bright room. For a moment I thought I was in the supermarket deli, trapped inside the display case—I'd been reincarnated as a bowl of Swedish meatballs. A woman's face appeared, full of freckles. I noticed a cloudy tube running into my arm. "You're all right," she said. "You're in the hospital. You had a little incident at work. Do you remember that? I'm Jeanine. I'm going to take your vitals."

I blinked, swallowed. My mouth tasted like vomit. She wrapped my other arm in a vest. It pinched. She was taking my blood pressure. I watched her move through a haze. Her scrubs had a pattern, dog bones and paw prints.

"Amy, you're awake." I discovered Doug standing at the foot of my bed. I wanted to tuck into the fetal position, I felt so powerless and exposed. "I just have to step out and take this call. But I'll be back. Take extra good care of her."

"Thank God, we were so worried." Another voice traveled from across the room—Roula. Seated in a chair in my hospital room as though she were a welcome guest and not my most hateful enemy. The violation sent flames through every part of my body, converging at my throat.

The nurse moved an object across my forehead. "Do you remember what happened?"

"Mm." I swallowed again.

"It was an accident?"

I nodded.

"So were you aware of the dangers of mixing bleach and ammonia? Two common household cleaners. It should really be one of the first things you learn, in your line of work."

"I— I was just trying to clean," I said feebly.

"Well, we all have forgetful moments," the nurse said. "But this is nothing to take lightly."

"It can be fatal," Roula said, because her presence here wasn't enough; she had to diminish me any way she could.

"You wish it was." It sounded like I might be crying, but I was too groggy to know for sure.

"I would never wish something like that." Roula braced her hands on the arms of her chair and gently rose to her feet. "I'll go. I'm sorry. I just wanted you to know I was praying for you. And I'll keep you in my prayers." She kept her head bowed. "Oh, and your bag. I picked it up. So you'd have it." She signaled to my backpack on the floor. I could only imagine what she'd done to it.

The nurse watched Roula leave, her lips parted as though she might speak. She turned back to me. "You're lucky your friend found you when she did. She probably saved your life."

"No," I said quietly. Her words tumbled around my brain. Roula had saved a life? And worst of all, it was my own. Now I knew I was crying. The nurse didn't acknowledge it—I appreciated that. All she said was, "That was pretty scary today, huh?"

She placed the tinny end of her stethoscope against my chest. "Take a deep breath. Another one, good." She took the earpieces out and said, "Can you tell me a little more about what happened? I just want to make sure I've got the story straight. That's part of my job."

I sucked my cheeks, trying to get some saliva into my dry mouth. "I was just trying to clean. There was something stuck in there. The toilet. And I guess I just got too focused on it, so I didn't realize."

"Okay, I understand."

Doug strode back in. "Sorry about that." He rolled his eyes at his phone and slipped it into a holster connected to his belt.

The nurse seemed to get the impression that she should leave. "I'm going to let you rest for a minute," she said. "I'll bring up something to drink. Juice? Okay. Press this if you need me."

Doug picked up the chair Roula had been sitting in and moved it beside my bed. "How are you feeling? You sure had us going back there."

"I'm sorry." It felt strange having him so close to my bed, but at the same time I wished he would reach over and hug me.

"Quite the dramatic exit! It's not every day we get a visit from an ambulance."

"The ambulance?" I shook with humiliation. An ambulance meant EMTs, maybe even one who had been in my training course, rushing up to find me passed out next to a flooded toilet, full of counterfeit goods . . .

"Don't worry about any of that. I just want you to take care of yourself. Let's make sure you get all the rest you need, huh? We can call this your last day—you only had one more week anyway, and this way you can take some time, regroup. Sound good? Amy?"

"That's okay. I want to finish."

"I don't want you to worry about that. You've been a huge help this summer. And we've got most people heading out on the cruise tomorrow anyway. It'll be a ghost town before you know it. A lot of our summer hires end up ducking out a little early, once things start winding down. It's no problem at all."

"I don't mind coming in one more week. Even longer, through the fall. I could keep up with the dusting and the floors and that kind of thing. You shouldn't leave the rooms unattended for too long. Mold could—"

"Listen, Amy, I'm glad you're passionate. But we've got Roula to take care of all that, and she's been with us for years now, so you see, I've got to defer to her. I've always liked you, you know that. You've gone above and beyond. And regardless of what happened today, the fact is that the season's ending and this was always meant to be a summer position, you knew that from the start." He checked his phone. "Look, I've got to get back. I'm glad you're okay, that's the important thing. Oh, and the bill, everything, that's all been taken care of. I figured you probably aren't on any insurance, and you've got enough on your plate."

"You didn't have to do that."

"That's okay. I know you're going to move on to bigger and better things after this. Just don't forget all us little people who knew you way back when. Stop in anytime, let me know how you're doing. I mean it." He touched my arm as he stood.

Once he was gone, I gasped for air—how long had I been holding my breath? I inhaled, exhaled, trying to concentrate only on that. Oxygen, carbon dioxide, oxygen, carbon dioxide. But as usual my brain rebelled. It insisted on taking inventory: no job, no friends, no apartment, no EMT certification, and no plan. It felt like the world was trying to erase me. I watched liquid move through the plastic tube into my arm. The nurse brought juice and crackers and I devoured them. Then I was overcome by fatigue and fell asleep.

I awoke to noise at the door, someone knocking and opening it at the same time, before I could respond. Gary lifted his hand in a reluctant, wooden hello.

"Doug called," he said. "He thought you might need a ride home. Guess he didn't know who else to call. I figured we should at least stop by and make sure you're okay."

"We?"

He gestured behind him, and a woman emerged. He hooked his arm around her waist and let the door close behind them. "This is Irina." She nodded blankly.

"Oh," I said. "Hi." She was a less sophisticated version of the woman in the picture, with brassy dyed hair, a tight skirt, and lips that seemed artificial. But for whatever reason, these things only made her seem more endearing and benign, nothing like the venomous man-eater I'd come to expect. What did I understand about her, about anything, after all? In spite of myself, I almost felt happy for them.

He whispered to her, then stepped closer and said in a muted voice, "Look, you didn't do this on purpose, did you? Because of—well, you know."

I felt a twinge behind my eyes and channeled all my energy into killing it. "It was an accident," I said at last.

The nurse entered and began puttering around my IV bag. Irina scrutinized her, along with the floor, the ceiling, the walls, the medical instruments beside my bed.

Gary was doing his best to appear calm, cool, and collected—as though he'd come up with that all on his own.

"Anyway, we're actually on our way to the Cape. Hank and Samantha are on their honeymoon, so they offered up their house for the weekend." He seemed annoyed that he couldn't fully enjoy rubbing this in my face, given my current condition. If Irina had ever considered me a threat, this scene certainly nullified it. "But it's not like I want you to be stranded here. We can wait if it won't hold us up too long." He said this more for the nurse's sake than mine.

"We just need to go through a few more things," she said. "Her vitals look good. We'll get a quick urine sample, then I'll get the machine in here and do a quick set of chest X-rays. If everything looks okay, she should be good to go. I'd say about an hour or so."

Gary scrunched his nose.

"It's fine," I said. "You can go. I have a ride. My friend Ward is coming."

"Guess we came all the way down here for nothing, then. Ah well, everything's exciting for Irina, even a trip to the hospital. She wants to see it all. This is her first day in the US."

"Oh, wow," the nurse said. "Welcome."

"Well then, we'll get out of your hair." He approached the edge of the bed. "We won't be back until Sunday night," he said. "So, you know, you can have until then."

◼

The room smelled like wool blankets and urine and the antibacterial gel they pumped from the hive on the wall. My mother's hospital room smelled exactly like this, but with a hint of coconut from her hand cream, which she was always asking us to lather on for her. Florence Nightingale criticized the way people act around death-beds, showering the dying with advice, urging them to get a second opinion, trying to cheer them up with fake optimism. Silly hopes and encouragements, she called it. But even that would have been better than how it was with my mother. Instead, I'd been indifferent and un-believing, too stubborn to offer a single word of hope or encouragement, even the silly kind.

I would use college as the excuse for why I couldn't visit or why I had to leave so quickly; I had a big course load and couldn't afford to fall behind. It didn't matter, I told myself, since she was hamming it up for the doc-tors anyway—we all knew how she could be. The queen of hyperbole and attention-seeking behavior, famous for her soap-opera sighs—of course she would be the one to get cancer. Now that she had the Big C to work with and a new, larger audience, who knew how far she would go. I'd picture her fainting across the bed the moment visit-ing hours ended, the gullible doctors pacing and wring-ing their hands as she whispered "No, please, don't worry about me," in the breathy voice of a practiced martyr. As time went on, that theory became less and less plausible, though I became more and more attached to it.

At one point, when she was getting worse and I said I had to go, I had a paper due the next day, my brother followed me into the hall. "Come on," he said. His face had no color in it. "You're killing her." And I knew even then that it was true. As sick as she was, it was me, I was killing her. And yet I couldn't not do it. It was as if time had already run out, she was already dead and I was already sinking into a life of misery, knowing I had been a thorn, a curse to the end; I was lower than the dirt that would rain down on top of her.

In the week after the funeral, Nnenna begged me to come with her to a chapel service on campus, just this once, just to try it. "It's really peaceful and relaxing, completely low-key. You could fall asleep if you want, no one would care. And if you decide you want to leave at any point, I'll go with you. I promise. Okay?" I sat comatose at my desk while she brushed my hair. "It might be nice to just get out and walk around a little. We don't even have to go in if you don't want to." She unlaced my shoes and set them by my feet. She brought my coat from the closet and held the sleeve open. But back then I was still foolish and arrogant enough to believe that faith was the enemy of intelligence. Now I can see why research shows religious people tend to live longer and recover from illness faster; if you're able to close your eyes and make a wish and believe that someone is listening, the ritual is not unlike an obecalp treatment. Still, not every obecalp can be successful, and not every prayer can be answered.

I turned to the empty chair Doug had pulled to my bedside. I tried to imagine my mother sitting there, watching me, her only daughter, the one the world was now trying to erase. For the first time in six years, it happened. The shapes of her hair and her shoulders took form, just the outlines first, then gradually filling in with color and texture until every detail was in its place. She was here, alive. I could feel the light whisper of her breath. She'd finally come back for me. I reached out, then caught myself, shrinking back into my pillow. The only reason for her to come back now was to gloat, to revel in the ultimate display of karmic justice: me lying in a hospital bed, defeated and miserably alone. I waited, shivering, gritting my teeth, terrified but also glad for her. She could finally unleash every last ounce of her wrath and scorn upon me. I deserved that and much, much worse.

But instead her hand moved, softly, slowly, to my forehead. She held it there, as though checking for a fever, gentle but unmistakable. I could feel it tingling all the way through my skull—like she was drawing something out of me or sending something in, or both. I opened my mouth. But then I saw there was nothing to say, nothing that needed to be said, nothing to be afraid of. My mouth closed, and I stopped shaking. I took what seemed like the first true deep breath of my entire life, as though I had been doing it wrong all these years. Warmth radiated out from her body, rising through the room. I felt it circle around me and cover me like a shell.

■

I thought about Peter, the most remarkable professor I ever had, while I lay on the bed under a spray of radiation. A technician had draped a lead apron over my legs and cranked the machine's arm down until it hovered a few inches above me. "Try not to move," he'd said, then disappeared around the corner with the cord. If Peter was right, if the things we do during a difficult time don't define us, then what does? I couldn't say I had a calling anymore. I couldn't say I had much of anything right now. But I could still do as the technician said: I could refuse to move—unflinching, unafraid—and lay bare all I held inside me. No matter what was exposed, I would not blink or turn away. I would probe deeper. As I lay there, I felt my body dismantling into its most basic parts, organs into tissues into cells. Then I held my breath and tried to reassemble in a slightly new and better way.

THIRTEEN

The X-rays came back clear. By the time they released me, I could hardly hold my head up, I was so exhausted. I did a lap of the parking lot, then walked back through the automatic doors. I spent the night in the ER waiting room, folded up in an upholstered chair, using my backpack for a pillow. The twenty-four-hour news channel flashed color and light, and the arms of the chair rammed into my sides. At one point a man jostled my shoulder, and I told him I was waiting for my sister, she was going to call when she was ready. In the morning, before dawn, I massaged the feeling back into my legs and stumbled out the door.

After forty minutes at the bus stop, I caught one heading in the direction of home. Well, what used to be home.

Even though Gary said they'd be away until Sunday, I couldn't bring myself to go back there. I tried to think of somewhere else to go. When we approached Magnolia Drive, I instinctively pulled the cord and headed for the bushes outside number 8. I'd never taken more than one berry at a time, but now I couldn't resist. I was famished and greedy and didn't know where I would have my next meal or even my next sip of water. I popped the ripest in my mouth, savoring each one. I'd never tasted anything so good. I loaded them into the front pocket of my backpack until it bulged.

I roamed, making expectant eyes at the houses as I passed, hoping one of them might take pity and open its doors to me. The streets were cool, dewy, empty. Not even the early joggers had ventured out yet. Just me and a bunch of dead worms that must've crawled out during the storm and then gotten fried by the sun. I took haphazard lefts and rights, rights and lefts, with no destination in mind. But when I finally looked up, I found myself on a familiar street, in front of a familiar building. The clubhouse, with its blue awning and white shutters, the parking lot glittering from a high-pressure wash. The alley by the employee entrance was deserted. Someone unlocked the employee door before the breakfast shift, but I didn't know when exactly. I tried pulling, and it gave.

Somehow I felt surprised to see the rosewood clock in its usual place on the wall, as though nothing on the hotel floor could possibly look the same as it had yesterday. The clock read 6:39. Roula wouldn't be in for at least another two hours. I entered the housekeeping closet. When I saw Roula's pots arranged on the desk, still glaringly, depressingly empty, I felt compelled to unzip my backpack. I transferred the berries into one of the pots. They almost filled it up. I stacked the other pots under it, to be sure she would notice. A pittance, after all I'd put her through. I felt mortified thinking of how I'd acted, how I'd twisted everything, trying to make myself superior. And still she'd decided I was worth saving. Making sure she never had to deal with me again—that was probably the best gift I could give her.

I heard voices in the hall and peeked through the cracked door. A young couple was exiting room 6, carrying big canvas tote bags and snuggling as they walked off, the tips of his fingers sinking into the back of her shorts. When their sounds had faded, I grabbed the keys off the loop in the closet and entered the room.

It felt weird to be inside, as though I hadn't spent all summer haunting these rooms, inspecting, polishing every inch. They'd left the sheets askew and a pile of Kleenex in the trash can. Through the window, I could see the cruise ship parked out in the harbor. It wasn't one of the mammoth ones you see advertised on TV with an indoor pool and a climbing wall and multiple theaters, but still grand and dignified, like a multitiered cake, each layer frosted white and lined with windows, and a deck sitting at the top. I knew from the flyer on the events board that it would begin boarding at 7:00 a.m. and would stop in Bar Harbor on the way to Halifax, Nova Scotia. The couple had left their things behind, so it seemed safe to assume they weren't planning to be passengers. Most likely, they were off to enjoy a romantic day on their private sailboat.

I entered the bathroom. I undressed, cautiously, so as not to disturb anything in the room. How bizarre, exhilarating even, to find myself naked here, to feel my bare feet against the cold tiles that I'd only ever touched through a layer of bristles or cloth or sponge. I had a brisk, glorious shower, using one pump of soap for everything, including my hair.

I brushed my teeth at the sink. I looked into the mirror, at the top half of my naked body. Water running off my chin, my wet hair molded to my head, the ends dripping. If the world wanted to erase me, why not let it, and then draw up a new version in her place? Maybe it wasn't an assault but an opportunity. I put on a clean pair of underwear and got the change of clothes from my backpack. I held them up: a nondescript T-shirt and a pair of athletic shorts, an outfit I'd worn countless times here this summer. I set them back down and walked into the bedroom.

I was going to have to borrow a few things. I wished there was another way, but I had limited time and so I needed to work with the situation at hand, as delicately and graciously as possible, and hope they would understand. In the closet I found suitcases, a nylon bag of golf clubs, and a few fancy dresses—too fancy. I knew now what I was meant to do, and to overdress for it would be a mistake. My mother once said that the poorest man in the room is the one in the most expensive suit. We were visiting Dad's family in Ohio, and had snuck into a holiday party at the hotel, just the two of us, giggling in a corner, judging everybody. That was a good time. In fact, there had been many, many good times.

I chose a pair of beige shorts from the suitcase and a blue shirt with embroidery around the collar. The shirt fit all right when tucked in but the shorts sagged off my hips, which stuck out like two horns—I must have lost a few more pounds. I didn't want to take a belt on top of everything else. So I unzipped a large pouch that said "Leave a little sparkle wherever you go" and gently foraged through the cosmetics and hair accessories until I located an elastic, which I used to gather the extra fabric. That left me with a bulge on one side, so I had to untuck the shirt and billow it out to mask it. Her loafers pooled around my feet; my sneakers would have to do.

I evaluated myself in the full-length mirror. I flipped my head, tousling my new short hair. Although it wasn't the most refined look, I still felt energized by it. A new person was taking shape before me, unfamiliar and unresolved. The core would always remain me, no matter if I passed an exam or saved a life or worked this job or another. But the rest was open-ended. This new me could have entirely different feelings and problems, different questions and struggles and dreams. There was so much to learn about her! It was both exciting and unsettling.

I stepped closer to my reflection. I needed just a touch of something else, to really distinguish her. I returned to the zippered pouch and sifted through shimmery tubes and glass jars, a metal eyelash curler, a set of brushes. I felt inspired by the pops of color, the wonderful clicking sounds they made as they shifted. I unscrewed a pot of cream foundation. If I had clean fingers and only skimmed the very surface, it wouldn't be the worst transgression. I dabbed a bit onto my face, concentrating on the purple sacs that had swelled up under my eyes over the past week. The tint was wrong for my skin, too dark and orangey, so I had to take a bit more to extend it down my neck and blend it in. She had a large palette of eye shadows in a spectrum of light to dark brown, and I tapped the spongy applicator into the middle box and swiped over my lids. She had an eyebrow pencil with a point on one end and a tiny brush on the other, and I alternated between the ends until I had two decent arches.

I stepped back to take in the full effect. The makeup looked rather clownish on me, but that was probably just because I wasn't accustomed to it. I remembered Nnenna once painting bright glittery swirls around my eyes for a "color party," her hands holding my head steady as she worked. I was trying to talk without moving my jaw, so my voice had a funny, stiff quality. I was telling her about the first time I experimented with lipstick. I'd gone out to walk to school with Angela, and the first thing she said was, "Wow, you're wearing lipstick," which devastated me. I tried to wipe it off when she wasn't looking, rubbing so hard my lips began to bleed. Nnenna laughed warmly. She blew across my skin to help it dry, making me tingle head to toe. "But you *were* wearing lipstick," she said. She couldn't relate, which I envied, but she also didn't judge, which made me love her even more wholeheartedly, unconditionally—even now. I tried googling her once, a year or so ago. I found she worked in an afterschool drama program for at risk youth. I wished her the best, wherever she was now. Maybe I would even write her an email someday.

The time was 7:14. I picked up the telephone on the bedside table and dialed my father's number. When his voice came on, a strange whimper came out of me, and I had to bite the side of my finger. It was an automated recording. "Dad, it's Amy. Sorry it's early, but I wanted to tell you to cancel the magazine subscription. If it's too late to get a refund, I'll pay you back for it. I'm not an EMT, I'm sorry. But everything's okay. And, I'm . . . Do you remember when Mom and I snuck into that party at our hotel, an office holiday party? And she ended up winning one of the prizes in the raffle? A little neck massager. She was so excited. Do you think you still have that around somewhere? Anyway, you can't call me back at this number, but I'll call you again in a couple days. And I'll explain everything. You don't have to worry. Okay. Bye, Dad."

Through the window, I could see members or guests who had been properly introduced filing down the dock and taking turns clambering into the launch boat. I put my dirty clothes into my backpack and then puffed out the sides and readjusted things, to make it look as full as possible. I folded my clean clothes neatly and placed them on the dresser. It certainly wasn't a fair trade. I pulled a ten-dollar bill from my wallet and laid it on top of the clothes. Then, after one last glance in the mirror, I marched down, eyes straight ahead, to join the line.

They didn't appear to be using any ticket system—on this secluded dock, among the gentle lapping of waves and sleepy conversation, any concern about Doug's so-called mosquitoes would have felt laughably out of place. But, speaking of Doug, he might be coming in early today, to sort out any last-minute issues before departure. I kept one eye scanning for him on the shore behind me. The other eye sized up the amount of baggage beside each person in line. I should've brought something else. I squirmed, desperate to find a use for my conspicuously empty arms. I tried mimicking the stance of the person in front of me, but a kid was clowning around, quaking the wooden planks under my feet and making it difficult to stabilize. I weighed the idea of returning to room 6 and swiping a suitcase, but I couldn't run the risk of bumping into Doug or Roula, or Jeremy. I had to push on.

The line moved quickly. Two launch boats did laps out to the cruise ship and back again, and one of the boys in polo shirts shepherded people along, motioning when the boats had reached capacity. Before long it was me, my turn. I didn't make eye contact with anyone as I stepped aboard and swung my backpack into my lap. The boat jerked into motion. As we coasted away from shore, I held my breath, but no one questioned me.

The ship towered above us, casting a cool shadow. A set of stairs ran from a side door down to a platform, where we were to disembark. "Permission to come aboard!" an older man next to me said, giddy as he hoisted himself up. An employee offered his hand to me, just as he did for everyone else. I squeezed it as I crossed the threshold, landing firmly, right foot, then left foot, on the platform. I followed the group up the stairs and into the belly of the ship, where staff members were collecting luggage and showing people to their cabins. "I travel light," I said when one began to approach. I smiled and twisted to in-dicate my backpack. "I'll just keep it with me for now. I'm anxious to get up on the deck and take it all in." He nodded with zero interest. "Up that way," he said.

The deck had a wide walkway along the perimeter, with a pool and lounge chairs in the middle. The veneer on the flooring felt slick under my sneakers. I stationed myself at the railing on the outer edge, my backpack lodged between my feet. People streamed up and down the tiers of the ship, but I didn't dare wander. Naturally, the worst-case scenarios came to mind: someone recognizing me, asking incisive questions, putting in a call to Doug or the authorities. But I refused to feed into them. And as I watched the launch boats fetch more and more people, lulled by the methodical back-and-forth, I began to feel oddly safe. Not because of the clothes and makeup, which hardly amounted to a disguise, but because I had no reason to analyze anyone else, and they had no reason to analyze me. What an extraordinary and unjustified privilege to be able to go from an elite university to a courthouse to a supply closet to a cruise ship without anybody raising an eyebrow.

Feeling confident, I turned around and propped my back against the railing to admire the deck. A woman stood nearby, middle-aged but with a ribbon tied around her ponytail that made her seem youthful and spirited. She was also alone. "Nice day," I said, striding up to her.

"Mm-hm." She covered her mouth. "Sorry. You caught me with my mouth full. Interested?" She pulled a bag of red licorice sticks from her purse.

"Oh, that's okay. Thanks."

"You probably find it appalling, this early in the morning, right? People always look at me like I have three heads. But it's all because of this cheerleading coach I had as a teenager. She was strict about our image, completely over the top. And she pounded it into our heads that if we were ever craving candy and absolutely *had* to have some, we should eat it first thing in the morning. Since that's better for burning calories. I ended up quitting the team, you can imagine. But by then, I'd already made a habit of it. Which of course is not at all what she had in mind." She wiggled the bag as if to entice me. "You could be my first convert . . . ," she said, making her eyebrows jump.

"Well. Why not." I'm not the biggest fan of licorice at any time of day, but I chomped through it with enthusiasm, like a good first convert should. "I think I could get used to it," I said, tonguing the gummy bits out of my molars.

She stuck out her hand. "I'm Meredith, by the way. I don't think I've seen you around before."

I met her hand, trying to think fast. "Florence," I said. Even if we no longer shared a calling, I could still pay tribute to her and all she'd done for me. "I'm new. So I haven't met many people yet."

"Are you here alone?"

"Yes."

"Me too. There are a few other ladies here—we all left our husbands and kids at home to fend for themselves. A fun bunch. We mostly came for the bottomless margaritas. You should find us tonight for dinner if you want. We'll be the ones drinking our weight in tequila."

"That'd be great, thank you."

"I'll save a seat." We heard a disturbance behind us, and Meredith whirled around. I turned as well, though hesitantly, my neck prickling.

A boy had gotten in the pool. His mother was kneeling at the side. She seemed infuriated rather than concerned, trying to keep her voice down as she reprimanded him. She alternated between a growl and a whimper, and though I couldn't make out the precise words, I could sense she was on the brink of a meltdown. Finally she reached in and grabbed his slippery arm, so that he dangled in the water. Meredith and I moved toward them, but just barely—our way of showing that we were empathetic but hoping not to get involved. We were everyday people, Meredith and I, with a healthy respect for the boundaries of other everyday people and no Hippocratic oath to fulfill, no need to be a hero.

A man came up behind, the father, and told her to let go. "Robbie, get out," he said with authority. Robbie planted his hands and rose up and out of the water like an acrobat. He looked scrawny in his dripping T-shirt, shorts, and sneakers. "Go change. Now," his father said, and the boy obeyed. The father eyed us, the scattering of spectators. "Nothing to see here," he said flatly, waving a hand, and we all turned away.

"Bet you're feeling glad you left your kids at home," I said to Meredith, but found she'd become engrossed in her phone.

"Sounds like my presence is required downstairs. A skin-care emergency." She went on typing as she spoke. "These women would commit murder if their facialists told them to. Not even kidding. Anyway, sorry. See you later?" She stepped away, eyes still on her screen, then looked up and smiled right at me.

"Definitely," I said. "See you soon."

Robbie's parents were walking nearby, speaking in low, stern tones. I faced the ocean and pretended not to eavesdrop. "The second you turn your back, a switch goes off," Robbie's mother said, her voice quivering. "And he loves every second of it, seeing me suffer like that. I don't know what else I can do. Honest to god, it's like he really truly hates me."

I peeked over my shoulder as they passed and caught the side of her face. Up close, I recognized her right away: she was the generous one who had once walked the length of the hotel floor to give me the gift of a peppermint.

A voice came over the intercom system. "This is Captain Perry Burkett here. It's my pleasure to welcome you folks aboard the *Sea Orchid*. We have officially weighed anchor here, as of eight twelve Eastern Standard Time. And it looks like we've got a beautiful day ahead of us, sunny skies and calm seas straight to Portland." I shut my eyes and breathed in. I was really doing it.

The boy, Robbie, reemerged in clean, dry clothes. He stood alone a few paces away, stabbing his toes against the side of the boat. I inched closer. He bent over the railing to gaze down at the water, so I did the same. We watched the ripples break and swing and blend, a perpetual shape-shifting. It looked chaotic and unpredictable, like something just freed from a cage. "So, you like to swim?" I asked.

He shrugged. "I guess."

"Not me. It's always made me nervous."

He seized the railing and thrust his chest over it, launching a mucusy ball of spit into the air. I lost track of the trajectory and hoped it hadn't curved back into a window. "It's not even scary," he said.

"I don't know," I said. "I guess it's the fact that you can't see what's under you, or behind. And you don't know what will be there when you pop back up. My mother made me take lessons. She knew it was important. But I was so stubborn. I hated to let go of the side."

He began to karate-chop the railing. "Hi-ya!" He gave it a roundhouse kick. Just when I thought he'd forgotten about me altogether, he said, "Seventy percent of the earth is water." He widened his stance and kicked again, with impressive flexibility. "And sixty percent of the human body."

I considered this. "Wow. You're right. That's true." I shouldn't be afraid of what was inside me. Earlier Robbie had tortured his mother with his reckless behavior, but that didn't make him rotten. People are more complicated than that. I considered offering some advice, about being kinder to his mother, but I trusted him, and her, that they would come together in their own time. She might never understand everything about him or the way he acted, but she would still love and forgive him, even when, especially when, he didn't deserve it. One day he might look back and wish he hadn't treated his own family worse than enemies, but over time he'd learn how to live with regret, and his family would understand, because they lived with it too.

Robbie was in the midst of another karate sequence when a boy ran up and jerked on the back of his shirt. "Come on," the boy said. Robbie took off. A moment later, I felt a sudden yet gentle push against my back. "Don't fall in!" he yelled, to spook me. Then he snorted and went galloping after his friend. I smiled as I watched them go.

Captain Perry Burkett came back on the intercom to invite everyone inside for a brief welcome toast, but I still wasn't ready to move.

So now I'm alone out here, holding the rail of the giant ship, as the sun melts the makeup off my face. Sparkles blink across the surface of the water, a dazzling show. They leave an echo at the back of my eyes, flashing yellow spots. I feel I could dance among them, without any effort at all. I am light and wispy as a moth. Even the weight of the world's dust has escaped from inside me and blown off with the breeze.

The land is just a stray mark now, the tip of a fingernail. I don't panic or pine for it, but I'm not running away from it either. Rather, ten times, die in the surf, heralding the way to a new world, than stand idly on the shore— Florence Nightingale said that. She has never stopped rooting for me, I'm sure of it.

I'm still young, and quite lucky. I don't yet have a bed to sleep in or a clean change of clothes, but in two days, I'll be in Halifax. Florence Nightingale said that people need variety: we suffer from seeing the same rooms, the same streets, the same walls, day after day. In Halifax, I won't see any of the same things. In Halifax, I can be and do anything. I can adopt a dog or join a swim team, grow flowers, ride motorcycles, make my own pastries or hats. But in the meantime, I have an unbeatable view of the Atlantic Ocean. The sun is shining, the wind is blowing, and Meredith is saving a spot for me at her table tonight.

ACKNOWLEDGMENTS

An immense thank you to Dee McNamer for your faith, generosity, and wisdom from the very beginning. This book exists because of you. Thank you to the teachers and classmates who read bits and pieces along the way, especially Alida, a brilliant reader and friend. To my first writing teacher, Joe Hurka: your encouragement made all the difference.

I am forever grateful to my agent, Sarah Bowlin, for your guidance and insight, and to my editor, Sara Birmingham, for choosing this book and making it better. I couldn't imagine two more talented or patient people to help me through this process.

Thank you to my remarkable parents. And thank you to Brian, for listening, for reading and rereading, and for everything in between.

ABOUT THE AUTHOR

KELLY MCCLOREY is a graduate of the MFA program at the University of Montana. She lives in Massachusetts.